A Border Agent Mystery

Best Wishes

Ray Summers

Illustration by Matt Butcher

Border Canyon

Ray Summers

ISBN-13: 978-1-7336745-0-8

Wynona Press
wynonapress@gmail.com
www.borderagentmysteries.com

This book is dedicated to
Janet Wynona Cloninger Summers,
my high school sweetheart and loving wife of 62 years.

Special thanks to freelance editor, advisor and friend
Rob Patterson
for his help in publishing this book
and launching the Border Agent Mystery series.

Prologue

Late Spring, 1963 – Nogales, Arizona

I was late for the gathering as I joined four or five other border patrolmen at a large round table in the dining area of a popular local restaurant. The U.S. Customs Service agent responsible for the impromptu meeting nodded a greeting to me and without pausing continued. "You can forget all the daily reports and bookkeeping stuff. Secretaries are gong to take care of all that for you. You're going to be issued a plain, unmarked government car, a $2,000 cash advance expense account and your job will be to be to catch smugglers. That's all, just catch smugglers."

The customs agent was explaining an organizational change in the service: uniformed customs port investigators normally assigned to ports of entry to investigate violations of cargo theft and port procedure were to be assigned plainclothes duties and assist local customs agents. In effect they would be apprentice agents, and all future customs agent positions would be filled from the custom-port investigator ranks. He was urging all of us to take the Treasury Enforcement agent exam in order to be ready when the new customs port investigator positions opened.

This man making the job pitch was a renowned if not – in border circles – famous customs agent. He was a native Spanish speaker capable of undercover roles as a Mexican when necessary. He had untold reliable sources of information and contacts on both sides of the border. He had dedicated years to cultivating and maintaining those sources. He had worked the length of the Mexican border for years. first as a border patrolman then as a customs agent. He was the perfect example of the dedication and efficiency required of a customs agent. I had often noticed him parked, just waiting, as I drove past on my early morning border patrol duty shifts. He would still be there when I went off duty that evening and again the next morning and all the next day. I saw him early afternoons, during evening duty shifts and during night duty shifts. With reliable information, he waited to spring his ambush on unsuspecting narcotics smugglers. That was what customs agents did: hunt, hunt, hunt. That was the job he was pitching and that was my job for the next twenty-six years.

– William R. Summers
Retired Senior Special Customs Agent

1

The scent of dust was in the car. The grey-haired man behind the wheel of the light-blue, four-door 1964 Ford LTD glanced up at the rearview mirror and the billowing brown plume behind him. Only heavy traffic would have ground the sunbaked West Texas clay into such fine powder. The thought caused Grady Matthews' hands to tighten his grip on the steering wheel.

The whitewalls of the car hummed across the pipe rails of another cattle guard, the third one since leaving the blacktop. The sound brought Grady's eyes down from the rearview mirror and back to the narrow winding road ahead. He was counting the cattle guards. There were five – he was positive of that – five cattle guards between the highway and the old ranch house at the end of the road.

The last one was on a hill overlooking the whole layout. Grady thought about the last time he had been there, twenty-seven, twenty-eight years ago. He'd been on a two-day surveillance, shorter than most. The burro pack-train had come early on the third morning. Twenty-five burros, a ton-and-a-half of paper-wrapped marijuana bricks and six smugglers... a long time ago. Nobody used burros anymore.

He wondered if the ancient house, the barn, two windmills and the sprawling system of corrals were still there. The canyon would be there: *La Pipa*, the Mexicans called it, the deep, narrow pipeline to and from the border.

Grady raised his boot from the accelerator and jammed it down onto the brake pedal. The LTD slid to a stop directly over the fourth cattle guard. He leaned toward the dust-filmed passenger's window and squinted out across an empty greasewood flat, past a low rise bristling with ocotillo sticks to a long copper-colored, flat-top mountain two miles away. Grady Matthews smiled. The butte, shimmering in the rays of the late afternoon October sun, was exactly where it ought to be. So the rest would also be.

He put the car in reverse, looked back, waited for the last of his dust cloud to drift by and slowly backed the car over its own half-filled tracks to a dry creek bed he had just crossed. He stopped, shifted again and drove northward off the road, up the rocky creek bed, bending cottonwood and willow saplings, maneuvering around drift logs and boulders for more than a mile before coming to a stand of tall mesquite trees. Turning left up a low embankment, he drove out of the creek bed and weaved through the big mesquites for almost a hundred yards, stopped near the western edge of the grove, turned off the ignition and got out of the car. The long barren butte he had seen from the cattle guard was now broadside, directly in front of him, only a quarter of a mile away. His eyes focused on the south end of the mountain where the brown perpendicular cliffs jutted up from the surrounding slope of rubble. From there he would be able to look down into the narrow valley beyond the ranch, or what was left of it and the corrals, especially the corrals.

He leaned back into the car for his hat. The wide-brimmed straw Stetson, tan trousers, white shirt and brown boots gave him the look of a typical Southwestern law enforcement officer. It was a look that suited him. He had been a federal officer on the Mexican border for over thirty years, ten with the Border Patrol, twenty-two with the U.S. Customs Service.

Retired now and recently widowed, he was wearing what he called his “town clothes,” wishing that the expensive hat he had just put on was one of his old curled-up ones. He hadn’t planned on a mountain hike when he left home that morning.

Grady glanced down at the brown calfskin boots. In the trunk of the car were jogging shoes that would spare the three-hundred dollar Tony Lamas a trip up the rocky slope and back. Moving with the agility of a young man, he stepped to the rear of the car, opened the trunk and took out a pair of grey, red and blue leather sneakers. Sitting down on the edge of the open trunk, he changed footwear.

When the last shoelace was tied, he stood, reached back into the trunk and pulled out a worn black pistol belt with a holster, handcuff case and an old-fashioned twelve-loop ammunition carrier filled with cartridges. The wide, heavy leather belt seemed to curl and buckle itself around his trim waist.

Again leaning inside the trunk, Grady opened a black leather briefcase and came out with a large blue-black Smith & Wesson .357 Magnum revolver. He dropped it into the holster on his right hip. As he snapped the keeper strap across the back of the revolver's hammer, he heard a noise behind him. Unsnapping the strap he turned to face the mesquite grove. Nothing moved.

After a moment of watching and listening, he glanced at the boots he had left on the ground, leaned over and picked them up. As he straightened, something struck the boots. He felt a searing pain in his stomach and heard the crack of a rifle.

Grady Matthews groaned, doubled over and spun away from the sound of the shot. The chocolate-brown calfskin boots tumbled into the trunk of the car.

2

The call came in on one of the embassy's special lines. If U.S. Customs Special Agent Ryan Shaw had not been so engrossed in his writing, he would have picked up on the first ring. But he was working on a final report, the last effort required to close a difficult year-long investigation into the illegal diversion of U.S. technology. In this instance, it had been radar tubes critical to state-of-the-art military air-traffic-control system.

Such items required State Department approval for export and were legally available only to specified friendly nations. Four of the restricted tubes had surfaced on the inventory sheet of a U.N. team following a spot check of Iraqi air installations near Samarra. In all five arrests had been made by foreign governments: one in Madrid, two in Frankfurt and two in South Africa. More were expected, but as far as Agent Ryan Shaw was concerned, it was over. Case closed, job finished. Customs attachés to U.S. Embassies weren't authorized to make arrests.

The phone rang for the third time. Ryan glanced at his watch. It was ten after five, Friday afternoon. The embassy office staff had long since departed, but the weekend duty agent should have been here by now. He glanced at the phone. The blinking light indicated the call was on a government line. That usually meant a call from stateside.

Expecting information on another case, he cleared the computer screen and picked up the phone. "Shaw," he said as he answered. He cradled the phone on his right shoulder, ready to take down names, dates and export license numbers. Instead, he stared at the blank computer screen in front of him and listened to the gruff familiar voice of Frank Marsh tell him about the disappearance of Grady Matthews.

As the message became clear, Ryan could feel a knot forming in his stomach, the dull aching kind that doesn't easily go away. Grady and Frank were like family to him. The three of them had spent ten years together on the Mexican border. He might as well be listening to his brother tell him their father had disappeared.

"DPS found his car yesterday afternoon at a roadside park just this side of Sanderson." Frank paused.

Ryan made no comment. He was remembering almost 20 years ago in Arizona, standing in front of Grady's battered wooden desk, right arm raised, repeating the customs special agent's oath of office. Frank had driven the seventy miles from Nogales to Tucson to give him the good news. The Pima County sheriff hadn't thought of it that way, had not been happy about losing another deputy to the feds, not even a green, twenty-two-year-old one.

"Hello... you still there?" Frank was almost shouting. Ryan straightened, blinking at the empty monitor screen in front of him. If anything had been found in Grady's car – blood, signs of a struggle, things scattered, anything – Frank would have said so.

"Yes, I'm still here. Where are you calling from?"

Ryan glanced at the lighted button on the telephone, confirming that Frank's call definitely had come in over a government line.

"Border Patrol," Frank answered. "I'm at sector headquarters in Marfa."

Marfa, Texas, twenty-six miles west of Frank and Joan's home in Alpine. They had left Arizona six years ago when Frank was selected to open the new Alpine Customs Office. A little over a year ago, the office had been closed and Frank had retired rather than move again.

"The Border Patrol helping?" Ryan asked.

"Doing everything they can."

"What about the locals?" There was a noticeable silence. Ryan could hear Frank take a deep breath before answering.

"Nothing in the car, at the house or anywhere else indicating foul play, so they're not doing much of anything – just filling out reports and making up happy-ending scenarios."

No evidence of foul play. Grady's car was just another stolen vehicle abandoned en route to Mexico. Grady was an old widower who may have decided on an unexpected trip – maybe to Mexico. That's the way the locals would see it, issue routine alerts and wait for something to turn up. Ryan didn't want to think about what might turn up, but weeks, months, even years could pass before it did.

Evidence and witnesses would be gone by then. He had seen it happen. He wasn't going to let that happen this time, not with Grady.

"I'm heading your way," Ryan simply said.

"Look forward to seeing you." Frank hung up.

Ryan slowly put the phone down and glanced at his watch. He had hauled enough stateside visitors to and from the airport to know that on Fridays, three flights, instead of the usual one, left Madrid for Kennedy International. If it was on time, the first one would be leaving in exactly one hour. He cleared his desk, scooping up notes and files into a side drawer, stood up and snatched his brown suit coat from the back of a nearby chair.

Ryan was tall, with blue-green eyes and flecks of grey in his thick, raven-black hair. At forty-two he exercised regularly to keep the muscular, athletic build he had taken for granted in his twenties and early thirties.

As he slipped his coat on, the telephone rang again. The blinking light signaled it was local. Probably a tourist wanting to know how much booze or how many cameras he or she could take back to the states or, maybe someone with a real problem. He finished checking his inside coat pockets for his wallet, government I.D. and passport. Then, as he leaned over and reached across the desk for the phone, the light stopped blinking and remained on. Someone had taken the call. The duty agent was here. He was off the hook.

Ryan glanced over his freshly cleared desk, stepped to the side door of his office, pulled it open and strode quickly out into the hall. If there was a cab in the usual place out front, he just might make the standby roster for that first flight to the U.S.

A half-hour later he scored the only seat available: first-class accommodations on the departing TWA flight for JFK, New York. His mind mulled the many possible scenarios and questions about Grady's disappearance; he hardly napped in the large comfortable seat and plush surroundings during the nine-hour transatlantic flight. The cramped coach seat for his six-foot frame from New York to San Antonio, Texas produced more speculation on his old supervisor's fate. Much of it was repeated pondering on what little he knew and what that might suggest.

Even to Ryan, a native of the Arizona-Mexico border, the western portion of the Texas highway map appeared uncluttered, incomplete, as if some cartographer had left out most of the highways, cities and towns. Alpine was in the center of a particularly large "unfinished" area four hundred miles west of San Antonio.

Ryan looked up from his map. It was just after midnight – early Saturday morning. The main concourse of San Antonio International was quiet, but most of the car-rental booths were still occupied by uniformed representatives. If he drove, he could be in Alpine by daylight. His other option was to wait, catch the next flight to Midland-Odessa at eight in the morning, then a commuter hop south to Alpine. He studied the map again, then folded it and headed toward the Budget rental car sign.

Six hours later he was still driving, staring at the lighted swath of highway ahead, rethinking Frank's telephone call again and again.

"Grady called sometime Monday morning," Frank had said, "left a message on the answering machine. Said he would see us that evening, but he never showed up. Joan and I waited all the next day, then drove over to Balmorhea and went through the house. Everything looked okay. His pickup was in the driveway so we reported him missing in Rose's Ford."

Frank hadn't given him much information to ponder during his flights and now an all-night drive to Alpine. But his mind still ruminated on every possibility Grady's disappearance might suggest from the mundane to tragic and suspicious.

As he shifted in the seat of the rented Caprice, something flashed in the darkness ahead.

He let up on the accelerator, gently depressed the brake pedal and the car began to slow. Frank eased to a smooth noiseless stop as pairs of glassy green reflections moved into the light of the high beams.

Javelinas.

Ryan lowered his window, cut the engine and watched. He hadn't seen a javelina since leaving Arizona seven years ago.

It was a big herd: three bristling boars, seven smaller sows and a hoard of grunting, half-grown piglets. They poured across the pavement, down into the bar ditch, under the barbed wire and into the greasewood darkness. Ryan sat in the middle of the deserted two-lane blacktop listening to the javelinas move through the brush. As the sounds faded, he leaned his head back, tired, no longer used to late hours and long drives.

His thoughts drifted back to the abandoned car. It had been found near Sanderson, well past Grady's intended destination... if Grady had left from his home.

Sanderson, Alpine and Balmorhea were all small towns. Alpine was the crossroads, with Sanderson eighty-five miles to the west and Balmorhea, where Grady lived, sixty-four miles northwest. Mexico was a hundred miles due south of Alpine.

Grady could have called the message in from anywhere. He could have been returning from a trip instead of beginning one. They would have to check on that. It was the only possibility of a lead he had been able to come up with. Too little information.

His eyes closed for a moment, but he caught himself, sat upright and reached around to massage the back of his neck. It wouldn't do to fall asleep in the middle of a highway, no matter how deserted it seemed.

He opened the door and stepped out into the predawn crispness, stretched and drank in the smells. The scent of the Texas desert was different from that of Arizona. He exhaled and took another breath: dew-moistened sage, prickly-pear blossoms, damp earth, javelina musk. Not quite Arizona but close, close enough for him to realize that he had missed it. He hadn't been back to the states since Rose's funeral two years ago. She had also been like family. Her funeral was the last time he had seen Grady or Frank.

Ryan walked around the car, pausing to stretch and do knee bends. The exercise and fresh air cleared his head. Back in the car, he started the engine, raised the window and drove on into the darkness toward the mountains he knew were now just ahead. As he topped a rise, flashing lights in the distance greeted him. He dimmed the high beams and slowed.

Vehicles with piercing red and blue revolving lights occupied the right lane of the narrow highway. A row of blinding, red phosphorous flares guided him into the left lane, past a black and white Texas Department of Public Safety cruiser, a green and white Border Patrol sedan and an orange-banded Brewster County EMS unit. A huge dual-wheel wrecker blocked the cordoned-off lane, its cable dangling into the darkness beyond a jagged gap in the highway guardrail.

A DPS trooper waved him on. Ryan eased past the big wrecker, a second Border Patrol car, two smaller flashing tow trucks and finally, the last spewing flare holding him on the wrong side of the highway. He eased back into the right lane and then pressed down the accelerator. The Caprice surged forward. The kaleidoscope of lights grew smaller in the rearview mirror. Whoever went over the side must have fallen asleep.

Ryan straightened in the seat and lowered the front windows an inch. The drone of the car engine rose to a higher pitch as he urged the Caprice up and around the base of the first mountain, beginning a 4,500-foot climb above the broken prairie. The eastern horizon now had a pink tinge to it, revealing mountain peaks on the skyline ahead. Alpine was half an hour away.

3

Ryan turned the Caprice into one of the marked parking spaces in front of a one-story, white-washed stone building. He switched off the headlights and engine and stepped out of the car. In front of him, above a large steamed-over window, twisted glass tubing spelled out CORNER CAFE in humming, ruby-red neon.

He looked up and down Alpine's grey, early-morning main street. Empty now, unlike the last morning he had been here two years ago. It had been fall roundup time then, when area ranchers pooled resources and worked cattle one ranch at a time – marking, branding, separating and shipping cattle. There were no empty parking spaces in front of the Corner Cafe that morning. Both sides of the street were jammed with pickup trucks and horse trailers.

Ryan glanced up at the humming red sign again, shivered from the morning's freshness, reached back into the car and pulled his brown suit coat from the front seat. It was wrinkled but probably looked better than his shirt. He slammed the car door and slipped into the coat as he stepped onto the sidewalk.

He had eaten his last real American breakfast here with Frank the morning after Rose's funeral. Inside, the cafe was larger than he remembered but still furnished with lime-green Formica-top tables and matching plastic-covered chairs. Large wooden booths lined the front and back walls. Across the room, a long counter with backless stools cordoned off the kitchen area. The cooking smells were tantalizing: bacon, sausage, eggs, gravy, biscuits and coffee.

A thin, red-haired waitress in a blue polka-dot bibbed apron looked vaguely familiar. A man in a grey delivery uniform was seated at the counter in front of her. Two elderly men in dark suits and ties occupied a booth near the front window. Ryan walked toward the row of empty counter stools, greeting the elderly men as he passed and nodding toward the delivery-man. The waitress met him with a pot of coffee, a thick white cup and a mumbled good morning. Ryan returned her greeting and asked if Frank had been in.

"Not yet." She turned to glance up at a large smoke-stained electric clock behind her. "But he'll be here any minute. You want to wait for him?"

Ryan said he would wait. As the waitress poured his coffee, he looked around the room again. Only three other customers, a far cry from the boisterous crowd of booted, rough-clothed men in dirty wide-brimmed hats who crowded the cafe during his last visit. Frank had known every one of them. In fact, Frank knew almost everyone in and everything about the Texas Big Bend country.

Six years ago, he had transferred in from Arizona to open the new customs office in Alpine. Frank and a handful of agents had then proceeded to stop the burro pack trains that for decades had moved tons of marijuana across the Rio Grande and up the narrow, winding canyons of the Texas Big Bend country.

Frank and his men had also put themselves out of business. Airplanes, filling the void left by captured burro trains, began flying the contraband into the U.S. Arrests and seizures in the Big Bend area dwindled, eventually drying up altogether, and the Alpine Customs Office was closed.

"Where are all the cowboys this morning?" Ryan asked the waitress. "It's about spring roundup time again, isn't it?"

"Oh...." She pulled the coffee pot away from his cup and appeared thoughtful. "They're working the Nine Points place by now, I think, or maybe Benson's down by Terlingua. They won't be up here for another week." She nodded, reassuring herself. "About another week," she repeated, and carried the coffee pot back to the warmer.

Ryan heard the door open and close behind him, then Frank's voice. "Good morning, Judge, Mr. Morris." Ryan swiveled the stool around and faced him. Frank didn't miss a beat. "Good morning, stranger. I wondered who had strayed this far off the beaten track in a rent car."

Ryan stood up. They shook hands and hugged – a big *abrazo*. Frank stepped back and looked at him. "Damn, that was fast! Didn't I just talk to you yesterday?"

"It might have been. All I'm sure of is that I was on a plane less than an hour after we hung up." Ryan made a downward motion with his hands. "And this is all I brought with me."

Frank frowned. "Just as well, probably got nothing but big city clothes now anyhow." Frank hugged him again. "Good to see you, partner."

Frank was a stout, compact man, not as tall as Ryan – almost a head shorter – and some twelve years older.

Ryan had known him long enough to remember reddish-blonde hair where gray now showed beneath the wide brim of his tightly woven straw hat. He would be fifty-four or fifty-five now, retired for almost a year.

He had opted for that rather than relocate when the office was closed. He and Joan had taken over her father's small propane-gas business.

"You boys ready for breakfast?" the waitress asked, slamming another cup down on the counter.

"You remember Ryan, don't you, Melba?" Frank turned to face her.

"Looks familiar. Been a while, hasn't it?"

"A little while," Ryan replied. He cut short further conversation by ordering eggs over easy, sausage, biscuits, and gravy. He hoped they would come soon.

"The usual. please, ma'am." Frank pulled a folded piece of paper from the pocket of his white western-cut shirt and tossed it on the counter as he sat down. "That's what was on the answering machine."

Ryan unfolded the paper. It was less than half a page of double-spaced typing:

Don't you folks ever stay home? I'm needing some help. I'll spring for supper tonight at Mingo's and maybe breakfast in the morning if you put me up for the night.

Ryan read it again and looked over at Frank. "No time on this?" He folded the paper and gave it back.

"Monday morning, sometime between seven and noon. Joan left the house at seven, and we met back there at noon." He put the message back in his shirt pocket.

"His car was found Thursday afternoon." Ryan made it a statement instead of a question.

Frank nodded. "Highway patrolman found it. Terrell County deputy called me. Joan and I drove right over, got there just as the tow truck was taking the car. The park is an old run-down, two-table affair. We looked around. I climbed the fence, made a circle... nothing. I went back the next morning with two helicopters and four Border Patrol trackers. Still nothing – not a scratch on the ground made by a human being. If Grady was ever in that park, he left on the blacktop, either on foot or in another car." Frank sipped his coffee.

Ryan raised his own cup and drank. He had visualized the search as Frank talked. Like Grady, Frank had started out in the Border Patrol. He was a good tracker. The border patrolmen he recruited to help were experts, or Frank would never have allowed them into the search area. If both they and Frank had come up empty, then there were no clues to be found at the roadside park. Grady's car was all they had.

"Where's the car now?"

Frank nodded satisfaction with the question. "Behind the Sheriff's Office in Sanderson. We're going over to look at it soon as we finish breakfast." He took another quick sip from his cup and stood up. "I'll make the call."

"You've already looked at it, haven't you?" The question was out before Ryan could stop it.

Frank again nodded his head and walked down the row of stools, said hello and slapped the shoulder of the man in grey as he passed behind him.

Ryan felt foolish. He had been working with strangers too long. Of course Frank had looked at the car. They had always done independent searches on suspect vehicles. Grady had insisted on it, and it always paid off. Either contraband was found that had been missed by others, or you slept better that night knowing nothing had slipped by.

Ryan sipped his coffee and took out the Texas road map. Sanderson was in Terrell County, a large county with only two towns, small ones – Sanderson and Dryden. What kind of a sheriff's office would a county like that have? Sanderson was an eighty-five-mile drive, one way.

He heard the restaurant door open and close behind him, but didn't look up. Out of the corner of his eye, he caught the silhouette of the delivery-man lowering his coffee cup, straightening and squaring his shoulders.

"May I have some change, please?" The voice was soft, feminine. Ryan looked up toward the cash register on his left. The soft voice belonged to a tall, dark woman in Levi's – tight Levi's – and a faded, long-sleeved blue denim work shirt. She handed Melba a bill and looked past him, over his head, around the restaurant. Her hair was black and straight, and hung loosely behind her shoulders. She was very dark with large almond-shaped eyes and dense arching eyebrows. *La Morena*, the Mexicans would call her – the dark one. Ryan stared hard at her.

She was beautiful. The woman turned her attention to the change being counted into her hand, smiled and thanked Melba, then turned away.

Ryan swiveled his stool around and watched her long stride take her quickly to several newspaper dispensers just inside the door. After depositing coins and extracting one paper, she moved to another dispenser.

The actual length of her hair was hidden behind a black, flat-brimmed hat suspended down her back by a long leather thong. Ryan wondered just how long her hair was. The inside thighs and seat of her new Levi's were stained with white, chalk-like marks left by dried horse sweat. Evidently she had been riding bareback, yesterday or perhaps last night. After withdrawing the second newspaper, she stepped to the door, pulled it open and walked out.

Ryan sat for a moment, staring at the door, then got up and hurried toward it. It was now full daylight as he stepped outside. The engine of a new turquoise-and-white Ford pickup was cranking up. As the truck pulled away from the curb, he could see the Mexican woman, *La Morena*, behind the wheel. She was alone, driving away without once looking in his direction. He watched the pickup until it turned left at the traffic light three blocks away, stared at the empty street for a moment, then turned and went back inside.

Frank was still on the pay phone at the back of the dining room.

Melba and the delivery-man were staring at him. The two old men were smiling.

Ryan ignored all of them and went to the newspaper dispensers that the Mexican woman had taken papers from: the *San Angelo Standard-Times* and the *El Paso Times*. Just below the mastheads of both newspapers, bold headlines announced that a U.S. Customs radar blimp had drifted into Mexico.

Ryan leaned closer to the plastic shield over the *El Paso Times*. “High winds snapped the cable of a Laredo-based radar balloon… found late Thursday near Sabinas Hidalgo, Nuevo Leon, Mexico.” Ryan moved to the other dispenser. Aerostat, the San Angelo paper called the balloon. “Larger than a Boeing 707 jetliner… anchored 15,000 feet above ground by insulated cable, equipped with 3,500 pounds of radar gear… 30-foot antenna… giving 182 miles of radar coverage in all directions… costing $18 million each.”

Ryan was tempted to buy the paper to also get updated on Bobby Kennedy’s campaign for the Democratic presidential nomination and the worldwide manhunt for James Earl Ray, the man accused of shooting Martin Luther King Jr. But for now all that concerned him was whatever had happened to Grady. He straightened up and walked back to the counter, wishing Melba would bring breakfast and wondering why such a beautiful woman would be interested in a runaway radar blimp.

4

Eastward from Alpine, the country sloped slowly downward for some fifteen miles, then rose again as State Highway 90 swung southward toward a narrow gap between two mountain ranges. Fifty-odd miles on the other side of the pass was Sanderson.

"The Glass Mountains," Frank pointed out, nodding toward the mountains ahead on the left. "Part of some ancient formation – a reef, I think, that surfaces again in the Guadalupes over by New Mexico."

Ryan glanced at the low mountains and nodded. He was usually interested in such things but was now feeling the two nights without sleep and the discomfort of Frank's new GMC pickup. It was wide with plenty of head and leg room but had been equipped with heavy duty springs for hauling large propane gas tanks that Frank now sold, delivered and installed. Without a load, his new pickup was a rough rider.

Frank had been telling him about Grady's pickup, the one still sitting in the driveway in Balmorhea. Ryan couldn't help wondering if it too was a rough rider. Maybe that was the reason Grady had taken his late wife's more comfy four-year-old LTD. Maybe he had planned a trip farther than the sixty-four miles between Balmorhea and Alpine.

"He still ropes all the time." Frank was off geology and back on Grady. "Hauls that old mare of his around to weekend affairs. In horse years, she's older than he is." Frank glanced over at Ryan. "They do all right, though, even on the fast little Mexican steers." Frank looked back at the road.

Ryan shifted on the red vinyl seat. Roping was more common ground for the three of them.

Frank used to say the only reason Grady had hired either of them was to be sure of a partner in the team roping events. Not entirely true. He had first met Grady and Frank at the weekend calf ropings in Sahuarita, just south of Tucson, but it wasn't until he became a deputy sheriff and began relaying information on marijuana- and heroin-smuggling operations that they had approached him about taking the Treasury Agent's exam. Ryan smiled to himself. No, it wasn't his roping expertise they had been after; it was his sources of information.

"Grady's still a good roper, still a damn good heeler," Frank said. "Del Norte Mountains back there on the right."

They were through the high pass and headed downhill again. Ryan didn't look back. He had found a tolerable niche next to the door and closed his eyes.

"Marathon." Frank's voice sounded distant. "You want to stop for anything?"

"No! Let's go on," Ryan said, opening his eyes. They passed several houses, a laundromat and a service station. Those made him wonder if there was gasoline in the tank of Grady's abandoned car. He didn't bother to ask. Frank wouldn't tell him; he would have to see for himself.

They passed a Dairy Queen, two more service stations and an old drive-in movie, and they were out of town. Grady would never have passed three service stations and run out of gas fifty miles later.

If the car was out of gas, someone else had driven it to the roadside park. He almost said as much but stopped himself. Frank had told him about Grady's friends, his good health, his traveling, his old pickup, his new pickup, his horse, his having no women in his life – but nothing about the car.

"I'm not talking about the car," he had repeated more than once. "You're going to look at it just like I did, just like the chief deputy did and just like the DPS team from Austin." Frank nodded his head in determination each time. "Then you're going to tell me about the car."

Ryan slumped farther down in the seat, leaned back and again closed his eyes. He would look at the car, but he was tired – in no shape to be looking for clues. He was glad Frank and the others had already gone over the car and found whatever there was to find. They would talk about it on the way back, make up and dissect scenarios. He folded his arms across his chest and let his head tilt forward, away from the vibrating backrest. He had slept only two hours on the flight out of Madrid – maybe. That was Friday night. Now it was Saturday morning here, afternoon or evening in Madrid. Two days and a night with two hours of sleep.

He straightened in the seat, leaned forward, flipped the visor down and settled back. The morning sun still streamed in, sapping strength wherever it touched him. He closed his eyes again and thought about a warm bath and clean clothes. New clothes, he would need something appropriate – boots, Levi's and a hat.

A hat. He thought about the black hat suspended down the back of the beautiful Mexican woman, covering her long black hair. He thought about her scuffed black boots with red stitching and deeply scalloped tops, and her new horse-sweat-marked Levi's.

Frank would probably know who she was. He cleared his throat and asked if he had noticed her in the cafe.

"Woman?" Frank sounded surprised.

"A tall Mexican woman, about thirty, in work clothes – Levi's and boots. She came in the cafe and bought some newspapers while you were on the phone."

"Didn't see her." After a moment he asked why.

Ryan explained about the runaway-blimp story on the front pages of the papers she had bought. Frank made no comment. Ryan waited, not sure if Frank was thinking about what he had said or waiting for more information.

"So what's the story on the blimps?" Ryan finally asked. "Are they finally up?"

"All three of them," Frank answered. "At El Paso, Marfa and Laredo, loaded down with sophisticated electronic stuff, not just radar. They got a lot of press and TV coverage. Sealed the border against air smuggling, plugged all the holes in existing military radar networks – that sort of thing."

Frank was quiet for a moment, then added, "I haven't heard of them catching anything yet." He shook his head. "They cost Customs a mint."

Ryan closed his eyes again. Maybe the Mexican woman bought the newspapers for some other reason. He thought about her avoiding eye contact with him, wondering what he would have said to her if she hadn't. He let his head tilt forward again and dozed until he felt the pickup began to slow.

"What kind of a sheriff's office does Sanderson have?" he asked without opening his eyes.

"Terrell County," Frank corrected, "about six full-time deputies, something like that, but only one on Saturday mornings. Let's go wake him up."

Ryan felt the pickup swerve off the highway and opened his eyes. They were in town, buildings all around, headed down an alley.

He must have really dozed off. Frank pulled up at the rear of a light-colored stucco building, opened the door and, saying he would be right back, stepped out. Ryan watched him walk to a nearby metal door studded with large rivets and push a button. A few moments later, the door opened, and Frank talked to someone inside. The door closed, and Frank came back to the pickup. "Car's over here." Frank motioned as he walked by the pickup.

Ryan got out and followed, glancing back as a hatless, blond young man in a tan uniform came out of the building. Jangling a large ring of keys, he caught up to them. Ryan introduced himself as they followed Frank to a large fenced-in lot with several cars and a wrecked horse trailer inside. The deputy unlocked a heavy iron double gate and pushed one side open.

"It's the blue-and-white one," he said, obviously unaware that Frank had spent the previous afternoon in the lot. The deputy handed him a set of car keys. "I'll be inside," he said, then turned and hurried away, shielding his face from the bright sunlight with his right forearm.

Frank shook his head as he watched the young man return to the studded door. "He's about the age you were when Grady sent me to Tucson to get you."

"Shanghai me, you mean." Ryan smiled.

Frank returned the smile. It was something an angry Pima County sheriff had once accused Frank and Grady of when Ryan resigned his deputy position to join the Customs Service.

Ryan turned, shading his eyes with his left hand, and walked around the LTD. Except for a hubcap missing from the right front wheel, it appeared to be in mint condition – no dents, scratches or rust. A hand-polished wax job glistened beneath a thin layer of fine dark-brown dust. Black powder around the white hood and trunk – grayish white on the blue areas around the door handles – marked the search pattern for fingerprints. Small, clean rectangular spots indicated that the search had been productive and numerous prints had been lifted.

Ryan peered through the driver's window. More white powder and angular clean spots on the blue interior.

Frank unlocked the door and handed him the keys. Ryan leaned inside. The odometer showed just over fifty thousand miles. The immaculate interior was like new. He commented on the car's appearance.

"Rose's car," Frank volunteered. "Bought it new for her when he retired. They used his pickup most of the time, except for long trips."

Ryan squeezed into the driver's seat, slipped the key into the ignition and turned it. The needle on the gas gauge showed empty. Someone besides Grady had driven the car to the roadside park.

He started the engine. There was still gas in the tank. Why hadn't they tried to make it on into town for gas? Ryan wiped the sweat from his forehead; it was like an oven inside the car.

Hurriedly, he checked the other gauges, the lights, brakes and rearview mirror, not sure what he was looking for, knowing some of it might mean something later. He cut the engine and looked around.

Nothing – not a scrap of anything on the floor, in the seat or ashtrays, or over the visors.

DPS boys took it all back to Austin with them," Frank said when Ryan opened the empty glove compartment. "I have Polaroids and a list of everything." Frank had mentioned the DPS team earlier.

To everyone but him and Frank, this had to be no more than an abandoned stolen car, something handled routinely by locals.

If a state forensic team from Austin had been over the car, Frank had stirred things up somehow. "And how'd you do that – DPS out of

Austin?" Ryan asked.

"They owed me, flew in yesterday after I talked to you."

Ryan shook his head. Old markers had been called. He had a feeling they would soon be looking at lab and latent-print reports from Austin. He got out of the hot car and walked around it a second time, then unlocked the trunk. The missing hubcap, covered with black powder and rectangular clean spots, lay to one side of a dusty whitewall tire. A powdered jack and a lug wrench also lay beside it.

Ryan leaned in and pushed on the tire. It was completely flat. He moved his fingers slowly along the tread until he felt something protruding from the rubber. He rotated the tire and saw that it was the splintered end of a large mesquite thorn.

As he felt along the remaining circumference of the tire, his eye caught the gleam of polished brown leather near the back of the left taillight. A pair of boots.

He picked them up as he straightened from the car trunk. The boots appeared to be custom-made and expensive – not new but well cared for and double-soled. Double soles – once the standard footwear for border patrolmen along the Mexican border. Grady had always worn double-soled boots.

Ryan ran his fingers over the frayed leather around a tiny hole in the top of one of the boots, then turned the boot over. There was a matching hole in the opposite side. Ryan frowned and glanced up. Frank nodded grimly and looked away.

Ryan examined the other boot. It was the same, a small puncture through both sides of the soft multi-stitched top. "That's a bullet hole," he announced, aware that Frank already knew that.

He heard himself say it again as his eyes welled up. Through the haze he could see Frank standing with his arms folded, looking out toward the mountains. He couldn't see clearly, but he felt sure Frank was crying too.

♦ ♦ ♦

From the sheriff's office, Frank drove to the highway and turned back toward Alpine. Four miles later, he turned onto an old strip of pavement paralleling the highway and followed it to the top of a hill.

"This is where they found it," Frank pointed out. "You were asleep when we came by before."

They both got out and stood beside the pickup. It was an old park, as Frank had described, and small, with only two concrete tables, stubs of two rock fireplaces and a rusty iron tower with no windmill. The hill was practically barren of vegetation, hard and rocky, but dotted with shallow pockets of fine gravel that would show a footprint if the light were right.

"Years ago, this was a rendezvous point for dope deals," Frank said. "Used to be two big cottonwood trees over there when the windmill was working." He pointed at two charred stumps just downhill from the rusty tower. "Los Alamos, it was called. Stuff bought in Ojinaga or Acuña was delivered here, well past the Border Patrol check points." He took a deep breath and exhaled, looking slowly around.

"We looked everywhere, both sides of the highway, up and down," he pointed, making sweeping motions. "Walked it out, two miles in every direction. It didn't happen anywhere around here," he said with conviction.

"What didn't happen?" Ryan asked louder than he intended. "Bullet holes through the tops of an empty pair of boots is a little confusing to me."

"I know." Frank's voice was soft. "The lab boys found them under the flat tire." He shook his head. "I thought they took them with the rest of the stuff." He was repeating himself. He had said the same thing as he carried Grady's boots from the car to the sheriff's office and again as he bagged them in a clear plastic evidence bag. They had left the boots with the deputy, along with a note requesting that the sheriff send them on to the DPS lab in Austin.

Frank took another deep breath and exhaled. "I don't know. I've thought about it and thought about it. It's pretty damn bizarre. I just don't know." He shook his head straightened, and focused on Ryan. "Let's get out of here."

They got back into the GMC. "All right, now talk to me," Frank said as he followed the side road downhill toward the highway.

Now they could talk about the car. Ryan started. “It’s only sixty-four miles from Grady’s house to yours; he uses his pickup most of the time, so why did he take the car?” Ryan went on. “Just because he wanted to? Because his new pickup was running bad? Or, you said he used the car for long trips; maybe he was going on to San Antonio or someplace else.”

“Go on,” Frank urged.

“Then why spend the night at your house, only an hour into the trip? Maybe he was on his way back from somewhere when he called and planned to spend the night with you before driving on to Balmorhea.”

“He called from his house, partner.” Frank nodded, looking at him and raising his eyebrows.

“The Border Patrol checked with the phone company for me.”

Ryan was quiet for a moment. That cut it down some. “So something happened to him between here and Balmorhea.”

Frank shook his head in agreement.

Ryan thought about the car for a moment, still their only source of leads. “Grady has obviously taken excellent care of that car – Rose’s car. Now it’s covered with dust and has a mesquite thorn in the tire. It’s been on a back road and probably through the brush. Why would Grady do that to a car he thinks so much of? If he had planned a back country trip, he would have taken the pickup, not Rose’s car.” He watched for Frank’s reaction.

Frank looked straight ahead, nodding his head slowly. “Joan and I checked side roads between here and Alpine yesterday until it got dark on us. The Border Patrol is doing the same thing today, between Marathon and the border.”

Ryan waited for him to continue. “You feel like working this highway some more?” Frank gave him an appraising look.

Ryan straightened. “Sure.” He glanced self-consciously down at his wrinkled white shirt and dusty brown trousers. He must look like hell, probably not smelling so good either. He ran a hand through his mussed hair. Frank would be laughing and teasing him about his clothes and appearance now if they weren’t involved in such an unpleasant task.

Frank looked back at the road ahead and said, "I've got Polaroid shots of the tire treads."

Ryan was quiet, thinking. There would be hundreds of side roads along the lengthy route between Sanderson and Balmorhea. He picked up his crumpled suit coat and took out the highway map.

Frank glanced at him again. "We've got a ways to go. Tell me something else."

Ryan leaned back as he unfolded the map. "I don't think Grady changed the flat tire or drove the car to the park."

Frank didn't seem surprised. Ryan hadn't expected him to. "The front seat was adjusted for someone with short legs, certainly not Grady.

"The gas tank is showing empty, also not Grady."

"Uh-huh." Frank nodded in agreement.

"The flat tire." Ryan noticed Frank lean slightly toward him, interested in this one. Ryan described the two cans he had noticed in the car trunk. "Compressed air and tire sealant. It was only a thorn in the tire. One can of that stuff would have aired up the tire and sealed the leak. That's what Grady would have done. Whoever changed the tire didn't know about the cans."

Frank nodded again, giving no indication whether he had noticed the cans of compressed air or not.

Ryan continued. "I don't think the car was driven very far after it picked up the thorn. The end of it was still sticking out between the treads."

"Wasn't driven at all," Frank said. "Wherever the car ran over the mesquite limb, it stayed there long enough for the tire to go flat. Then someone took the tire off and tossed it into the trunk on top of Grady's boots." Frank's jaw muscles tightened; he took a deep breath and exhaled. "We need to find where that happened."

So far, neither of them had mentioned the unmentionable. They had talked as if Grady was going to show up unharmed, be found wandering along some highway or in some strange city with no idea of how he got there.

Ryan decided to leave it that way. He looked down at the map. "A hundred and forty-nine miles of highway between Balmorhea and

Sanderson," he said. "A lot of side roads, maybe heavy traffic over some of them."

"Maybe none over the one we're looking for," Frank said defensively, then conceded it was a long shot. "But it's all we have," he added.

A car covered in brown dust and a big mesquite thorn weren't much to go on.

Ryan looked ahead at the jagged mountaintops, then out the side window at the grey desert scrub flashing by. Something that would lead them to Grady might be behind any scraggly cat-claw bush, in the mountains ahead or sixty miles on the other side. The chances of finding it were less than slim, but not looking for it was unthinkable.

Frank interrupted his thoughts. "That gate on the right," he pointed. "That's the last one Joan and I checked yesterday." He glanced at the large rearview mirror outside his window and slowed the pickup. A quarter mile farther up the road, he turned across the highway into two ruts that led across the bar ditch to an aluminum stock gate. It was locked on both ends with thick rusty chains and several intertwined padlocks. Without getting out of the truck, they could see that no traffic had passed through it for quite some time.

"A lot of mesquite around here," Frank observed, looking across the flat brush-land. "None of it very big, though." He backed out onto the highway and drove on. The next side road was on the right, behind a cattle guard, well-traveled and dusty, but the dust was grey, not brown.

They returned to the highway and drove on toward Alpine, checking and exploring side roads until they reached Marathon just after noon. At the Dairy Queen, they ordered burgers and fries.

"What's this number?" Ryan asked as he looked over the list of items taken from Grady's car.

He passed it across the table to Frank. "There, under the notebook heading."

Frank leaned back, focusing on the paper. "It's a number from Grady's pocket notebook we found over the visor. It was on the last page all by itself. DPS thinks it's a trailer license number, a farm or ranch trailer. If it is, it's five or six years old and they're having problems checking it. Texas farm and ranch trailers don't have to be registered if they're used only to haul the owner's stock or produce." Frank handed the list back to Ryan. "Might be something."

When they finished eating, Frank bought a small foam ice chest at the Shamrock station and filled it with soft drinks and ice. By five that afternoon, all the drinks were gone. By seven, they were drinking the melted ice. When darkness finally came, they were still ten miles from Alpine.

They would start again at first light, split up, utilize the rented Caprice and cover twice the area they had today. Tomorrow the tire tracks and other signs they were looking for would be six days old.

5

The sheet and pillow case had a strange but not unpleasant smell. Ryan rolled over on his back, took a deep breath, and exhaled. The trunk was open and Grady's boots were suspended above it, slowly turning, hanging from an invisible string. The bullet holes were clearly visible. Suddenly there were gunshots, more bullet holes appeared in the boots, and someone shouted. "Time to roll out."

There were more knocks on the bedroom door, then it opened. "Time to get up." It was Frank.

Ryan opened his eyes and glanced toward the un-shaded window. It was still dark outside, almost as dark as the unlighted bedroom. "What time is it?"

"After five. Hurry up!" Frank flipped on the light. "We've got something new." He stepped back into the hallway, pulling the door closed behind him.

"What?" Ryan called after him, but there was no answer. He sat up on the edge of the bed, squinting against the glare of the ceiling light, wondering what Frank was talking about and what had happened to the previous evening.

Frank must have called Joan from the cafe yesterday morning. That would explain why she had not been surprised when he walked into the kitchen behind Frank last night. The savory aroma of homemade chili was the first thing that had greeted him. The bear hug and kiss came seconds later. Joan's Texas-style enchiladas were one of his favorite meals, something he had been looking forward to last night and something he had missed. Ryan thought about it. They had visited for a few minutes, drank a beer, then Frank had showed him to the guest room and bath.

Ryan remembered showering, shaving... how good it had felt to be clean and to lie down on the bed. That was the last thing he remembered – lying down on the bed.

He stood up, went into the small bathroom, washed his face, combed his hair and returned to the bedroom. He had clean socks, underwear and T-shirts, the only clothes of Frank's he could even attempt to wear. The shorts were big in the waist, the T-shirt short, but both were wearable. He put them on, picked up his wrinkled trousers and white shirt. He hated putting them back on, but there was nothing else.

The telephone on the nightstand caught his eye. He should have called the embassy yesterday and let the duty officer know where he was. He finished buttoning his shirt and picked up the phone. Frank was on the line. Ryan replaced the receiver. He wouldn't be missed until tomorrow, Monday, but he needed to call sometime today.

Sitting down on the bed, he pulled on one of the clean socks Frank had tossed at him the previous evening.

Suddenly, the door opened. "You ready?" Frank asked. "We've got a couple of stops to make."

"What about Grady?" Ryan pulled on the other sock and slipped his feet into the now-scuffed and dusty wingtip oxfords.

"Come on," Frank said impatiently. "I'll bring you up to date in the car."

Joan was waiting at the curb behind the wheel of her white, late-model Chrysler New Yorker. The motor was running. "Good morning," she greeted Ryan as he opened the door behind her. In the dim light she looked the same as she had twenty years ago when Frank first introduced them at the Border Patrol Christmas party in Nogales. Her blue eyes still sparkled, and her smile still came easily. "We decided to eat without you last night." She laughed as he closed the door.

"Sorry about that. I barely remember laying down on the bed."

Frank opened the door and slid into the front passenger seat. "He was in the restaurant at Lajitas Monday afternoon." He slammed the door and turned to face Ryan as Joan pulled away from the curb. "Grady was looking for his horse." Frank paused as he tugged on the seat belt.

"Last weekend, somebody stole his old dun mare. That's what he meant when he said he needed help." Still working on the seat belt, he glanced at Joan. "Tell him about the phone call." Ryan leaned forward.

"A customs inspector called from Presidio last night," Joan said. Presidio was the Texas border town Ryan had often heard weathermen announce as the hottest spot in the nation. It was a hundred or so miles south of Balmorhea. Joan slowed to make a left turn. "The inspector is someone Grady worked with years ago."

"Jim Benton, another old Marfa sector border patrolman," Frank interrupted.

"Anyhow..." Joan crossed a highway and entered another residential area, "he said Grady had been there at the port of entry, Monday around noon, putting up a reward poster for his horse." She stopped in front of a large, white, two-story frame house where a yellow porch light was burning. "The inspector had been off for a couple of days and had just heard that Grady was missing." She left the motor running and got out of the car.

"Grady must have left Presidio just after lunch." Frank took over as Joan hurried up the walk to the front door of the big house. "I called the cafe owner in Lajitas last night and found out Grady was there about two or two-thirty, put up a poster, visited a while, then left."

"Where is Lajitas?" Ryan felt inadequate having to ask.

"Ninety-five miles straight south, almost on the river. Nothing between here and there but the old store at Terlingua."

Ryan had never heard of Terlingua either, but if it was the only thing between Alpine and the Rio Grande, he had the feeling he would know all about it before the day was over.

Joan returned and got into the car. "He's not coming." She handed Frank a ring of keys. "He said to take the tags off of everything and leave them on the counter by the cash register and to drop the keys off at the cafe."

Frank nodded. The porch light went out as Joan made a U-turn in front of the house.

"Then we look between here and the border today," Ryan offered as he leaned back against the seat.

"Right, and instead of splitting up, I think we'll stay together in the truck."

Two vehicles would cover more ground. Ryan was about to question the change in plans when Joan spoke up. "I think you should call the sheriff and let them do something." She swung the car onto the main highway toward town.

"Grady doesn't live in this county, and his car wasn't found in this county," Frank said defensively. "And it's Sunday. Brewster County is broke, and the sheriff won't authorize overtime, not even regular time, to look for someone who, as far as he is concerned, was never in his jurisdiction. He made that perfectly clear Thursday night when I told him Grady's car had been found."

It was quiet – very quiet. Joan drove through the green traffic light and on down the dark, deserted main street of Alpine. She sighed and shook her head. "Frank, what are you up to?"

"Nothing." Frank shrugged. "Nothing."

It was quiet again for a moment, then Frank spoke in a low, serious tone. "There's a place I want to look at, that's all, a place Grady knows about. He was a border patrolman working this whole area before I got out of high school, before either one of you even started school. He knows this area." He took a deep breath. "And... there's a place he told me about when I got the Alpine job. I don't know why he would have gone there to look for his horse, but he might have. I want to look there first, that's all. Not up to anything." He shrugged again and raised his eyebrows. "You can come with us if you want to."

"No, I have things to do in the office, and you need to make some gas deliveries today or tomorrow." She stopped the car in front of a darkened store a block from the Corner Cafe.

Frank held up the keys Joan had brought back from the big white house and jingled them.

"These are the keys to Steiner Brothers Western Wear." He nodded toward the store. "You can take anything you want and pay for it later." He handed Ryan the ring of keys. "Be sure you get some good walking boots."

6

A footprint that could have been made by Grady's left boot was next to the iron-pipe gate fifty miles south of Alpine. It had, in turn, been stepped on by a smaller, slick-soled boot. Both tracks were several days old.

The gate was locked with a length of heavy chain and a large brass combination lock. Frank held the lock in his left hand, staring at the small digital wheels on the bottom. "New lock," he said.

"I still have a key for the old one." Ryan handed him a ball-peen hammer he had taken from the large tool chest mounted behind the cab of the pickup. Still holding the lock, Frank struck it a light blow with the hammer. Nothing. He tried again, turned it over and struck the other side. "Never been able to do this," he mumbled, handing Ryan the hammer and moving to one side.

Ryan pulled the lock toward him, tightening the chain. No combination lock would have stopped Grady, not even a large expensive one like this. He could open any of them with a fist-sized rock. Ryan struck the side of the lock, and it popped open, undamaged. He unhooked the lock from the chain and swung the gate open. Frank drove through.

Ryan pushed the gate closed, slapping at the dust on the sleeves of his blue denim shirt and the thighs of his Levi's. The new unwashed clothing felt big and stiff. A washing tonight would soften them up and bring them down to size. As he reached for the chain, his eye caught spectacular sunburst patterns in the dust, tracks left by the soles of his new boots. He threaded the lock shackle through the loose chain and glanced over at the other footprints:

Shallow, faint, dust-filled depressions where two people had stepped, four... five... maybe six days ago. If the large track on the bottom was Grady's, Ryan didn't want to think about what they might find farther up the road. He snapped the lock closed and walked to the pickup.

Frank drove slowly away from the gatc. They were headed west, away from State Highway 118 into a wide, flat basin surrounded by jagged peaks. The dirt road was narrow, winding, washboard rough and dry. Traffic had ground the baked surface into a dark brown powder that settled into passing vehicle tracks, obliterating all traces of tread design.

Ryan reached for the Thermos of coffee on the seat between them and felt the two leather pistol cases Frank had tossed onto the truck seat that morning. "Take your pick," he had said.

One of the cases, a black sheepskin, contained a glistening black Army model 1911 .45 semiautomatic pistol. Ryan remembered when Frank had sent it away to have the special black chrome applied. The finish was worn now, almost to bare metal on the right side where Frank's trouser belt had held it, out of sight, under a shirt or jacket for the major part of his law-enforcement career. The black pistol was Frank's.

Ryan zipped the cover back around it and then opened the brown pistol case: Another .45, new or almost new, with an unobtrusive green Parkerized finish.

"Accurized, target barrel, sighted in for six o'clock," Frank had said. "There's a full clip of ammo and a round in the chamber."

Ryan pulled the large Thermos of coffee across the seat toward him. Frank was saying that the ranch they were on belonged to an old smuggler.

"Señor Hilario Naranjo-Gaitan." He glanced at Ryan. "Lalo for short, of course. Old Lalo Naranjo. That's what he's known by around here. Across the river he's Don Naranjo." He turned to the road ahead.

Ryan unscrewed the cup from the Thermos, knowing there was more story on the way.

Frank handed him a large battered plastic mug from the clutter of items bouncing atop the dashboard. "There's a ranch house fifteen miles ahead, at the end of this road. An old house, old barn and so many pens the place looks like a feed lot."

He slowed the truck, braked to a stop and waited, watching the side mirror until the dust passed; then he rolled the window down and peered out at the road. "Dual wheels," he announced. "No wonder we can't find a car track. Trucks have chewed this road to pieces."

The window up, he drove on, quiet for a moment, as if thinking about what he had just said.

"So what's with the heavy traffic?" Ryan asked, then remembered what the waitress had said. "They're working cattle down here someplace. Is that it?" He nudged Frank's arm with the scarred and chipped coffee mug.

"Not here." Frank took the coffee. "Never any cattle on this place, not to be rounded up anyway, not for thirty or forty years." He took a sip from the steaming mug and glanced at the big side mirror outside his window, then back to the road ahead. "I'm going to slow down, keep the dust low until we find out what all the traffic is about."

Ryan gave him a puzzled look.

"The Mexicans call this place *La Pipa*," Frank said. "That's exactly what it was – a pipeline."

Frank sipped at the coffee again, then rested the mug on his leg. "It's the Border Canyon Ranch to everybody on this side of the river. Both names come from a deep, crooked canyon with sides so steep cattle and horses can't climb out of it. Most places, neither can a man." He paused, shaking his head.

Ryan poured his own cup of coffee and listened.

"The canyon is twelve miles long. The old ranch house and pens are on this end of it the Rio Grande on the other." Frank narrowed his eyes. "There's a good crossing there, where it meets the river gorge. A solid rock bottom. Most of the time, the water's only belly deep on a cow. Once a herd was crossed and started up the canyon, one man could handle one or two hundred head. There was no place for them to go but north through *La Pipa* to the pens."

Frank raised the mug off his leg as they bounced across an iron-rail cattle guard. "The family that owned this place originally, the Talberts, made a bundle during Prohibition, letting Mexican booze smugglers use the canyon. Then during World War II, they became millionaires smuggling cattle. Thousands of head came up through the border canyon. Nobody cared much." Frank made a face. "The Army needed beef, and people around here got all the meat they wanted without ration stamps."

The road turned rocky, sloping upward toward a long, slow rising ridge a mile ahead. Frank speeded up and again checked the long side mirror outside his window.

Ryan looked back. The harder ground had thinned the rising dust to a barely discernible haze. A ribbon of dark-brown powder had settled along the lower edge of the rear window.

Ryan stared at it. The dust was the right color. They had both noticed that at the locked gate. He turned to face the road ahead and sipped his coffee. They just might find... something they really didn't want to find. Then what? Notify the sheriff. And what kind of sheriff's office did Brewster County have? One strapped for funds, according to Frank. That translated to undermanned and undertrained. Better if a Texas Ranger and the DPS lab were on the scene first, if that were possible. It would be Frank's call. He knew the players and would know how to handle them.

As they reached the top of the ridge and started down the other side, Frank was telling him about the death of the Talbert family patriarch and how the widow had moved to Dallas to live near a son and daughter.

"She died a year later, and the kids sold out to Naranjo. Lots of talk about that," Frank added in a low voice. "Even today, forty years later, any time the ranch is mentioned, you still hear about the Talbert kids selling out to a Mexican criminal who can't even set foot on this side of the river."

They were at the bottom of the slope and back on the brown earth plain. Frank slowed, checking the dust cloud again. "When Grady worked this area as a border patrolman, Lalo Naranjo was running stolen cattle south into Mexico and marijuana north through this place."

Ryan was watching the road ahead, but he could see Frank glance in his direction.

"Grady told me all about Lalo and his *La Pipa* ranch when I took the Alpine job." Frank paused a moment, thinking, then shook his head. "I don't know why he would have come here on his own. His old mare wouldn't be worth all the trouble to send her down the pipeline to Mexico. I just know that he would have driven past the gate on the way up from Lajitas."

"Good enough," Ryan remarked and finished the coffee in his cup.

The dust was the right color, and the old boot print was the right size. That was more, much more than they'd had last night. Frank slowed for a cattle guard made of large pipes spaced too far apart. It made for a rough and noisy crossing.

"When I got here, Lalo had a ton of marijuana a week coming out of this place," Frank recalled. "Crossed it on burros, twenty, sometimes thirty to a train. From the ranch he trucked it on to Chicago." Frank grinned. "They were sitting ducks once they entered that canyon. We would put a horseback team in behind them and just wait at the ranch for the pipeline to deliver them. We got five loads before they switched canyons. It turned into a real game then, sometimes took us a month to find them when they changed canyons."

Frank was smiling, the first time Ryan had seen him really smile since his arrival. "We finally ran them out of burros." Frank laughed. "Lalo was shipping them in by train from all over Chihuahua." Frank's laughter faded, and it became quiet.

Ryan waited. He had heard most of that before, but he had gone on foreign assignment before Frank retired, and they hadn't talked much when he came back for Rose's funeral.

"Did you ever get him?" Ryan asked.

Frank was still smiling. "Lalo? No, he never comes to this side, not that anyone knows about. There are federal warrants out for him dating back to the Twenties – FBI, immigration, customs. Four new indictments for narcotics smuggling while I was chasing him. Nope, never got him," he said wistfully. "They closed the office and I retired." He shrugged. "The burro trains had disappeared by then, and Lalo had switched to airplanes. All we did was force him into the 20th century."

Juniper and mesquite brush, heavy with brown dust, had become thick on both sides of the road. Frank slowed the pickup. "We're going down into a dry creek bed just this side of the ridge." He pointed ahead. "Watch close on your side."

The truck nosed down and slowly approached the dry creek. They both saw the vehicle tracks, or what was left of them, at the same time. Ridges of ground-up earth bordering the road had been flattened. In the creek bed, morning sunlight reflected from gravel and rock pressed flat by vehicle tires.

Frank turned the pickup off the road. Rocks tossed up by the deep tread of the pickup's new tires thumped and clanged against the undercarriage as Frank followed the seemingly glowing vehicle trail up the creek bed. "I know where this track is going," he said through clenched teeth as he maneuvered around a sharp bend and plowed down a stand of already-bent cottonwood saplings.

Ryan's voice was low. "We haven't talked about what we're really looking for."

Frank was quick to respond, almost snapping, "Let's don't. We know what it's going to be. Let's just look"

They were on the trail now, getting close. Ryan could feel it. So could Frank. Not excitement this time, not the exhilarating feeling that came near the end of a successful chase... but dread – sickening, painful dread.

Ryan lowered the window and watched the right bank for signs. For almost a mile he wondered about Frank's remark that he knew where the tracks were going. Finally he broke the silence and asked.

"Right here," Frank replied, swerving left up the low embankment and stopping as soon as the pickup was clear of the creek. In front of them a long, low, flat-top mountain lay just beyond the grove of large mesquite trees they had stopped in.

Ryan was staring at the big mesquites. This was the place where Grady's tire had gone flat.

Frank opened his door and stepped out. "The ranch house is on the other side," he said, looking toward the butte. "There's a game trail going up the slope and around this end."

He pointed to the high cliffs on the south end of the butte. "From there, you can look down on the whole outfit, see everything, and nobody can see you."

He turned his attention to the pressed gravel and earth a short distance away. "Came out of the creek back there," he pointed, "and went straight into the trees." His voice broke. He cleared his throat, swallowed and reached back into the truck for the pistol cases.

He tossed the brown one to Ryan, unzipped the other, took out the black .45 and tossed the empty sheepskin back onto the seat. "Let's take a look." He shoved the .45 into the waistband of his Levi's, positioning it just back of his left hip as he walked into the grove toward the butte.

Ryan followed, slipping the other pistol into his waistband in the same cross-draw position Frank used. The treadless depressions led them to the far edge of the grove. Dead leaves, twigs, yellow mesquite beans and sparse dry grass covered the ground where the trail ended.

They circled in opposite directions, eyeing the area carefully under every possible light condition. It was too neat. The mat of dead leaves should show something – an impression of the jack base, the flat tire, a knee print... something. Even the hard, rocky creek bed had revealed enough to get them this far.

Ryan widened the circle southward, going deeper into the grove, and found a severed broom-sized willow branch. He picked it up and walked back to Frank. "Swept!" he said, tossing the branch aside.

Frank was standing in the center of the area they had circled. He nodded agreement and took a step forward. There was a strange look on his face. "Hold out your hand."

Ryan put his hand out, palm up. Frank dropped a small heavy object into it. "Something they missed," he said dryly. "So did we."

Ryan looked down at the steel lug nut. Neither of them had noticed it missing from the right front wheel of the Ford LTD, but they both knew that's exactly where it had come from.

7

The butte rose a hundred feet above the slope of rubble that had once been part of the ancient, mottled-brown volcano core. Ryan leaned against the base of its sheer east wall, breathing hard, looking south along the trail waiting for Frank's signal. He pulled the wide brim of his Stetson straw hat lower and glanced down at the jumbled slope of boulders now between him and the distant mesquite grove. It had been a steep quarter-mile climb, and he was feeling it. In Madrid, he was a regular on the embassy's roof-top track, made most of the grueling three-night-a-week workouts for the tough Civil Guard patrol officers at the National Police training center and bicycled frequently with two Scotland Yard attachés from the nearby British Embassy. But none of it was mountain climbing, and the search for missing radar tubes had kept him away from home port the better part of the last six months.

He took a deep breath, eased himself down on a nearby boulder, straightened his legs, and flexed his toes. The new boots were tight across the instep. Reddish brown, oil-tanned pull-ons. They would stretch, as the hat had done. Warmed by the sun, its fibers had softened, and it now clung comfortably to his head.

He studied the grove below. Fifty yards by one hundred at least, and they hadn't missed an inch of it. Nothing there.

His eyes moved past the grove. They had worked back to the road on foot and found two round-toed shoe or boot prints in the creek bed, pointed toward the grove, too small to be Grady's but probably the right age. Nothing else. Not another human sign in the grove, around it or on the trail coming up to the butte. He caught a movement out of the corner of his eye and looked up. Frank was motioning for him.

Ryan stood up and moved quietly along the base of the butte, joining Frank at the south end, and together they rounded the corner. Crouching, following the sheer walls to the west side of the slope, Frank led him to a low breastwork of boulders in front of a shallow depression in the west wall.

Below, past the stacked rocks, Ryan could see the ranch. It was a half mile away, on the near edge of a long, narrow, almost treeless valley of tall grass. Frank handed him the binoculars. The house was old, as Frank had said, a large adobe, with cracked and peeling concrete stucco, a rusted metal roof and a large front porch. It was surrounded by four huge cottonwood trees. On the far side of the house, a windmill churned in the light breeze.

No vehicles or people were in sight.

North of the house, about fifty yards, stood the barn. Old and large, single-story with grey walls of peeled upright cedar logs. Several sheets of new metal glistened from the otherwise rust-streaked roof. On the near side of the barn, another spinning windmill, corrals and horses. The nearest corral was full of horses. Ryan stared at them for a moment, then lowered the glasses and looked at Frank.

"I don't know what they're doing here," Frank said, "but Grady must have known about them."

Yes, Ryan thought as he looked back through the glasses, if Grady had found out there were horses here in the old smuggling pens, or even thought there might be, he would have come looking for his stolen mare. "He was down there," Ryan said aloud.

"Yes," Frank replied.

"There's three or four duns in the bunch." Ryan panned back and forth over the horses. "His mare branded?"

"Freeze brand, small white flying M on the right foreleg. You want to take a look?" Ryan thought about it, watched the horses a moment longer and looked carefully around the barn, then back at the house. "I don't think anybody's down there." He panned up the empty road leading to the ranch, then back to the house, lowered the glasses and looked at Frank. "Let's wait. I want somebody to talk to."

Frank nodded and gave him a look of approval. "So do I," he said in a low voice, then shook his head. "I can't figure what the horses are doing here," he repeated. "They're just grade horses, not worth more than slaughter price on either side of the border."

Ryan raised the binoculars again and pointed them toward the barn. Frank would know about that. He would know about the price of horses, beef, sheep, wool, goats, mohair, new trucks and used trailers; the cost of feed; and everything hashed over at the cafe, service station or the outlying ranches when he delivered propane. The horses in the corral looked to be in good shape, but as Frank had observed, none of them would win any prizes. Beyond the barn and the horses were the empty pens Frank had said made the place look like a feed lot. He was right. The maze of pens ran almost the width of the narrow valley. They were old and made of native unpeeled cedar poles jammed horizontally between pairs of upright posts to form a thick, dam-like wall. Labor-intensive, but popular along the Mexican border where material was free and labor cheap. Ryan had seen such corrals all his life.

He moved the glasses down, back to the horses, and counted heads. "About twenty," he said.

Passing the binoculars to Frank, he crept back toward the smooth lava wall, brushed gravel aside and sat down from his squatting position. He took off his hat, leaned back, put his head against the cool rock cliff, took a deep breath and closed his eyes. A moment later, he heard Frank step over beside him, clear gravel and rocks out of the way and sit down.

"They don't look like Mexican horses," Frank commented. "They're not Mexican horses," Ryan volunteered, eyes closed, head resting against the cliff. "Too fat."

Frank exhaled loudly. "I just don't know what's going on here."

Ryan made no comment. His eyes were closed, and he was relaxed, not sleepy and tired as he had been yesterday, just relaxed. He and Frank had waited like this before, many times. It had never crossed his mind that they would ever be doing it again. He shifted his shoulders into a more comfortable position.

It was relatively cool on the shaded earth next to the huge solid core of night-cooled lava rock. The clean scent of wild grasses and the distant tolling of the pumping windmills drifted up the slope on a light breeze. If it weren't for its unpleasant purpose, he would be enjoying this surprise visit to a past life.

Ryan cracked an eyelid and looked over at Frank. He was stretched out on the rough ground, arms folded across his chest, a flat rock for a pillow and his hat over his face.

Beyond the wall of rocks in front of the grotto, he could see the jagged, haze-grey mountains to the west, like the ones forming the San Rafael Valley east of Nogales. He could almost imagine that they were there now, and that later they would drive back over the Washington Camp Mountains to Nogales.

He would pick up Nancy, and the two of them would meet Frank and Joan, Grady and Rose, and head across the border for enchiladas, margaritas and iced buckets of Bohemia and Carta Blanca. He could almost imagine that, but not quite. Nancy belonged to someone else now.

The sound of an approaching vehicle came suddenly, then faded just as quickly. Frank immediately sat up and moved to the rock barricade. Ryan crept up beside him. A pickup truck, coming fast, topped a rise about a mile away from the ranch, and the sound of its engine reached them again.

Frank had the binoculars on it. “Driver and one passenger,” he said as the truck swerved north ahead of its dust cloud and followed the road along a low ridge. Ryan could see the pickup was a late model, light tan over dark brown. Too far away to tell the make. “No one in the back,” Frank said.

The truck made a final turn toward them and clanked across a cattle guard and down the side of the ridge. As it skidded to a stop in front of the house, Ryan decided it was a Chevrolet or a GMC.

A small, thin man got out of the pickup and, without closing the door, bounded up onto the porch and out of sight. It was only a brief, distant glimpse with the naked eye, but something about the figure stirred Ryan’s memory – the angle of his hat, the way he moved, something.

“My God,” Frank said quietly, almost to himself. “Goddamn it, I should have known... I should have known.” He thrust the binoculars toward Ryan. “Here, take a look. See anybody you know?”

Ryan took the glasses and aimed them at the front of the porch. "He's still inside," he said, looking toward the pickup, then back to the porch. "Who is it?"

"Someone who was looking for you a couple of weeks ago."

Ryan moved the binoculars away from his eyes and stared at Frank. "Looking for me?" Slowly, he raised the glasses back to his eyes just as the little man appeared. Ryan watched him, standing on the porch, arms folded, head cocked to one side in a strange, familiar way, staring at the pickup as if talking to someone. It hit him like an electric shock.

"Joe," Ryan said aloud. "*Guero* Joe Montez." He let the binoculars down and stared at Frank. He felt his jaw go slack and his mouth open. He shook his head in disbelief.

"Come on," Frank said. "Let's go find out what the hell happened to Grady."

8

Ryan and Frank crept away from the rock cover to the other side of the mountain and retraced their path north along the base of the butte. They were moving fast.

The image in the binoculars would not leave Ryan's mind, nor the question that had immediately formed there: What did blonde, blue-eyed "*Guero*" Joe Montez, the best, most prolific informant he'd ever had, have to do with Grady's disappearance? He hadn't thought of Joe for a long time, or anything else that might remind him of the border and Nancy.

Joe had come to Alpine to work for Frank five years ago when Ryan was temporarily detailed to the Treasury Law Enforcement Training Center in Washington, D.C..

Frank went past the trail leading down to the mesquite grove and continued on along the cliff wall. Ryan followed, ducking an overhang of rock and a spike-studded ocotillo limb.

It was the year-long D.C. assignment that had cost him Nancy. The thought was still unpleasant, but for the first time it failed to generate the hollow ache that usually followed the slightest thought of her. That both surprised and pleased him.

At the north end of the butte, the trail nosed down the east side of the long jumbled slope at just enough of an angle to keep them below the skyline from the ranch. Near the bottom Frank stopped, removed his hat, and peered over the ridge. Ryan, a few feet behind, waited a moment and did the same.

The barn was less than a hundred yards away. The tan-over-brown pickup, no longer in front of the house, was now parked before them, near the east end of the barn. Frank motioned. Ryan followed on down the slope into a shallow arroyo.

Keeping low, they pursued its zigzag course for several uncomfortable minutes before Frank again stopped, removed his hat and cautiously raised his head over the shallow embankment.

After a long look, he squatted lower, leaned back against the gravel arroyo wall and whispered, "Corrals are between us and the barn now." Ryan nodded, waiting.

"We can go straight to them without being seen, then around this way" – Frank made an encompassing motion with his left arm – "and get to the barn and pickup without opening gates or climbing fences."

Ryan nodded, removed his hat and scanned over the embankment. The high, solid walls of the old stacked-post corrals were only thirty yards away. He pulled his hat on and scrambled out of the arroyo. Frank followed.

Reaching the corrals, they moved south along the ancient posts to the end of the enclosure. Ryan peered around the corner. The pickup was a hundred feet away, broadside, front facing toward the corral, between them and the east end of the barn.

Ryan pulled back. "Somebody's in the pickup," he whispered.

Frank peered around the corner. "Damn it! I don't think its Joe.

"It's not... different hat," Ryan whispered. "But he could come back any minute and just drive off."

Frank pulled the .45 from his belt. "Let's don't wait for that to happen."

Ryan drew his pistol. "Let's go."

Pistols at ready, they rounded the corner and sprinted toward the pickup. Nothing inside the truck moved. Almost upon it, Ryan realized they were about to surprise a large cardboard box with a hat lying on top of it. Frank saw it at the same time, and they slowed to a walk.

Ryan looked over at Frank and smiled. Frank grinned back. They moved on up to the pickup.

The tall box on the passenger side of the seat was closed. The hat on top was brown felt, misshapen and slick where dirty hands had tugged on the front of the brim – a work hat. On the floorboard, a duffel bag leaned against the door, surrounded by six empty Lone Star beer cans and a crumpled white Dairy Queen sack. A small gasoline can was in the bed of the pickup, tied behind the driver's side of the cab.

The barn was only a few yards away. Large double doors were propped open with heavy cedar posts. Doors at the far end of the barn were also wide open. No noise or movement came from inside. Ryan and Frank glanced at each other.

"He must be out back with the horses." Ryan said.

Frank nodded agreement.

They shoved their pistols back under their belts and strolled casually around the pickup, through the open doors and into the barn. It was a large, low-walled structure with no loft. Bales of freshly cut coastal Bermuda hay, stacked to the rafters, filled a large portion of the corner on their right. As they walked past the hay, a small door opening toward the corrals on the south side of the barn became visible.

Someone outside cleared his throat. A figure suddenly loomed in the doorway, a small man holding a long hay hook in each hand. At sight of them, he yelled and jumped back through the door. Ryan hurried to the opening and called out "Joe!" as he cleared the door. Across the corral, the little man had already climbed the six-foot-high fence, and was about to drop out of sight on the other side. "*Soy* Ryan!" he yelled

The little blonde man hesitated and looked back. Ryan yelled again, this time in English, "It's me, Ryan."

"*Cuate*?" Joe Montez turned and straightened atop the thick fence. *Cuate*, the Spanish word for twin, an even more affectionate term than *hermano* – brother. Only Joe Montez had ever called him *Cuate*.

"It is you, *Cuate*." The little man smiled and shaded his eyes. "And Mr. Frank." He jumped down from the fence and came toward them, fanning his face with an open hand. "You scare the hell out of me."

"Is anyone else here?" Ryan asked in Spanish.

"No, only me." Joe quickly closed the distance between them and wrapped his arms around Ryan's waist. "Long time, *Cuate*, long time," he said in English. Ryan felt himself squeezed several times.

He hugged back. "Long time, Joe."

Joe held on to him for a moment, then gave a final pat and pushed himself away. "Long time," he repeated quietly, looking at the ground and wiping his eyes with the back of his hands. “Hey, I’m looking for you last week,” he said in an exaggerated tone, looking up at Ryan.

His eyes were moist. He seemed embarrassed, took a deep breath and glanced quickly away to Frank. “I’m looking for him last week, no?”

“Two weeks ago,” Frank corrected and offered his hand.

Joe stepped forward, then paused, pointing at the pistol in Frank’s belt. “Ah, Mr. Frank,” his smile broadened, “you said you not working anymore.” He began to shake his finger at Frank as his mouth twisted into the crooked, sideways smile peculiar to Joe Montez. “You said you not working anymore,” he repeated.

Frank stepped forward, grabbed the pointing finger and forced a handshake. They both laughed.

“Okay,” Joe said, turning and pointing at Ryan’s pistol with his left hand. “You working, too. Now we gonna do something.”

Frank let go of Joe’s hand and stepped back.

Joe shook his finger at Ryan. “We going to do something big, *Cuate*, bigger than anything ever.” Ryan gave Frank a questioning look. Frank folded his arms across his chest and leaned back against the barn. Joe had last worked as an informant for Frank, but it was Ryan the little blonde man belonged to.

“What is it we’re going to do, Joe?” Ryan asked calmly in Spanish. Joe would sulk if he thought he was being pushed. “Big! Something big this time,” Joe said in Spanish and motioned toward the corral. “First I have to feed the horses. For two days they have had nothing but water.” Joe glanced behind him, then around the corral.

“Feed the horses!” Ryan heard himself blurt out, then caught himself. Joe Montez had to be handled a certain way. “Joe, what’s going on here?” he asked in a forced, calm tone.

“You mean the horses?” Joe gestured toward the corral behind him. His crooked smile had faded.

“Yes, the horses. What’s going on?” Ryan repeated, this time in Spanish.

“Okay,” Joe looked around, then walked to the hay hooks he had dropped and picked them up. Walking past Ryan toward the barn, he said in English, “I’m looking for you last week.”

He turned toward Frank and shrugged. "Two weeks ago... I'm looking for you, or Mr. Frank." He stopped at the small side door, turned to face them and switched back to Spanish. "Mr. Frank said he wasn't working anymore and didn't want to know anything." Frank pushed himself away from the barn wall, nodding in agreement.

"And he said you were still in Spain." Joe paused for a moment and looked toward the corrals. "First I must feed the horses. They have had nothing but water for two days." He turned and walked into the barn. Frank and Ryan followed him inside. They each brought out a bale of hay, carried them to the corral holding the horses, and dropped them near two other bales Joe had carried out before they surprised him.

"What do you have them penned up for, anyway?" Frank asked, looking at the horses. "Why don't you just turn them out into the trap? There's plenty of grass and water out there."

"They had to get shoes," Joe replied in English. "They had to get shoes first." He put his bale of hay down, pulled out the hooks and walked back to the barn. Ryan and Frank remained, breaking bales open and tossing sections of hay over the fence. Joe returned with another bale. They broke it open and tossed it over the fence.

"*Cuate*, you know about Lalo?" Joe asked in Spanish as he wrapped loops of bailing wire from the hay around a corral post. Joe was ready to talk.

Ryan switched to Spanish. "Yes," he answered. "Frank told me about him."

"It's hot." Joe motioned for them to follow and led the way back into the dim barn. He stuck a hook into one of the stacked bales of hay and yanked it down onto the packed dirt floor. He did the same with two more, jammed the hooks into the stacked hay and sat down on one of the bales.

"The horses belong to Lalo." Joe took a deep breath and stared down at the floor.

"He is going to cross something with them. I think it will be cocaine."

"Cocaine?" Ryan pushed one of the downed bales of hay closer to Joe and sat down in front of him. They spoke in Spanish.

"*Si*," Joe nodded affirmatively. "I think so. There is a man from Colombia. Lalo is going to cross something for him, something big, something that will take all the horses." He gestured toward the door leading out to the corrals. Frank positioned the other bale of hay slightly behind and to the right of Joe and sat down. It was where he had always sat, or stood, when another officer was doing the questioning. It was where he had sat nodding, shaking his head or giving other signals when Ryan first joined the team and was learning the business of asking questions. Frank knew the Big Bend country and many of the people on both sides of the river. Ryan was glad he had taken up his old position.

"The Colombian is camped across the river," Joe was saying. "He has airplanes, big airplanes that bring the *contrabando*. Cocaine, I think."

"Airplanes are bringing cocaine, and then they cross it with horses?" Ryan hadn't intended the question to sound as skeptical as it did. Joe didn't seem to mind.

"Not before." Joe shook his head. "Before, other airplanes came for it. Airplanes from here" – he pointed to the floor – "came to the airport in Mexico and picked up marijuana, pills and heroin." Joe looked over his shoulder at Frank. "No?"

"That's right," Frank explained. "Lalo has his own airstrip, out in the middle of nowhere. When we put his pack trains out of business, he built the airstrip. After that, he never crossed anything himself. Planes flew in from all over the country, picked up what they wanted and flew it right back into the U.S., a regular doper's shopping mall. There was nothing to stop them."

Joe turned back to face Ryan. Frank winked, meaning there was more they would discuss later.

The blimps. Ryan thought about the customs radar blimps. They had stopped the illegal air traffic, and now old-fashioned pack train smuggling was returning to the border. "What do you have to do with all of this?" Ryan was looking straight into Joe's pale blue eyes.

"Nothing," the little man shrugged. "Not for a long time." Again he glanced back at Frank. "I helped Mr. Frank. I loaded the airplanes and wrote down the numbers and gave them to him."

Frank nodded agreement.

"Mr. Frank retired," Joe turned back to Ryan, "then the Colombian came. His name is Rodrigo. He has his own men, Peruvians – all of his men are from Peru. He doesn't trust Mexicans or Colombians, and for sure, he doesn't trust me." Joe pointed to himself. "Rodrigo doesn't like me, so Lalo gave me the pool hall in Ojinaga. I run the pool hall for Lalo." And run a few girls, and deal a little heroin, pills and grass. Ryan had the picture.

Frank could fill in the gaps later. Right now, he wanted to get to Grady. "Joe, if you're running Lalo's pool hall in Ojinaga, what are you doing here?" He saw Frank's nod of approval.

"I'm telling you." Joe sounded irritated and stomped his foot. "Two weeks ago, Lalo told me, 'Go to Fort Stockton and get Conchas."

"Felipe?" Frank interrupted.

"Yes, Felipe Conchas." Joe nodded affirmatively and glanced back at Frank. "That's when I came looking for you."

Frank nodded until Joe turned back toward Ryan, then he winked again. Ryan could skip the questions about Conchas.

"Lalo told me to go get Conchas. He said we were going to pack it out again like before, so I came to find you or Mr. Frank, to tell you we can do something."

"Go on." Ryan leaned forward, staring harder at him. "I found Conchas in Pecos. They had him in jail for fighting in the bars and for shooting deer." Joe pointed at a half-dozen deer hides tacked flesh-side out on the opposite wall of the barn. "He's been shooting them here, too. He sells them in Alpine. They make good tamales." He smiled his crooked smile and patted his stomach.

Ryan stared, unsmiling.

Joe's smile faded. "I paid his bail and took him to Lalo." He paused, glancing back at Frank. "That's all I knew until last night." He straightened and turned back to Ryan. "Last night Lalo came to the pool hall. He told me that Conchas was dead – that he had a wreck and everybody was killed."

"Who was killed?" Ryan asked.

"Conchas and two men from Fort Stockton. They had come to shoe the horses. They hit a deer and went off the road. Everybody was killed."

Joe brightened and stood up. "Last night, Lalo told me I am the boss now, like before. He said, 'Go find some help, take the horses and cross the cargo for Rodrigo.'"

Ryan was thinking about the wreck scene he had passed early Saturday morning between Fort Stockton and Alpine. A plunge off that bridge into the dark arroyo certainly could have been fatal. He felt Frank's eyes on him. It was time to ask the question.

He looked up at the little man now standing in front of him. "Joe, sit down," he said quietly, motioning with his hand. When Joe was again seated on the bale of hay, Ryan spoke slowly in Spanish. "Joe, last Monday, six days ago, sometime in the afternoon, a man came here to the ranch. No one has seen him since. Something happened to him here..."

"A blue and white Ford?" Joe interrupted.

"Right." Ryan took a deep breath. "A blue-and-white Ford. What about it?"

"I drove it." Joe squinted and looked thoughtfully upward for a moment, then down at his hand, counting fingers with his thumb. "Wednesday... I came here to the ranch." He looked up at Ryan. "Lalo called on the telephone and said, 'Conchas needs help. Go help him.' I came here, and Conchas said, 'Drive the car to Los Alamos.' I drove the car, he met me there, we left the car and came back."

"Did he say anything about where the car came from, or why he wanted you to drive it?"

"I asked him what the car had in it and why we were taking it to Los Alamos." Joe looked back at Frank, shaking his head. "Nobody uses Los Alamos anymore."

"What did he say?" Ryan prodded patiently.

Joe turned back and squinted at the floor. "He said he didn't know. I asked where the car came from. He said he didn't know that either. He said Lalo told him to take it to Los Alamos and leave it."

Ryan and Frank stared at each other. There had to be more. "Was that all he said about the car?" Ryan asked.

Joe shrugged. "He didn't want to talk about it, so I didn't ask anymore. When we got back, I got in my pickup and left, went back to Ojinaga."

"Where was the car when you got here?"

"There, in front of the door." He pointed toward his own pickup.

"Was Conchas here alone? Anyone else here at the ranch?" Ryan asked the only question left, hoping for something, anything else.

"He was alone. There was nobody else."

Ryan stared at Joe. Shortly after becoming a deputy sheriff, Ryan had stopped what probably would have been a fatal beating of Joe Montez by two other deputies. As a result, Joe had become Ryan's informant. The little blond Mexican was a dope dealer, smuggler and con man with no scruples as far as Ryan knew, except that in all the years they had worked together, Joe had never lied to him or Frank. There was no reason to doubt him now.

Ryan stood up, gave Frank a disappointed look, shoved both hands into the pockets of his new Levi's and walked slowly toward the large open doors, staring at but not seeing Joe's new tan-and-brown GMC pickup outside.

He heard Frank ask where the horses had come from. Joe replied that Conchas had gathered them from various West Texas sale barns.

Ryan's fingers found the lug nut from Grady's car. He pulled it from his pocket and stared at it. From the moment he had received Frank's call at the embassy he had focused on Grady's disappearance. There was little he had been able to do. Frank had done it all, brought them this far, to what would have been the end of if Conchas hadn't smashed into a deer and gone through the guard rail.

A deer had killed Conchas. The irony of it did not escape Ryan as he walked toward the row of taut, dry deer hides Conchas had tacked flesh side up on the barn wall. He looked carefully at each one. A bullet hole was easy to see from the flesh side, even a small one, but there weren't any. The deer had all been hit high, in the neck or the head. Conchas had been a good shot.

"What kind of gun did he have?" Ryan asked in Spanish.

"Twenty-two," Joe answered. "A Marlin, long barrel, shoots like this." He made a levering action under an imaginary rifle.

A .22 had probably made the holes in Grady's boots. Ryan rolled the lug nut back and forth between his fingers. What they had now was just enough to get the local sheriff's office involved. There would be a search of the area and a lot of publicity. Whatever was going on here with the packhorses, whatever Grady had stumbled into, would be called off by the smugglers, and Joe's fingerprints would surely be among those lifted from Grady's car.

Ryan turned away from the deer hides. Besides keeping Joe out of trouble, he didn't intend to spend the rest of his life wondering what had happened to Grady. Frank would feel the same way. That brought him to the only thing they had left: Lalo Naranjo. Naranjo would know what happened to Grady. Conchas must have told him. But Lalo Naranjo was in Mexico and never came to this side.

Frank was asking something about a new airstrip that the Colombian named Rodrigo had built. Ryan walked back to the hay bales where Joe and Frank were talking. There was no question that Frank had done it all up to now, brought them this far, but Frank couldn't do what had to be done next.

"Joe, tell me again what you're supposed to do," Ryan demanded in a loud voice, interrupting Joe's description of the airstrip and Rodrigo's camp.

The little man looked up from the bale of hay he was sitting on, obviously startled at the almost-shouted question. He swallowed, straightened himself. "I have to cross Rodrigo's cargo," he said in Spanish.

Ryan put his foot on the bale of hay in front of Joe and leaned forward. "But what do you have to do first?"

Joe looked puzzled.

"Get some help." Ryan answered his own question. "Lalo told you to get some help, no?"

"*Si.*" Joe stared up at him.

"Well, how much help do you need?" Ryan was talking fast in Spanish. "Two men, three or maybe only one good one?" He looked past Joe. Frank shook his head and winked as if he had an eye full of pepper.

9

One hundred forty kilometers southwest of Alpine, at the foot of the Sierra Hermosa de Santa Rosa and the edge of the desert brush lands known as Las Lomas de Peyotes, life had come to its normal early-afternoon standstill in the small town of Melchor Muzquiz, Coahuila, Mexico. Nothing moved beyond the coolness of thick adobe walls or the shade of tall, lush pecan trees along the Rio Sabinas north of town. It was *siesta* time.

Inside one of the small adobes overlooking the river, the latter of two persistent houseflies that had been worrying the face of Customs Comandante Julio Antonio Suarez-Benevides was finally dispatched with a folded newspaper. The *comandante* relaxed. The paper fell to the floor, and he wallowed his head deeper into the fresh white-cased pillow. A customs *distrito comandante* along Mexico's northern border doesn't work very hard, but he worries a lot – even if his *distrito* is remote, sparsely populated and relatively untouched by commercial traffic. Comandante Suarez was trying not to worry, trying not to think of the new trouble he might be in. He was trying to sleep, escape the reality that he was still in such a godforsaken place.

It had been more than three years since he reported to the huge white-stucco federal building in Monclova and officially received his assignment as *comandante* of a customs *distrito* that had been hastily and especially carved out for him, a customs district along the Rio Bravo that contained not a single port of entry – not Piedras Negras, not Ciudad Acuña, not even the small isolated crossing points of Boquillas or La Linda were his.

To support himself and his twelve inspectors, there were only the inland traffic checkpoints along a 250-kilometer dirt-and-gravel road running west from Muzquiz to Altares, an adobe and tarpaper village below the big bend of the Rio Bravo. He had been given a sentence, not an assignment, a sentence of undetermined duration.

He struggled now not to think of it, something he did every night and every siesta. Today, he was succeeding, drifting, almost asleep but for the distant sound of a motorcycle. He groaned pitifully and pulled the pillow over his head. There were no motorcycles in Muzquiz, but there was a 1954 GMC six-cylinder pickup with two exhaust manifold gaskets burned away. It was his district's only official vehicle. But today was Sunday. He breathed deeply, lying to himself that the loud pickup was destined for someplace other than the *comandante*'s house, that it would not soon stop out front and that big, loud Inspector Miguel Ramon-Sanchez would not pound on the front door, yelling that something was *importante*. He did not want to see Sergeant Ramon today, tomorrow, the day after or ever again. He was drifting, almost asleep.

There had to be a way out of this place. Uncle Felix would have had him out long ago – if only he hadn't died. Uncle Felix had been angry, very angry when he learned of the trouble; but he had stood by him, saved him, saved his only nephew's very life and arranged for the appointment to another government position in Muzsquiz. Even the influence of those serving on El Presidente's Cabinet has its limitations, and Captitan Julio Antonio Suarez-Benevides of the elite Coast Guard Intelligence Unit in Tampico had taxed that influence to the limit. It had been Muzquiz or nothing.

The motorcycle sound was louder. The *comandante* pulled the pillow tighter against his ears and drifted back to the realm of half-sleep, where the red-and-white shrimp boat and the three very large state policemen were always waiting.

The policemen had come for him early one morning at his condominium overlooking Tampico Bay. They had put him into a large silver limousine and driven him to a private yacht tied up at one of the exclusive clubs on the outskirts of the city. The three policemen had escorted him aboard the yacht and left him in the company of a tall, well-groomed, polite young man in dark tortoise-shell glasses.

The man had invited him to breakfast. While they were eating, the young man explained that the red-and-white shrimp boat and its cargo, five thousand pounds of freshly-harvested Cienegas de Flores marijuana, belonged to *La Bolsa*, "The Pocket," street name of Felipe de Andaz-Mercedez, mayor of Tampico and brother-in-law to the governor of the state of Veracruz.

The young man in dark glasses said that *La Bolsa* was very upset that Captain Suarez had stopped, searched and impounded his new boat. He said that all but a few pounds of its cargo had mysteriously disappeared.

Under his pillow, former Captain of Coast Guard Intelligence Julio Antonio Suarez-Benevidez's face twitched, and he made soft whimpering sounds as he again relived the things that had happened to him before he could get word to Uncle Felix.

"*¡Comandante! ¡Comandante!*" The hoarse bellow preceded a loud pounding on the door. "*¡Comandante! ¡Importante!*"

Comandante Suarez tore the pillow from his head, sat upright on the edge of his narrow metal cot and looked around the sparsely furnished room. For a few seconds now, he would feel relieved, happy to be the customs *comandante* of the Muzquiz *distrito*, content with only poor campesinos to prey upon and very grateful to his deceased Uncle Felix.

He wiped his forehead and rubbed the small of his back. A bed, a large king-size bed. A *comandante* should have a decent bed... if it would fit. He glanced around the small two-room house.

"No!" he said aloud. He would not be in Muzquiz long enough to justify the trouble and expense of new furniture, a large refrigerator, larger quarters.

"*Comandante! ¡Jefe! ¡Importante!*"

"*Pasale!*" Suarez yelled at the door. There had to be a way out, back to Tampico, back to life.

The door swung open, bouncing hard against the adjacent wall, and a very large man in olive drab uniform took a long, dust-stirring step into the room and saluted. "*Importante, Jefe,*" Customs Inspector Miguel Ramon-Sanchez repeated.

Suarez, seated on the edge of his cot, wearing only white jockey shorts, returned the salute, his eyes already on the short machete in the inspector's left hand. "Another one," the commander commented as he smoothed back his coarse, straight black hair with one hand.

"Where did it come from?" He stood up and took a pair of army green trousers from a nearby chair.

"The same place, *Comandante*, La Morita." La Morita, three huts near the western edge of his jurisdiction, where the primitive, sometimes-impassable road from the Chihuahua border country crosses another unimproved track coming south from the Big Bend area of the Rio Bravo.

"Well, who had it?" Suarez asked sharply. *Hijo*, everything had to be dragged from these desert *campesinos*. He stepped into his trousers and pulled them up.

"Duarte, Jefe, Rene Duarte, one of the vaqueros from El Rancho Merced."

"And...?" Suarez asked impatiently. Buttoning his trousers, he answered the question himself. "He got the machete from his daughter who went to a dance at some camp in the mountains, *correcto*?"

"No, *Jefe*, he got it from his sister."

Suarez inhaled slowly, exhaled and glanced at Ramon's blank face. "Put it down," he nodded toward a chest of drawers next to the door, "and wait outside." Inspector Ramon placed the machete where he was told, saluted, backed out and gently closed the door behind him.

Suarez walked over to the chest, pulled open the top drawer and took out a clean pair of socks and an undershirt. The machete in front of him was, like the others, short by machete standards, only the length of his forearm, and, like the others, had a bright yellow wooden handle. He put on the undershirt, tossed the socks onto the bed across the room and picked up the big knife. He turned, facing the window, slowly rotating the blade in the sunlight until he could see the small letters stamped into the blue metal near the wooden handle. Colombia.

This was the third such machete his men had found... well, the third one his men had turned in... during the past two weeks.

Barefoot, he carried the machete into the small room he used as an office and placed it on a small table with the other things from Colombia. Three machetes now, two multicolored sleeveless dresses, a pair of women's hand-tooled leather sandals and six lace shawls.

All from the La Morita checkpoint. All found in vehicles coming east on the Chihuahua border road.

There were rumors of a large camp and drunken parties, *pachangas*, somewhere in the mountains west of Sierra del Carmen. Word was that anyone bringing women to the camp was welcome and well-rewarded. Suarez walked back into the front room, sat down on the side of his cot, and pulled the socks on.

He had paid little attention to such stories until the items from Colombia began to show up at the checkpoint. Then he had done something foolish, something that could cause him more trouble.

He pulled a shiny black boot onto his right foot, hobbled across the room and opened the front door. "Inspector! *¡Vengate!*" Leaving the door slightly ajar, he limped back to the cot and sat down. Carefully the door was pushed open. Inspector Ramon stepped into the room and again saluted.

"*Si. Comandante.*"

Suarez did not look up. "Where is the man you sent into the mountains last week? Has he deserted? Is he lost or what?" He pulled the other boot on and sat upright on the cot, hands on his knees, waiting for an answer.

"I don't think so, *Jefe*," Ramon replied solemnly. "Inspector Contreras is a good man. He is from Altares and knows the mountains well. His family is here in Muzquiz, his wife and children and his mother. I don't think he would desert them."

"He probably found the fiesta camp and the women, got drunk,and decided to stay."

"I don't think so, *Jefe*."

The Comandante walked to a nearby closet and removed a clean, sharply-pressed, olive-green shirt from a hanger. He had hoped to get more information on the rumored mountain camp, have something concrete to report to his supervisors in Monclova. Instead, he would now have to report one of his men missing, missing for over a week, after being ordered on an unauthorized investigation by his *comandante*. There would be trouble over this. The comandante thought about that as he put his arms through the starched shirt sleeves.

Perhaps this would be as bad as the trouble with the red-and-white shrimp boat. It would depend on what had happened to the missing man and what official or officials were involved in whatever was going on in the mountains.

Suarez pulled a dark brown tie from the closet, tossed it over his shoulder and, stepping around Inspector Ramon, walked across the room to a narrow door that led to a small bathroom.

He finished buttoning his shirt and opened the door. On the back side was a full-length mirror. He stepped closer and went to work on his tie. A nest of Colombian drug smugglers, that's what it was. Had to be, if there actually was anything to the rumors of a secret mountain camp. He raised his chin to better see his progress with the tie. How much cocaine would be involved in such an operation? It had to be cocaine if they were Colombians. How much money? He finished the Windsor knot, smoothed his straight, raven-black hair with the palms of his hands and frowned.

Officials would have to be involved. As the customs *distrito comandante*, he should be involved, should be receiving something if Colombian drugs were being smuggled into the United States through his district. And where was his missing man? Slowly, Suarez moved his hands back to the perfectly crafted Windsor. He grasped the knot and yanked the tie from around his neck, picking the knot apart as he turned toward the door.

"Inspector, take the pickup to the cantina and bring back the yellow van Hector uses to haul liquor." He stripped off his uniform shirt as he walked to the closet. Hector would give them the van, or he would never bring another load of liquor through a checkpoint in this district.

"And make him put a...." Suarez glanced at Ramon's immense bulk and corrected himself. "Make him put two cases of Tecate and a chest of ice in the back." He opened the door for the inspector. "Then come pick me up. We will see about this secret camp ourselves."

10

The rented Caprice slowed as it approached the outskirts of Alpine. It wasn't yet noon and already, according to the radio, the temperature was in the low eighties. Ryan reached over and tuned up the air conditioning until fog spouted from the air vents. He glanced at his watch: 11:20 a.m. Still time for another stop before meeting Frank and Joan for lunch.

The trip had been a short one by West Texas standards, only fifty-two miles to Border Patrol Sector Headquarters, on the outskirts of Marfa, and back.

"Helping look for Grady," he had said to the Chief after identifying himself as a customs agent and friend of Frank Marsh's. "Just checking in." Was anything going on that his and Frank's nosing around might interfere with?

Any agency working the border cleared their operation with the Border Patrol unless they wanted a green-and-white Jeep driving up in the middle of it. The Chief would know if Customs or the state had anything going on in the area.

"Nothing," the Chief had said, and immediately had offered up the tracking team again that had concluded their search for Grady's car tracks between Marathon and the border early Saturday evening. Ryan had thanked him and declined, saying that he and Frank had finished up between Sanderson and Balmorhea and were probably going to work south between Alpine and the border.

The Chief introduced him to two of his assistant chiefs, several patrol agents and the radio dispatcher. "Be nosing around the area for a few days with Frank," he had repeated to them, mentioning nothing about the horses, Lalo Naranjo or the Colombian drug smuggler. Ryan didn't like misleading them, but the Chief himself would be in trouble if he knew what Ryan had planned and failed to report it.

The main street of Alpine was wide, with high curbs and angled parking on both sides of the street. Ryan turned into one of the faintly-marked spaces across from Steiner Brothers Western Wear, got out and crossed the street to the store.

Inside, he introduced himself to an elderly, balding man behind the counter. "I'm Ryan Shaw, a friend of Frank Marsh...." He didn't get to finish.

"The feller who needed clothes so bad," the old man chuckled. He introduced himself as Robert Steiner, and turned toward the cash register. "Got your bill right here." Looking down through large gold-rimmed bifocals, he sorted through a pile of receipts on the counter.

"I want to thank you for letting me in Sunday morning. I appreciate it," Ryan said sincerely, "and there's a few more things I need." Without waiting for a reply, he turned from the counter and moved briskly about the store, selecting items and stacking them on the counter: a lined denim jacket, two pairs of Levi's, two long-sleeved denim shirts, six pairs of socks, underwear and a long yellow stockman's rain slicker. He put the last of it on the counter and pulled a leather badge holder from his shirt pocket.

"That it?" the old man asked, lowering his head to stare through the top half of his glasses.

"I think so," Ryan replied, extracting an American Express card from behind the leather pad holding his gold-plated customs agent's badge. The old man stared at the badge.

"Most people buying that kind of outfit usually get some gloves."

"You're absolutely right." Ryan glanced around the store.

The old man pointed toward the front without taking his eyes off the badge.

Ryan handed Mr. Steiner the credit card, folded the badge case, and walked to the glove display near the front of the store. He picked out a pair of buckskin roping gloves marked large, thrust his right hand into the soft leather and made a fist. Tight. He pulled the glove off and tried an extra-large size. Too loose. He retrieved the large pair and tucked them under his arm, found another pair marked small – Joe would appreciate a pair of the fancy palm-padded gloves – and took them back to the cash register.

Mr. Steiner smiled when Ryan tossed the two pairs of expensive gloves onto the pile of clothing. He punched the prices into the register. "Going to be here permanent?" He leaned over the counter to write on the credit card invoice.

"Just visiting," Ryan said.

The old man stopped writing, slowly looked over the pile of clothing, gave Ryan a skeptical look, then went back to the invoice.

Ryan ignored the look, and his gaze drifted out the front window to the True Value Hardware store across the street. That was convenient. It would save him another stop. He signed the invoice and gathered the two large paper bags with twine handles stuffed with his purchases in front of him.

"Thank you, sir," the old man said as he stapled the receipts together and dropped them into one of the bags, "Come back to see us."

Ryan knew that Mr. Steiner had already had a good day, but he wished him one anyway.

Outside, he crossed the street, opened the car trunk and tossed the bags of clothing in next to three cardboard boxes of supplies he had purchased in Marfa. He closed the trunk lid and went into the hardware store. A bell on the door jingled as he entered. It was cooler inside than it had been in the western-wear store.

"Help you?"

"Yes," Ryan turned toward the checkout counter on his right. A large, dark-haired young man sat on a stool behind the cash register. "Which way are the pocket knives?"

"Right over there," the clerk said over a bulging lower lip packed with chewing tobacco. He pointed toward the middle of the store as he spat into a large Styrofoam cup. "Other side of the axes and hatchets." He put the cup down and followed Ryan to an island of wood and glass display cases. "You want a big one or a little one?"

"Oh, maybe something in between," Ryan said, moving slowly along the first glass-topped case. There wasn't much variety, mostly stock knives, thick and hard on the pocket. He looked up. The young man was big; six-four or -five, two-hundred-sixty pounds at least. Just out of his teens, maybe. "I'm looking for a single blade," Ryan said, "thin, easy to carry but big enough to do something with. I had a knife like that, a Kershaw. Got any Kershaws?"

"Nope." Big Boy sounded like he needed to spit, pointed to an adjacent display case and hurried back toward the front of the store.

Ryan moved around the corner and saw the knife: a thin, medium-sized lock-back with red, yellow and black stripes on its handle, single blade. He leaned over, squinted but couldn't make out the manufacturer's name. Big Boy was back with his spittoon cup. He moved fast for his size.

"Let me have a look at this stripe-handled knife."

"Yep." Big Boy squeezed through the narrow opening between the display cases. "It's a Schrade brand." He stooped behind the display case and placed the colorful knife on the counter along with two others all in small blue velvet-lined boxes. "These other two are by the same guy." He moved the three small boxes across the counter to Ryan. One knife was larger and the other smaller than the striped one that had caught his eye.

"Snake patterns," Big Boy affirmed.

Ryan removed each knife from its cushioned box, examined the blades. "These are all Schrade knives," he commented.

"Guy over at Fort Stockton puts the fancy handles on 'em. Snake patterns. He's done a diamondback." Big Boy pointed to the largest knife, large enough for the artisan to work three realistic black and gray diamond patterns into the handle material.

"Copperhead," Big Boy thumped the smaller box of the three, "and the coral snake." He pushed the brightly colored knife toward Ryan.

A series of red, yellow and black bands seemed to encircle the knife's handle, narrow yellow always separating the wider black and red.

"They got the same kind of poison as a cobra," Big Boy offered. "Did you know that?"

"Yeah, I've heard that."

Big Boy nodded. "Same as a cobra... but they don't have any fangs.

They have to chew the poison into you." He continued nodding for a moment, staring at the coral knife. "Guy's working on a big folding hunter now." He picked up the cup and spat into it. "It's going to be a python."

"Interesting, but I'm not a collector." Ryan stared down through the glass. Everything else was too big or a sheath knife. He picked up the coral-snake knife, palmed it in his right hand and with his thumb and middle finger eased the blade up far enough to push it fully open with his thumb. "Ring this one up for me." He pushed the empty box across the display case, folded the blade and dropped the striped knife into his pocket.

He glanced at the next display case: handguns and binoculars "How are you fixed for .45 ammo? Got any jacketed hollow-points?"

"Yes, sir." Big Boy straightened from replacing the knives and Ryan followed him to nearby wall shelves stocked with ammunition. "Couple of boxes of .45 hollow-points and two cartons of those Remington .22s." Twenty boxes of .22 caliber long-rifle shells: always good trading material in Mexico. Just may come in handy. Flashlight, spare batteries, small diamond-embedded knife sharpener and three Zippo cigarette lighters plus replacement flints and lighter fluid ended his shopping spree at Big Boy's hardware store.

Ryan loaded the two heavy bags from the hardware store into the trunk, got into the car, backed out and drove east along the main street. He couldn't think of anything he'd forgotten.

It was all done, even the embassy call. He thought about that for a moment. They would have missed him today. Maybe not Friday, or over the weekend, but today they would have been looking for him. He had called the duty agent last night, said there had been a family emergency. He would have to explain in detail later, catch some flack for leaving Spain without notifying anyone, but for now he was covered.

Two blocks past the Corner Cafe, he paused at the traffic light and made a right onto State 118, bumped across the Santa Fe's main-line tracks and drove past the church with the tall steeple Frank had described. "South end of town," he'd said, "on 118, out toward the ranch, El Tecolote serves the coldest beer and best damn tamales in the Big

Bend country."

And that's where he found them. Joan's big white Chrysler and Frank's grey GMC, parked on a wide caliche parking lot in front of a small, weathered adobe building. Brilliant pink-and-turquoise letters over the door informed those who read Spanish that this was El Tecolote, "The Owl" cafe.

Other cars were in the parking lot indicating a large crowd, but Frank and Joan had the broad concrete-slab patio to themselves. They waved from one of a dozen small metal card tables under a long brush-top ramada extending from the north side of the small restaurant.

Ryan pulled up next to Frank's pickup. Frank stood up, snatched a bottle of beer from the bucket of ice on the table in front of him and threw it just as Ryan opened his car door. Ryan scrambled out, slammed the door shut and caught the spiraling brown bottle.

Frank laughed and walked to a window on the patio side of the cafe. Holding the cold bottle at arm's length, Ryan twisted the cap off and let the foam flow over his hand onto the ground. Leaning over, he sipped at the cold froth as he walked to the shaded patio. Frank ordered a dozen tamales at the window as Ryan pulled a chair from under the small metal table.

"Beer's good," Ryan said as he sat down across from Joan.

"Are you still going?" she asked softly, raising her eyebrows.

Ryan looked at her for a moment, then past her at Frank, waiting at the window, then down at his bottle of beer.

"Come on, Joan, I used to do this all the time."

She leaned forward, both arms on the table. "These are Colombian cocaine traffickers. They murder presidents, attorney generals, governors, even candidates for the offices. They blow them up or mow them down with machine guns, and they'll do the same thing to you." She leaned back. "Don't do it. Please don't go over there." She folded her arms and stared at him, eyes and face pleading.

Ryan stared across the table at her. She was a remarkable woman. He had thought that before, many times. She was strong, caring and sensible, exactly the kind of woman Frank should have.

Joan had raised all of their children, four of them, almost

singlehandedly while Frank was occupied enforcing immigration and narcotics laws along the Mexican border.

Ryan knew of no secrets Frank and Joan had from each other. She had always known what he was doing. She knew everything that was going on now, everything he and Frank knew about Grady, Lalo and the Colombian drug trafficker Rodrigo. They had talked about all of it last night, well into the early morning hours.

Frank slid a rusty metal tray with paper plates, plastic forks, a bowl of salsa and a bundle of tamales wrapped in newspaper to the center of the table. Ryan opened the package and, with a fork, raked several tamales from the steaming pile. He flipped two of them onto a paper plate and pushed it toward Joan.

Frank looked at his wife, then at Ryan as he scooped three tamales onto a paper plate with his fingers. "Come on," he frowned. "We did all this last night. I don't like it either."

He took a drink from his bottle of beer and looked back at Joan. "We can't do it your way. He can't just call customs headquarters and say, 'Hi, this is Agent Shaw, assigned to the American Embassy in Madrid. I'm down here on the Mexican border working a really big dope case.'" Frank shook his head. "He would spend the next week in D.C. trying to explain all that, then there would be weeks of paperwork and meetings, begging for clearance to work in Mexico. Customs, the State Department – everybody gets a say-so."

Frank shook his head again. "You're not going to get clearance for an undercover investigation in Mexico based on the word of a snitch. Not going to happen. Even if it did, the State Department would have to notify the Mexican government and get their approval."

Frank stopped, glanced at each of them. "We did all this last night," he repeated. "It's now or never. He wants to go... he's going." He popped half of a tamale into his mouth and started shucking another.

Joan stared at her husband. "You'd be going too if everybody in Mexico didn't know you."

Frank stopped chewing, stared at his plate. "Yep," he said wistfully. "I guess I would."

They ate and drank in silence after that, listening to the blare and throb of mariachi music from the jukebox inside the restaurant. The scent of scorched grease and mesquite coals wafted down from the restaurant's stubby rock chimney.

Ryan waved a fly away from his face and took a drink of the cold Mexican beer, savoring its mild, pleasant bite. "Beer's good," he remarked quietly, realizing he had already said that several times and that it wasn't only the beer that was good. Frank and Joan, the patio, Mexican music, cooking smells, even the logos on the metal folding tables and chairs, Pepsi, Corona, Carta Blanca, all took him back. "We haven't done this for a long time," he said. His eyes went to the empty chair beside him, the chair where Nancy would have been sitting. He could see her long blonde hair and her bright blue eyes plus hear her laughter.

"What happened to her?" Joan's voice seemed to come from far away.

Ryan blinked back to the present. The chair was empty. He blinked again. It was still empty. He took a deep breath. "She left... went away..." he answered, staring at the vacant chair, "while I was in Washington on the training detail." He looked out toward the distant mountain peaks, at the ruffled streaks of white above them. "About the time I left on that little mission" – he took another deep breath and exhaled – "Public Health decided to close all their border offices." He shrugged.

"She took one of those research jobs she was always talking about. Went overseas to Barcelona." He glanced over to check their reactions.

He had never told either of them his reason for taking the Madrid assignment.

Joan looked sympathetic. Frank tightened his lips and shook his head.

"It took a little over a year to shake loose from the D.C. detail and wrangle an overseas assignment." He looked back toward the mountains. "By the time I got there, she was involved with another doctor, a Swede." Ryan emptied the beer bottle, tossed it into a nearby garbage can and reached for another. "They got married last year, and he took her home to Sweden."

Joan reached across and touched his arm. "I'm sorry. The two of you were wonderful together, so happy."

"Yes, we were." Ryan twisted the cap off the fresh bottle. "No way it was going to last, though." He shook his head. "She was a doctor, and I was a customs agent." He smiled a humorless smile and took another tamale from the pile. "We both passed up things, you know... opportunities, just to stay in Nogales." Ryan took a deep breath and wrinkled his forehead. "We did pretty good. Made it last as long as we could."

The tamale broke in half as he shucked it. He broke it again and popped a bite into his mouth. "Good tamales."

It was quiet again for a while. Frank broke the somber mood by asking Ryan about his trip to Marfa.

"Good," Ryan answered. "There's a dispatcher on twenty-four hours a day, two planes available, and they know all about me."

Frank turned toward Joan. "Just so they'll know who they're talking to in case he needs some help in a hurry."

Joan shook her head without comment and poured beer into her glass, took a sip, closed her eyes and began nodding in time to the music.

"Chief says there's nothing going on in his sector," Ryan added.

"Told you so," Frank said. "The state narcs don't venture off the pavement. If they were working anything around here, everybody on both sides of the river would know about it. Messing up something they're working on is one thing you don't have to worry about."

Ryan nodded. "You bring me anything?" he asked.

Frank reached into his shirt pocket and pulled out a thick fold of bills. "$300." He handed it to Ryan. "Saddle, rope, bridle, chaps, old sleeping bag and a couple of odds and ends are in the back of the pickup."

Ryan stood up and pushed the money down into the pocket of his Levi's. "Let's load it in the car." He finished off his beer and tossed the bottle into the trash can. "Time for me to get moving." He avoided Joan's eyes.

Frank remained seated, turning sideways in his chair. "That little store down the street...." He pointed toward a small building across the highway and half a block away. "It belongs to Lalo's daughter, Rosa Galvez."

He looked at Ryan. "Never had anything on her, don't think she was ever involved in any of his illegal doings, but she doesn't need to see me loading stuff into your car."

Ryan loaded the saddle, sleeping bag and other gear into the back seat of the Caprice and returned to the patio. He offered Frank his hand. Frank squeezed it, smiled uncomfortably and let it go. Joan sighed, hugged him, and patted him. "Hurry back."

Ryan walked quickly to his car, got in, started the engine and backed up, heading the car south. He waved once, pulled out onto the highway and drove past the store belonging to Naranjo's daughter.

It was another old adobe with cracked concrete stucco. Faded red and green letters on the side and front, spelled out "Galvez Grocery." He turned his attention to the highway ahead, passed a speed-limit sign – 55 miles an hour – made himself comfortable, pressed down on the accelerator and checked the rearview mirror.

A new turquoise-and-white Ford pickup had just pulled off the highway behind him, stopping in front of the old store with the faded signs. It looked like the truck the Mexican woman had driven away from the cafe early Saturday morning. Ryan touched the brake pedal, hesitated. What if it was her? What was he going to do? No time for that now.

He looked back at the highway ahead, moved his foot back to the accelerator, and pressed it down. Newspapers with radar-blimp stories... now she was at the store belonging to Naranjo's daughter – if that was her back there. He let it go. He had a cover story to make up, gear to pack, horses to move and Lalo Naranjo and a Colombian smuggler to think about. He reached 65 miles-per-hour and found some Mexican music on the radio.

Damn, she was a beautiful woman.

11

In the crossroads village of Paso de San Antonio, Chihuahua, Mexico, one-hundred-twenty-five miles south of Alpine, Customs Comandante Suarez emerged from the side door of a large, weather-ravaged adobe building. Holding a chipped blue-and-white enameled washbasin in one hand and a small frayed cotton towel in the other, he paused in front of the doorway, squinting against the mid-afternoon brightness.

The room, furnished him by the owner of the dilapidated hotel, had come complete with one of the half-dozen young girls the owner referred to as his nieces. The "niece" who had accompanied the *comandante* to his room just after lunch had departed less than a half-hour later, the *comandante* having fallen asleep quickly this siesta without once thinking about Tampico, the red-and-white shrimp boat, or the young man with tortoise-shell glasses.

Suarez raised the small towel and dabbed at the sweat beads forming on his forehead. His eyes searched the top of a jagged mountain range on the cloudless eastern horizon, settling finally on what he believed to be the general direction of Muzquiz. At least there were trees, shade and running water in Muzquiz. He was having second thoughts about his investigation. It had moved too fast and brought him too far.

Yesterday, just as he and Inspector Ramon had arrived at the checkpoint in Altares, a truckload of illegally cut firewood had pulled up.

The driver, a short, thin middle-aged *campesino* with large round eyes, had an arrangement with the checkpoint customs inspector and would have been gone in another minute. It was exactly the sort of situation Suarez had come looking for. The woodcutter, Vicente

Morales, had been eager to talk to the *distrito comandante* about anything other than the cord of green live oak and ponderosa pine he had taken without permit from the nearby Sierra del Carmen protected wilderness area.

Vicente had rubbed his chin, looked at the ground and said he was very sorry, that he knew nothing of a camp in the mountains. But there could be one, he had said, nodding slowly. Something was going on. He was sure of that.

Several times now, in his back-road wanderings for firewood, he had seen a bus, a small white bus filled with women, winding its way northward through the mountains between the village of Paso de San Antonio and the border. He did not know where the bus was going there was no road, only tracks, many tracks. It was very strange. Something was going on, but Vicente didn't know what. The driver? Yes, he knew the driver of the bus, knew him very well.

The woodcutter's information had taken them 30 miles farther west, into the state of Chihuahua, well beyond any jurisdiction of the Muzquiz customs *distrito comandante*, to the village of Paso de San Antonio and Señor Casio Esteban-Martinez, owner of the establishment serving as village service station, cantina, restaurant, general store, hotel and... other things.

Señor Esteban had been expecting them. That had not surprised Suarez. All goods sold in the Esteban establishment had to pass through customs checkpoints. A man in Señor Esteban's position would know when a *distrito commandante* was in the area, even if he was out of his own jurisdiction, out of uniform and driving a borrowed van.

A large family to support, that had been the theme of Señor Esteban's opening small talk. Suarez's blunt question to that had the intended effect. It caught the businessman off-guard, let him know that the visiting *comandante* knew something of what was going on in the mountains north of Paso de San Antonio.

"Si," Esteban answered. His large family included the young prostitutes he managed. And, yes, he reluctantly confessed, his attractive "nieces," some of their girlfriends and girlfriends of the girlfriends, did accompany him when he took supplies to a distant camp in the mountains. Señor Casio Esteban, owner and operator of all enterprise in Paso de San Antonio, had talked freely after that. He was the sort of man who knew when it was time to talk.

The camp was not far from the Rio Bravo, in a deep, narrow canyon. The parties, the *pachangas*, took place almost every night on a huge ledge jutting from the north wall of the canyon. That's where he took the women. That's where the man in charge lived, a man from Colombia named Rodrigo. Business with Don Rodrigo had been very good. Recently it had doubled. More men had arrived – more small, rough-looking men from Peru.

"*Peruanos*," Esteban had said last night, "*Mas Peruanos*." Rodrigo was from Colombia, but his men, even the pilots, were from Peru. They all had machine guns and semiautomatic pistols.

Comandante Suarez left the doorway of the hotel and walked toward a small open shed that contained the water supply for the Esteban enterprises, three canvas-covered 55-gallon steel drums.

Airplanes, Esteban had said, sometimes as many as three large airplanes, were parked on the airstrip in the canyon below the ledge. There was a bulldozer, two tractors and several pickups, but no army vehicles... and no soldiers. That had Suarez puzzled. No soldiers, no Mexicans at all except for three cooks and a few caretaker laborers? An illegal operation of this magnitude with no military protection? That was very strange.

Suarez untied the sisal rope around the nearest water barrel and pulled back the folded brown canvas. He took a rust-pocked dipper from a nail in the wall of the shed, plunged it into the half-empty barrel and slowly brought it up.

Last night he had ordered Esteban to have his bus and a load of women ready to start for the camp this afternoon. His plan had been to take the women to the camp and see for himself exactly what was going on, but now he was remembering a red-and-white shrimp boat, three very large state policemen and some of the things that happen to lesser officials who interfere in the business of higher officials. Perhaps going to the ledge camp was not such a good idea. None of this was his business. The camp was not in his district. Nothing from the camp was passing through his checkpoints, nothing of consequence anyway. He should call it off, return to Muzquiz and forget everything he had learned, or... he could make a report, report everything to his superiors in Monclova. He could do that. Let someone else, someone authorized to conduct such investigations, find out what was going on, take the risk of offending involved officials, take the blame... or the credit.

Suarez looked down at the small rust hole in the bottom of the empty dipper. He had let all the water run out. He submerged it again. The water in the barrel was cloudy, a light brown, like the water in Muzquiz. He ladled it into the badly chipped blue-and-white enameled washbasin and set the basin down on a wooden shelf attached to the shed. The lavatory in his Tampico condominium had also been blue, sparkling light blue porcelain with chrome faucets, hot and cold, polished every day by a housekeeper. The water that had flushed his toilet there had been crystal clear.

The *comandante* leaned forward and washed his face in the clouded water, straightened and dried himself with the coarse cotton towel. If there were no soldiers, no army protecting the camp, then maybe there were no government officials involved at all. That would be valuable information... very valuable, especially if it were reported to just the right person.

The *comandante* daubed his face once more with the stiff ragged towel and tossed it onto the ground. The woodcutter's information had been good. He would send word to let Vicente Morales pay something extra and keep the wood. For the first time in three long, miserable years, Customs Distrito Comandante Suarez felt a small glimmer of hope.

12

The brown-and-tan short-bed GMC pickup made a right turn off State Highway 118 and stopped in front of the locked gate. Ryan pulled up behind it. He had overtaken Joe several miles back.

The small blonde man got out of his pickup, waved and sauntered up to the gate. Ryan waved back, feeling guilty. He and Frank had left Joe completely in the dark. Never told him the Ford LTD belonged to Grady and that finding Grady was their real objective.

They had let Joe go on thinking they were working a straight narcotics smuggling case. Ryan was not comfortable with this deception and again found himself considering telling the little man the truth. Again, he decided against it.

Despite the loyalty and friendship Joe had demonstrated over the years, he was a paid informant. At times he had been paid very well. There was always the possibility that he might not agree to this high-risk, unofficial operation for friendship's sake alone. Joe Montez was their only link to Naranjo. He would have to be kept in the dark for now.

Joe pushed the gate open, got back into his pickup, and drove away. Ryan pulled up inside the gate and stopped. As he waited for the dust from Joe's pickup to drift away, he turned his thoughts again to what had occupied him since leaving the Tecolote Cafe.

The background story he had used years ago should still work: cowboying around Arizona, prospecting in Mexico, then easing into other, more profitable things. He could add that he and Joe had worked pack trains together in the past; that Joe called, needed help, offered a lot of money, so he'd hopped a plane to San Antonio. Sounded okay. He would run it by Joe when they got back to the ranch. They could iron out the rough spots and toss around a few old names.

The dust cleared. Ryan got out of the car, walked back to the gate and pushed it closed. This time there was no fake driver's license, checkbook, social security card or anything else to back up a phony name. He would have to use his real one. That should present no problem. He had kept his Arizona driver's license up to date, had never worked the Texas border, and no one knew him here or on the other side of the river.

Ryan pulled the heavy chain through the welded pipe gate and locked the ends together with the same combination lock he had tapped open the morning before. He turned the lock end-up, dialed the numbers Joe had given him, 0-9-1-6, and yanked it open. *Dies y Seis de Septiembre,* the Mexican independence holiday. He smiled. They should have tried that one yesterday before resorting to the hammer. He scrambled the numbers, snapped the lock closed and walked toward his car.

He had no plan regarding Naranjo. Too many variables now. He was certain only of the outstanding federal warrants for Lalo Naranjo and knew that if Naranjo were on this side, arrested and in jail, bargains could be struck, charges dropped or reduced in exchange for information on narcotics smuggling and... missing people. Naranjo would be at the Colombian's camp sometime tomorrow to see the horses Conchas had purchased and the men Joe had recruited.

Ryan stepped into the Caprice and drove toward the ranch. He would get the horses to the camp. That was as far ahead as he could plan for now.

♦ ♦ ♦

Ryan left Joe sorting supplies on the porch of the old ranch house, drove to the barn, carried Frank's riding gear inside and dumped it on the floor near the small side door. He pulled the hooks out of the stacked hay, dragged two bales out into the empty corral, broke them open and distributed the sections.

Standing in the open gateway leading to a small twenty-acre pasture, Ryan whistled. He waited a moment and whistled again, louder than the first time. According to Joe, the late Mr. Conchas had acquired the packhorses on short notice from various West Texas sale barns. Some of them had probably been pets and might come to a whistle.

As he walked back toward the barn, a big dun gelding and two sorrel mares trotted into the corral. By the time he returned with two more bales of hay, the corral was full of feeding horses.

Ryan dragged the bales to the center of the corral, left them, walked to the open gate, pulled it closed and glanced at his watch. Almost three. Joe said Naranjo had been insistent about starting the horses down the canyon at sundown.

He made his way through the horses to the two bales of hay he had just dragged in, stripped off the wire and scattered the sections. He moved back to the gate nearest the barn, twisted the loops of wire around a post and turned to look at the horses. He had studied them briefly yesterday, especially the three duns, looking for Grady's flying M brand on a foreleg. He hadn't found it.

He was looking for something else now, a saddle horse to take him into Mexico and back, a big strong one that might have to carry a double load on the return trip.

All the animals appeared healthy, active and in the ten-to-fifteen-year-old age range. A zebra-striped grulla gelding was big, but his short, thick neck and large feet gave him a clumsy look. One of the dun mares looked good, also two geldings – a tall blood bay and a seal brown. The seal brown stood beside the only paint, appearing almost black in the shade of the high corral. He was heavy, muscular, with dark hooves, but there was something about his eyes. They were small, a little dull – unintelligent.

The blood bay was alone at one of the hay sections. He was tall with high withers, probably a good runner. He ate with his ears back, twitching his tail and tossing his head at passersby. Ryan had a feeling he felt the same way about people.

The dun mare was big and deep-chested, with dark points and well-defined stripes on each foreleg. Her hooves were jet black, and she seemed alert. She shared a section of hay with two smaller sorrel mares and a stocky big-footed palomino gelding.

Ryan was about to move toward her when a sleek, rose-gray mare approached the group, ears flattened, and head tossing. The dun mare and her peaceful group gave ground and dispersed, leaving the hay section to the pushy grey. She was probably the leader of this bunch, certainly a candidate if it hadn't been settled yet.

As Ryan watched, the grey mare was joined by a large dark stallion colt, about two years old. The mare pinned her ears and snaked her head at him. The colt hesitated, stepped back momentarily, then, tossing his own head, confidently moved up to the section of hay. The mare ignored his second approach, and they ate peacefully side by side. Ryan was certain the big youngster was her colt. He wondered why Conchas would have bought the stud colt for a packhorse operation. That was asking for trouble.

Ryan went back to the barn, returned with the riding gear, dropped it just inside the gate and moved out among the feeding horses with Frank's curb-bit bridle over his right shoulder. He patted the dark colt's bulging shoulder as he passed, admiring him, but wondering again why he was here. A big stud colt among a green pack string would be nothing short of disaster.

He made his way quietly to the dun mare, put his hand on her back, moved it slowly up to her black mane and slipped the reins around her neck. She offered no resistance. He placed the bit into her mouth, the headstall over her ears, then buckled it and led her back to the gate.

The sound of a vehicle engine came through the open side door of the barn.

Ryan ignored it, thinking Joe would have finished sorting groceries and trail gear by now and be coming for the paint gelding he had already claimed as a mount.

Talking quietly, Ryan positioned the thick riding pad across the mare's back, slowly lifted the heavy roping saddle and settled it down on the pad. The mare stood quietly, ears cocked forward, staring through the gate slats toward the barn. Ryan, continuing the quiet words, reached under and pulled the girth toward him. It was too short for the mare's deep chest. He let it swing back, moved around the mare's rump to the other side.

The dun nodded her head, snorted, pawed at the base of the cedar pole fencing and stared again at the open barn door. As he reached for the billet anchoring the girth, Ryan's eye caught a slight movement at the barn door.

"Come, get your horse," he called out in Spanish without looking up, "and try him out."

"Actually, I want two of them," replied a soft feminine voice in English, a voice he had heard before. "The big bay and the blaze-face sorrel."

Startled, Ryan looked up, across the seat of the saddle. From under the flat brim of her black hat, *La Morena* stared back at him over the top slat of the gate. "The bay is over there in the corner." She pointed.

Ryan stared silently at her. What was she doing here? "Get the horses for me, please."

It didn't sound like a request, even with the "please" tacked on.

"You going to ride both of them?" Ryan moved easily into his undercover role. An old muleteer wouldn't be ordered around by some strange woman, no matter how pretty she was.

He lengthened the girth by two holes and walked slowly around the mare toward the gate.

La Morena took a step back. "These are my grandfather's horses. Get the bay and the sorrel."

"Your grandfather's horses?"

"Yes, my grandfather's horses," she said. "Don Lalo Naranjo. Are you are working for him?"

"I sure am." Ryan stepped toward the gate.

"Then you are working for me." She took another step back. "Are you going to get the horses for me or not?"

"Right now, ma'am," he said, still staring over the gate. "Going to get both of them for you right now." He turned back to the dun mare and ducked under her neck to the other side.

La Morena moved back to the gate. "And what is your name?"

"Shaw, Ryan Shaw." He pulled the girth tight against the mare's chest.

"My name is Yolanda."

He secured the latigo, put the stirrup down, swung back under the mare's neck, and stepped toward the gate again. "Nice to meet you, Miss..." He touched the brim of his hat and waited. She didn't correct him, neither did she volunteer a last name. "Miss Yolanda." Tugging the cuffs of his new roping gloves, he leaned over, tossed Frank's battered chaps aside and picked up the lariat.

"The bay and the blaze-face," he said. Yolanda was a pretty name. It suited her.

"Sure you want the bay? He acts a little..."

"Rope him." Her brown eyes widened, and she raised her chin ever so slightly. She had not backed away from the gate this time.

Well... he was supposed to be the hired man. Ryan stepped away from the gate, rolling the loop in Frank's worn lariat until it was the proper size. He draped it over his right shoulder and moved toward the center of the corral, thinking that it had been a long time since he roped a horse – or anything else.

Sensing a stalk, the horses scattered before him. The bay Yolanda wanted snatched a last bite of hay and moved warily to the far side of the corral, crowding behind a mass of already-milling, head-tossing horses.

Ryan slipped the loop from his shoulder and took four coils of lariat from his left hand. He flipped the stiff loop to his right side, opening it, then across to his left and waited, feeling Yolanda's eyes on his back.

The herd closed around the tall bay, momentarily pinning him. Ryan brought the loop across to his right, then forward, above his head and released it, all in one smooth, sweeping motion. He knew instantly it was a good throw. The loop arched across the corral, straightening the four coils thrown with it, hovered an instant above the bay gelding, then dropped around his neck. Ryan snapped the loop tight. The gelding surrendered immediately, and Ryan led him to the gate.

Yolanda tossed a halter and lead rope over the gate. Ryan haltered the bay, secured him to a corral post, re-coiled the lariat and went for the sorrel. Another good catch and he led the other horse back toward the gate, wondering again why she wanted two horses.

Yolanda stepped into the corral, and Ryan's eyes went straight to the dark walnut grips of the revolver protruding from a holster on her right hip. He hadn't noticed it when she was on the other side of the gate. He stared at it. She offered him another halter. He took it and turned to the sorrel.

The pistol appeared to be a Smith & Wesson .357 combat Magnum, but Smith & Wesson also made a .22 caliber on the same frame He would need a closer look to tell which it was. She might handle Magnum rounds all right, certainly the lighter .38 specials that could be fired in a .357. Maybe this wasn't a .22.

Ryan opened the gate, and Yolanda led the two haltered horses out. "Hold it open a minute, please." She gave a low dovelike whistle and walked on toward the barn. The rose-gray mare and the dark stallion colt trotted through the gate after her.

"Thanks," she called back over her shoulder. "And the pistol you keep staring at is only .22 – for snakes and things."

13

Ryan rode the dun mare in figure-eights around the corral. She responded quickly to heel and toe cues and to the lightest touch of a rein on her neck. He liked the mare, but it was Yolanda and the .22-caliber pistol that were still on his mind.

A .22 had probably put the holes in Grady's boots. How involved was she was in her grandfather's business?

Ryan circled the mare back to the gate, leaned over, unlatched the gate, pushed it open and rode through. The dun mare sidestepped perfectly as Ryan pushed the gate closed and latched it. He patted the dun on the neck and praised her. She had been someone's good horse.

He found Yolanda and Joe at the west end of the barn. Joe was in the back of Yolanda's pickup, handing down small cartons of lard. Yolanda was distributing them evenly in ancient, rawhide panniers hanging on either side of the big bay gelding. Each carton had been sealed inside a zip-lock plastic bag in preparation for the pack trip. There was easily 150 pounds of lard being loaded.

Ryan dismounted, tied the dun to a post and joined them. At least he and Joe had taken time to go over their story before Yolanda showed up. In the pickup, near Joe's feet, were two medium-sized cardboard boxes of ammunition. Most of it appeared to be .22 caliber.

"You want the ammo on the other horse?" Ryan asked. "The ammunition, duffel bag and sleeping bag go on the sorrel," Yolanda replied without looking in his direction.

Ryan walked past the horse Yolanda was loading to the blaze-face sorrel tied near the barn door. Another pair of rawhide containers were hitched to the horse's packsaddle. Ryan led him back to the pickup and began loading ammunition. All of it, the thirty ten-box cartons of .22

bullets, fifteen boxes of 12-gauge shotgun shells and eight boxes of .30-30 had been reinforced with clear packaging tape. "You planning a big hunting trip?" Ryan asked.

Yolanda glared at him, took four more plastic-encased cartons of lard from Joe and loaded them into the rawhide basket. "For the store," she said, as if that explained everything. She carried more cartons to the opposite side of the big bay, loaded them and returned. "My aunt's store across the river in La Mula," she said. "Some things are hard to get in Mexico. But you already know that, don't you?"

Ryan did not miss the sarcasm in her remark. Maybe his remark about the ammunition had sounded the same way. He decided he would just be quiet until he and Joe had a chance to talk.

"I don't know why she is here," Joe whined an hour later as he and Ryan packed their own trail gear, food and clothing into new brown nylon panniers hanging from the big-footed palomino. "Lalo told me I am the boss. She has been gone a long time – two maybe three years. I used to see her sometimes at Lalo's, but she never has anything to do with these things." That, and "*es nieta de Lalo*" – she's Lalo's granddaughter – was the only explanation Ryan could get out of Joe before Yolanda rode up to the porch on her rose-grey mare.

The dark stallion colt stood beside his mother tossing his head and pawing the ground. "Is he coming along?" Ryan nodded toward the colt.

"He won't be any trouble," Yolanda answered.

Ryan stared at the colt for a moment, looked at Yolanda and, shaking his head, went back to packing. Yolanda watched as Ryan and Joe lashed their two sleeping bags atop the load of supplies and mounted up. The three of them then led the loaded packhorses back to the barn and turned them into the corral with the others. Yolanda rode to the other side, threw the gate open and led the horses out. Ryan and Joe brought up the rear. It was dusk as they rode away from the ranch.

The valley quickly funneled them into a narrow canyon. The floor was rough, littered with large boulders. The horses were forced into a single column, and progress slowed as they maneuvered around the huge, jumbled rocks. The high canyon walls seemed to close in overhead, giving Ryan the impression that they were in a tunnel, or what had once been one, the jumbled rock being the remains of its roof. It was not a comfortable feeling.

The clean, washed look of the smooth boulders gave warning that here, inside *La Pipa*, the pipe, was no place to be during a heavy rain. Ryan was relieved when, an hour later, the canyon widened to fifty feet or more and was clear of the large rubble. The overhead moon was bright; occasionally, when the canyon ran straight, it gave him a glimpse of Yolanda at the head of the column of horses. The moon also revealed the stallion colt moving along the column, tossing his head, nipping and harassing the other horses, like a wild stallion moving his herd. To Ryan's surprise, the colt was actually helping move the horses along.

♦ ♦ ♦

It was well after midnight when they reached the river. They had waited north of the highway bridge for more than an hour, until the moon had set. The bridge was State Highway 170, between Lajitas and Presidio, seventy-five feet above the canyon floor and two miles north of the Rio Grande. They had passed under it on rough, hard ground under cover of darkness and had ridden the two miles to the river.

Ryan waited now on the dun mare in the darkness, smelling the cool, fish-scent of the Rio Grande and watching the lantern-light silhouette of Yolanda and her mare move across the narrow opening ahead, stringing a riata. Joe was closing off the canyon behind. The horses would then be confined to the cordoned-off area.

Above the steep canyon walls, the sky was a long strip of brilliant stars. Ryan was thinking about Yolanda. He had tried to imagine her shooting Grady. That was hard to do.

Not that she wouldn't shoot someone – he had no doubt about that, given the right circumstances. She was not shy about taking control of a situation, as she had done with him at the corral and when she had assumed command of the packhorse operation. There had been no declaration of authority. She had simply started giving orders, and he and Joe had complied. She was making all the decisions now. The question was, for how long. Was she coming back with the loaded pack train? Ryan had considered that and decided it would simplify things considerably if she did.

Yolanda finished up ahead, tied the end of her riata to the east wall, rode back to the lantern hanging from a cottonwood limb and began unsaddling her mare. Ryan heard Joe's paint gelding come up behind him. "We got 'em now, *Cuate*. Come on, get something to eat," Joe said as he rode by.

They would wait now, according to Yolanda's timetable, here in *el parque*, the park, as she and Joe called the grassy mouth of the narrow canyon, until daylight before crossing the river and making the steep climb out of the river gorge.

He watched Yolanda pull the saddle from her grey mare, end it up on the grass and turn to the two packhorses she had tied to a small cottonwood. She was a competent, experienced horsewoman... and a smuggler. Was she a murderer?

Ryan nudged the dun with his right heel and rode up to the lantern with the packhorse carrying his and Joe's gear. Joe and Yolanda were removing cartons of lard and ammunition from the panniers. Ryan dismounted, tied the horses and helped with the unloading. When the containers were light enough, he and Joe lifted them off the packsaddles and lowered them to the ground.

By the time they had unloaded their own packhorse and unsaddled, Yolanda had a fire going under a big cottonwood tree. Ryan walked toward her carrying a small grocery bag Joe had handed him. "How much farther to the camp?" He leaned over and placed the sack on a large flat rock.

"Not far." She was kneeling before the fire, hat hanging down her back by the leather thong. "About two hours." Her dark eyes and long black hair glistened in the firelight.

Ryan kneeled down across from her and emptied the sack onto the smooth rock: two bags containing tortillas and cooked beef. "We going by the store on the way?" He had been wondering about the merchandise delivery.

"I'm going to the store." She broke a small dry limb across her thigh and tossed the two pieces into the fire. "You're going on to the ledge."

"The ledge?"

"The ledge," she stared at him across the fire. "Rodrigo's camp. Your good friend, your *cuate*, hasn't told you about the camp?" The question was sharp.

Ryan shook his head. "Nothing about a ledge." He opened the bag containing a dozen flour tortillas and offered them to her.

Still staring at him, her eyes narrowed, she took a tortilla and spoke in a normal tone. "In the morning, after we cross, I am going up river to La Mula." She raked coals from the fire with a stick and tossed the tortilla on them. "You know where that is?"

"No," Ryan said.

"Eight kilometers." She nodded up river and flipped the tortilla over. "You and Joe go on to the ledge camp." She looked up at him. "Get some rest. There are new packsaddles and harnesses. Get them ready. I will be there sometime tomorrow with these two packhorses and three others. The day after tomorrow, we load up and leave after dark." She snatched the tortilla off the coals.

So, she was coming back, Ryan thought. He tossed a tortilla onto the hot coals, unwrapped another package, and offered her the meat it contained. Life had suddenly become much simpler. Lalo Naranjo would deal for his granddaughter, tell everything he knew about Grady's disappearance. All Ryan had to do was wait until they were back at the ranch with the load of cocaine and arrest her.

He thought about his next question and saw no harm in it. "And how many times are we going to do this?" Yolanda peered into the darkness toward Joe, then looked back at Ryan.

"Your friend doesn't tell you much, does he?" She picked up a small canteen and drank from it.

"He told me he was recruited just a few days ago himself and that he needed help. So here I am." Ryan pulled his tortilla from the coals.

"I got some chilies and onions," Joe said joining them, placing a coffee pot, canteen and a paper sack beside the fire as he sat down.

"Jose, tell your compadre, your *cuate*, how long this job is going to take." As she reached across for another tortilla, Yolanda said quickly in Spanish. "Maybe he has something better to do."

Joe looked surprised. “I don’t know,” he said in Spanish. “Lalo told me to take the horses and cross Rodrigo’s cargo. That’s all he told me. That’s what I’m going to do.”

Ryan did not understand her hostility toward him. She had seemed that way from the beginning. He did not want to provoke her, not now. He would stop asking questions. He knew all he needed to know. “I don’t have anything else to do,” he said slowly in Spanish. “I’ll pack for you and Joe for as long as you want. I was just curious, that’s all.”

“Well,” she said in English, looking first at Joe, then at Ryan. “It’s a big job and it’s going to take a long time.” She leaned over and picked up the empty coffee pot.

Joe reached into the paper sack, took out a two-pound bag of coffee. Yolanda poured water from the canteen into the coffee pot. Ryan watched her, thinking that the job was not going to take as long as she thought.

14

Inside the large tent on the ledge, late morning sunlight gave a fluorescent glow to the light-green canvas. The Colombian lay motionless on his big bed, listening for the noise that had awakened him. Only the distant, monotonous drone of the diesel engine that powered the electric plant could be heard. Sergio Rodrigo-Cabrera rubbed his forehead and glanced on either side of him. The girls were gone – two of them he thought, maybe three. The bedding was gone too, heaped somewhere on the floor, no doubt. Only a pillow remained. He doubled it under his head and stared down at his nakedness, at the fine white crystalline granules clinging to the thick black hair on his chest. He brushed clumsily at them with both hands.

From outside came the loud chinking noise that had awakened him. "Mexicans," he muttered.

Covering his ears, he rolled to the edge of the bed and stared at the sunlit canvas wall. The silhouette of the horse outside pawed impatiently at the hard ground. He had standing orders that the mare be saddled and brought to him every morning after breakfast... after breakfast... not while he was sleeping, not when he didn't feel like riding.

Rodrigo sat up on the edge of the bed and held his head, waiting for the dizziness to pass After a moment he stood up, snatched a towel from a nearby table and unzipped the doorway. The movement made him dizzy again. He paused, holding the canvas flap until the light-headedness passed, then strode naked out past the overhang of the canyon wall into the bright sunlight, toward a shower stall of new unpainted planks perched on the edge of the cliff.

"Take the mare away," he shouted in Spanish at two old men lounging in the coolness of the overhang. "And tell the cooks to fix my breakfast." As he did every morning, Rodrigo turned at the shower stall and walked west along the length of the big ledge to the wide packed-earth ramp that angled fifty feet down to the canyon floor. Two large stone corrals stood below, just past the bottom of the ramp. Empty! Still no packhorses!

He stomped back to the new shower stall, stepped inside and turned on the hot water.

Mexicans! How long does it take to bring twenty-five horses thirty kilometers down the canyons to the ledge? The question made him pause for a moment. How long had it been since Naranjo told him the horses were being gathered and shod? He adjusted the water temperature, stepped under the spray, shook his head in the warm water and couldn't remember. Whenever it was, the horses still weren't here and that meant another day in this godforsaken canyon.

He turned to let the water run down his back. Where were the horses? They should have been here by now. How long since Naranjo had said it would be only a few days? He shook his head. He had already tried to remember that.

Rodrigo squeezed shampoo from a plastic bottle onto his head and scrubbed it into a lather. He would remember in a moment, remember everything, as soon as his head cleared. It was the powder, the cocaine that was making it hard to remember things. He would stop that today, stop using the cocaine once and for all.

He had known others who became too fond of and too careless with their own merchandise. That wasn't going to happen to him. He was too smart.That would be stupid, to let such a little vice ruin everything now, after all the hard work and expense, the incredible expense.

A fortune gone, and being in this godforsaken place for three... no, two... only two months? Had it been only two months? Two miserable months? Too long, whatever it was, long enough that even the endless parade of young girls had grown monotonous. Long enough that he now understood why people paid so much for so little of the white crystalline powder.

He would stop using it today.

Rodrigo stepped back under the tepid water and rinsed the thick lather from his hair. Had he just ordered the horse taken away? Yesterday he had. He could remember that, and the day before. He hadn't ridden for quite a while, hadn't felt like it. He peered through the translucent cascade of water and saw the mare being led away. "Stop!" he shouted, moving from under the water to the open end of the stall. "Leave the mare, take her to the shade, *alla en la sombra*."

He would ride after breakfast, again this afternoon, and after breakfast tomorrow. He would take no more of the white powder, smoke no more of the strong sinsemilla marijuana.

There was too much at stake.

He unwrapped a new bar of soap and sniffed the wrapper before tossing it over the wooden planks of the stall. The black Cayman Island girls liked the sweet smell and bright pink color of this soap. Slowly, he rubbed the engraved bar over his body. It slipped from his hand and skidded across the wooden floor. Rodrigo leaned over, reached for the bar of soap and drove a small splinter under the nail of his right index finger. He straightened, staring at the protruding sliver of wood. "Goddamned Mexicans!" he muttered in thickly accented English.

He plucked the splinter with his teeth, spat it out and held the bleeding finger under the warm water.

Goddamned American blimps! He could be in Barbados or Martinique now if it weren't for the radar blimps.

Rodrigo turned the hot water completely off and let the cold spring water, piped from the back of the ledge, take his breath away. It always cleared his head. He wasn't really angry about the American radar blimps, not anymore. They were going to be very good to him. The blimps had shut down his operation completely, still had him shut down, but they had done the same to everyone else, stopped all smuggling flights across the border.

Rodrigo smiled. Cocaine that had flown freely into the United States over the Mexican border had backed up in the Colombian jungles. Street prices had soared, in New York, Chicago, Houston, Dallas and other large cities, doubling, then tripling within a week. Stepped-up enforcement campaigns by Colombian federal police and military made it impossible to warehouse the merchandise until alternate routes into the U.S. could be established.

Still smiling, Rodrigo turned to let the icy water run down his back. He had been in perfect position, had already known of an alternate route. Old Naranjo had talked of it often enough: burro pack trains, river crossings, dark winding canyons. It was the opportunity of a lifetime, and he had jumped at it.

On credit, and at discounted prices, he bought everything the other traffickers had on hand and could process before government troops closed them down. At the same time he constructed the new airstrip and moved his operation from Naranjo's old landing field twenty miles inland to within pack-train distance of the border. His planes never stopped flying, and the stockpile grew with each flight.

Now he had it all. Soon it would be across the border, trucked to an insulated hangar on a ranch near Amarillo, Texas, and slowly doled out to hungry American wholesalers for whatever price he decided on. Yes, the American radar blimps were going to be very good to him.

Rodrigo turned off the water and stepped out onto the sun-warmed flagstones that formed a small terrace along the cliff's edge. Daubing the cold water from his face, he stepped nearer the brink. On his right, to the west, he could see all of the two-thousand-foot runway, stretching up the canyon, a hard all-weather runway of packed river gravel and clay.

The equipment that had built it was a quarter mile away, parked along the south wall of the canyon: A big D12 bulldozer that had carved its own road through the mountains, three dumptrucks, a small road grader, a backhoe and a roller. Directly across the canyon, a hundred yards away and also under the protective slope of the south wall, three large twin-engine, turboprop planes glistened in the sunlight, staring back at him: two Beechcraft King Air C90s and one Aero Commander, all equipped with state-of-the-art navigational equipment and auxiliary fuel tanks giving each a maximum range of over twelve-hundred miles.

To the left of the airplanes were four pickups, two military-style Jeeps, and the yawning entrance of a low-ceiling limestone cavern that now contained the largest cache of cocaine ever amassed anywhere in the world. Sergio Rodrigo stood naked in the warm sun and smiled. It was all his.

A small man dressed in khakis and a bright red-and-blue headband left the shadows of the cavern and circled its entrance, making himself and the short-barreled Uzi submachine gun, suspended under his right arm, visible from the ledge. Rodrigo was looking for the guard, saw him, but gave no evidence of it.

He knew there were others, out of sight, just inside the cool cavern. All of his men were here now, twenty in all. The last of them had arrived unexpectedly early yesterday in the two King Airs. He did remember that. They had narrowly escaped a military raid on the last of his own processing camps. There would be no more flights from the Colombian jungles, not for a while.

Glaring hawklike from the ledge, he looked eastward along the south wall, at the camp of brush huts almost a half mile away. Mexicans! Four old men and their wives. Naranjo's people that he had evicted from the ledge, all too old to work, even to properly care for his horse.

He turned from the cliff and looked about his own camp atop the ledge. Plenty of Naranjo's people here, too, from La Mula, the tiny village near Naranjo's ranch. Four errand-runner handymen: one a self-proclaimed expert in electrical work plumbing and diesel engines; his helper; and two others in charge of the runway equipment and vehicles. Three cooks: Marta, a plump grey-haired señora and her two look-alike daughters, Catalina and Isabel. All spies for Naranjo – the old people down the canyon and these on the ledge. A situation he had avoided in Colombia by recruiting all of his men from Peru.

It would be only a matter of time until Naranjo's Mexicans reported that the flights from Colombia had ceased. The merchandise on hand must be gone by then. If it were even suspected that his sources had dried up, that the huge cache of cocaine in the cavern would in all likelihood be the last to pass through the province controlled by Lalo Naranjo, Rodrigo had no doubt that the old smuggler would have it confiscated by his ally, General Pagazos, the local military zone commander.

No, Naranjo must never know about the problems in Colombia, reason enough in itself to stop sniffing the fine white crystalline powder.

He could do that.

But there would still be the women. He smiled, then frowned. That had been a mistake. Allowing outsiders into the ledge camp. He enjoyed the spirited young señoritas, the mariachi bands and the all-night revelry as much as his men; but it had been a mistake, the result of sniffing the white powder too often.

He had told himself it was to keep the men here in the camp and out of trouble in the surrounding villages. But it was for himself also that he had encouraged the Mexicans to bring the women and music. Now, too many – far too many people – knew about the ledge camp.

The modern kitchen, plentiful food, drink, gifts, the strange Peruvian men – it all must be the gossip of surrounding villages. He was relying too much on Naranjo's military connection. It worried him.

Rodrigo looked back down into the canyon at the new runway, the airplanes and the entrance of the cavern containing his cocaine. Without the horses, it would all be for nothing.

The once-orphaned child from the slum streets of Barranquillas, Atlantica, Colombia, concluded his morning bath ritual in the usual manner. Whipping the damp towel around his neck, he strolled casually back under the overhang to the shiny chrome-trimmed restaurant cookstove and inspected the breakfast being prepared for him.

The mother-and-daughters cook team, as they did each morning, pretended to ignore Rodrigo's nakedness. The youngest managed a guarded glance as she scooped the last bits of sizzling chorizo from the grill with a wide spatula and dropped them into a white serving bowl. Her sister finished spanking a small ball of dough to the proper thinness, tossed it onto her portion of the grill and caught a glimpse of Rodrigo's bare white skin as she leaned over to flip another half-cooked tortilla speckled-side up. The mother was just closing one side of the huge double-door refrigerator when shouts came from below the ledge.

"*¡Caballos! ¡Vienen caballos!*"

Rodrigo hurried to the brink of the ledge. A crowd of his Peruvians were on the runway in front of the planes, shouting and pointing up the canyon.

"*¡Caballos! ¡Caballos, Jefe! ¡Vienen los caballos!*"

Rodrigo squinted up the canyon. There, between the runway and the north wall, across from the bulldozer and backhoe, a long string of horses was coming fast, their varied colors blending perfectly with the brown and red tones of the canyon.

The packhorses at last! Rodrigo pulled the ends of the towel, making it tight against the back of his neck, and watched the line of horses approach.

Naranjo's little blonde Mexican was in the lead, behind him only one other rider, at the rear of the column. Two men and how many horses? There should be twenty-five. Twenty-five and he could be gone in two weeks. The small blonde man, "little white rat," Rodrigo called him, waved at the men lined up in front of the planes, others in front of the cavern, then up at the ledge as he passed.

Rodrigo waved back, then, realizing what he had done, lowered his arm and scowled at the three cooks and two of the handymen who had gathered nearby on the rim. He looked back into the canyon and counted. Only sixteen packhorses. The four guards he was sending with the first load would each take a horse, leaving only twelve to carry cargo on the first trip.

He looked farther up the canyon. Empty!

Rodrigo folded his arms, tightened his jaw muscles and watched the horses pass below. God damned Mexicans. Twenty-five packhorses were to be the minimum, what had been agreed upon, what he had been promised – not sixteen. They could take his riding mare, take Lalo's prized ranch stock, buy more, do whatever had to be done, but there were going to be twenty-five horses packing cocaine out of here.

Angrily, Rodrigo turned his attention to the last rider. He was tall and big-boned, like the dun horse he was riding. The wide brim of his straw hat covered his face until he looked up and raised a hand in greeting.

Rodrigo felt a jolt go through his body. An American? A goddamned American? Had that ignorant little white Mexican brought a goddamned American here to the ledge?

15

Ryan was surprised to see a naked man up on the ledge, but he knew who he was. Even from fifty feet below, he could see the surprise, then the anger in Rodrigo's face. He turned his attention back to the horses ahead, still feeling Rodrigo's eyes on his back. He knew it would not be long before he met the Colombian.

Just past a gravel-and-earthen ramp leading down from the ledge was a large stone corral. Four men had fanned out across the runway to guide the horses into its wide-open gate. Joe and the lead horses were already disappearing inside the high stone walls. Across the runway, short dark men in new khakis and brightly colored headbands stared surly from under the noses of three large airplanes. Rodrigo's men. Peruvians, Joe had said, fifteen or sixteen in all, twice the number Joe had told him about.

Two of the men, machine guns dangling from shoulder straps, straightened from their slouched positions behind a waist-high stone barrier that guarded the entrance of a cave.

Ryan returned their sour looks and peered into the funnel-shaped opening. It was deep and dark. Nothing of its interior could be seen. He glanced back at the three aircraft, parked tail to wall just west of the cave. Big, long-range turboprops, the kind a South American cocaine smuggler would need. Above the airplanes was the solid rock overhang.

For most of the last two miles, the overhang on both sides of the canyon had crept inward. The runway, the aircraft, equipment and the ledge itself were all but hidden from the air.

Ryan was awed by the Colombian's ingenuity and audacity. Within a few miles of the U.S. border, he had constructed and concealed a complete airport facility. The last of the horses turned into the stone corral and Ryan followed them in.

A wall ran north and south just inside the gate, dividing what appeared from the outside to be one large corral into two smaller ones. The corral walls, three feet thick and six feet high, were made up of large, gray river stones, each carefully placed and shimmed with pebbles and small stone chips. Although he could easily see over it on horseback, the solid enclosure immediately made Ryan uncomfortable. He felt trapped.

He rode to the only other gate, a connecting one in the east wall, that led into the other corral.

He dismounted, dropped the dun's reins, opened the cedar-pole gate and slipped through to the other side. It was much like the other corral, but this one had water.

A large pipe protruding from the canyon wall spouted water into a long stone-and-masonry water trough. The overflow at the far end gurgled along the ground for only a few feet before disappearing into the sand and gravel. Ryan walked over to the flowing pipe. It was rusty and encrusted with minerals. Long ago it had been driven into a flowing spring in the limestone wall to divert the water into the trough. He rinsed his hands, splashed water on his face and drank.

There was a slight mineral taste, but it was good, and cold... much too cold for horses to drink after the warm morning trek. He took off his hat, drank from the pipe again, moved his head under the flowing icy water and held it there. Rodrigo would be coming soon.

The cover story he and Joe had gone over yesterday no longer seemed as believable as it had sitting at the kitchen table in the old ranch house. He wasn't even sure it had worked on Yolanda. From the look on Rodrigo's face, he wasn't going to listen to much of anything anyway.

Ryan stepped back from the trough and shook his head, flicking some of the cold water from his face and neck; he straightened, smoothed his hair and stared across the corral at a gate in the east wall. It would let him and the dun out toward the mouth of the canyon.

The wide valley, a half mile away, would take them to the river, probably less than five miles away. If there were no crossing place, he could leave the horse and swim.

According to the map and briefing Frank had given him, the highway would be only a few hundred yards from the river. He could catch a ride to Lajitas, call Frank, and always wonder what had happened to Grady. No!

There was a plan now, a good plan, a good chance to find out about Grady – if he could just get past Rodrigo. He pulled his hat on, opened the gate and walked back into the other corral. Joe had cut out the horse carrying their gear, tied him to a snubbing post in the middle of the corral and was rummaging through one of the panniers. The men who helped pen the horses stood quietly in front of the gate they had closed behind them. Ryan saw that they were old, dressed in faded Levi's and crumpled straw hats.

"*Gracias*," he said as he led the dun toward them. As he drew nearer, he realized that they were even older than he first thought. Only two looked to be under seventy years of age.

Their clothing was old, too, frayed and patched. They had the dusty, unkempt look of outdoor living about them. They smelled of wood smoke and old sweat.

"*Cigarros,*" Ryan heard Joe shout from behind as a gold-and-white carton of cigarettes sailed through the air. One of the old men caught it just as the wide gate behind him was yanked open.

Rodrigo rode into the corral on a prancing chestnut sorrel mare. His silver-mounted Mexican saddle flashed in the bright sunlight as he passed in front of Ryan, then Joe, and crowded the loose horses against the far wall. Four khaki-clad men carrying short-barreled machine guns rushed into the corral and fanned out in covering positions.

Ryan stepped back to the dun's left shoulder, putting the animal between him and all but one of the machine guns. The old men retreated to the nearest corner of the corral. Joe picked up the reins of his paint saddle horse and started toward Ryan, but Rodrigo circled back on the high-stepping mare and cut off the retreat.

"You don't have enough horses, Blanco," Rodrigo shouted in rapid, strange-sounding Spanish. The sorrel mare tossed her head and pranced nervously in place. "And who is this?" The new saddle squeaked as

Rodrigo turned, pointing a rawhide quirt toward Ryan.

Again, he shouted something in the strange dialect. This time it was completely unintelligible. The mare tossed her head and began a tight circle. "A *gringo!*" Rodrigo shouted as his mount completed the revolution. "That's what you call them here, no? *Gringos*! You brought us u*n hijo bastardo gringo*!"

Ryan understood that part. He felt his face flush and his thoughts turned to the .45 pressing butt forward against his left hip... under his belt and buttoned shirt. Not the best quick draw position, not with four Uzis already trained in your direction. He remained motionless, hands in front of him, his eyes on the man glaring down at him.

Rodrigo's mare made another circle, her frightened eyes rolled back, toward the flashing spur rowels not quite touching her as Rodrigo pumped the heavy stirrup leathers against her ribs.

Not the time for anger, Ryan thought, not the time for anything stupid. Rodrigo had just told him something.

Not enough horses, he had said. Not enough horses! That's what this was really about. He might not like a *gringo* being brought into his camp, but it was horses he had mentioned first. Yolanda had said the job would take a long time.

Ryan turned slowly toward the dun mare, checked the girth and stepped up into the saddle. He turned her around and moved up alongside Rodrigo's smaller mare. He would make it short and simple. "Señor Rodrigo, I don't believe we've met," he said in Spanish. He was close enough now to be safe from a machine-gun burst.

"My name is Shaw, Ryan Shaw. "I'm a muleteer, a packer, and I'm a good one." He nodded toward Joe without taking his eyes off Rodrigo. "Señor Montez is also a muleteer. You can see that these are good strong horses, all shod, ready to go to work."

Rodrigo's new saddle squeaked again as he shifted uncomfortably, glancing behind him at his four gunmen.

Ryan continued. "There are more just like these on the way." His peripheral vision picked up three more Uzi-armed men as they came through the open gate to his left.

Rodrigo took a deep breath and glanced confidently around as the new arrivals spread out on either side of him.

Ryan went on unabashed. “Señor Montez and I take good care of the horses we handle. We give them good feed, keep shoes on them,and don’t let their backs get sore. We’re ready to haul all the cocaine your airplanes can fly in here.”

Rodrigo stiffened at mention of the word “cocaine.”

Ryan’s voice took on a harsh sound as he finished. “We can do that for you, Señor Rodrigo. Or you can get somebody else to pissant it out of here on a short string of crippled horses or burros....”

Rodrigo’s face turned angry again. He backed the mare away, and she began her tight nervous circle again.

Ryan felt like a target. His face muscles began to twitch as he watched the sorrel turn Rodrigo around in slow motion. The Colombian seemed confused, glaring from the machine guns to Joe, the old men, then back to Ryan. How desperate was he to get his cocaine across? How much did he dislike Americans? Suddenly, Rodrigo jerked cruelly on the reins and moved the sorrel back alongside the dun.

“Come to the camp tonight,” Rodrigo muttered in English. “We will do something special for such talented experts.” He aimed the mare toward the gate, leaned forward, hit her with both spurs and was gone.

Ryan took a deep breath, looked at Joe and winked. It was all he could manage for the moment. The little man gave an awkward salute but didn’t smile. Ryan leaned forward, pressing both hands on top of the saddle horn to stop their shaking.

16

Ryan watched from the back of the dun mare as Joe and the four old men scattered hay. It was still too soon to let the horses in to water, but they could eat. As they finished with the hay, one of the old men glanced up at the sun and spoke quietly to the others. They in turn looked upward, then moved toward the gate.

Joe motioned with his arm. "Cuate, come on. We've been invited to lunch." Ryan was hungry. He quickly got down, pulled the saddle, thick pad and bridle off of his horse and headed toward the gate. One of the old men waited and opened it for him.

Ryan nodded as he carried the gear past him. Outside, he stopped, shifted the saddle to his left hip and offered his hand. "Ryan Shaw."

"Juan Bejarano." The old man said as they shook hands. Ryan thanked him again for helping with the horses.

"*De nada.*" Juan took the heavy pad and bridle from atop the saddle.

"There are packsaddles and equipment here for the horses, no?" Ryan asked in Spanish.

"*Si,*" Juan replied, "Many saddles, fine new saddles from Colombia, there in the cavern." He pointed across the runway. "*Con la carga blanca.*" With the white load.

Ryan asked how much "white load."

"*¡Mucha!*" Juan closed the gate behind them. "The cave is full of it. *¡Mucha carga!*" He shook his head.

Juan rounded the outside corner of the stone corral and led them past a huge stack of baled hay to a long narrow sotol-thatched hut, a *jacal*, backed against the north wall of the canyon.

Joe and the other old men were waiting in front. They looked up as

Ryan and Juan approached. Ryan nodded to them and looked inside, over the hut's half-wall, at four large cots made of burlap and poles, a large plywood table, three metal folding chairs and a small propane cook stove. Apparently this was to be their quarters while at the ledge camp. Not fancy but tolerable. The three cots were bare, apparently unclaimed. The old men must be housed elsewhere.

Beside him, Joe's saddle hung from a rope attached to the arbor framework. Other lengths of rope dangled nearby. He hoisted Frank's heavy saddle, pulled the end of a loose rope down through the gullet, then up, around the horn, and secured it with a slip knot. As Ryan lowered the saddle to hang from the arbor, he looked up. The east wall of the stone corral cut off his view of the cavern entrance, but most of the large recess that funneled down to it was visible. He remembered there had been two armed men behind the fortified passage when he passed by with the horses.

Ryan turned to the others and introduced himself to the three old men he hadn't met.

Lunch was a half mile down canyon from the corrals. Ryan and Joe were ushered into an open area between two of the four brush huts making up a small encampment under the overhang of the south canyon wall. Ryan was introduced to the four wives, and the men seated themselves at a large makeshift table made from an old door. Señora Bejarano and the three other women served the food: meat-and-potato tacos made with thick corn tortillas cooked on a large sheet of metal suspended over a bed of hot coals.

"Miguel and Felipe cut wood for the Peruvians," Juan Bejarano said in reply to Ryan's question about what they did. "Marcos has a boat. Sometimes he fishes."

"We used to have goats and sheep and a few cattle," said Miguel, who looked the oldest. And we lived on the ledge until Rodrigo came." All the men nodded agreement.

"They took the animals, took our houses. Now we live here." He made a sweeping gesture.

"We will go back when Rodrigo leaves," Felipe quickly added.

"Yes," Juan agreed, a bitter tone to his voice. "The ledge belongs to us. We will go back when Rodrigo leaves." There was a long silence, then Ryan asked Juan if he helped out with the woodcutting and fishing or if he was *el mero gallo*, the boss. That amused everyone, including the four women.

"I catch snakes," Juan said proudly when the laughter subsided.

Ryan tried to keep the smile on his face as he carefully eyed the taco in his left hand.

"*¿Por que?* What do you do with them?" Joe quickly asked, looking down at his own taco.

"Rodrigo and the others," Juan replied, "l*os Peruanas*, they pay ten dollars American for *los reyes*, the king snakes, l*os indigos*, the blue ones, and *los cascabels*, the rattlers." He wrinkled his leathery face into a smile, showing large, evenly-worn, white teeth.

"*Si, si*," Joe turned to face the old man. "*¿Pero, por que?*"

Why? What do they do with snakes?"

"They make them fight," Juan said, still smiling. He made motions with both arms and hands, simulating striking and writhing serpents. "They get drunk, make bets and throw them into the pit up there. He nodded up the canyon with his bare, grey head. "Up there on the ledge." He grinned, exposing the large white teeth again. "I found a good one this morning." He looked at the other men. They nodded their heads in agreement.

Ryan glanced at Joe, who wrinkled his brow, shook his head and looked relieved. They finished their third taco as the old men reminisced about the days when they worked for Don Naranjo and every week had a burro train going up *la pipa* to the ranch.

After lunch Felipe, Miguel and Marcos stretched, yawned, excused themselves and wandered off toward the other *jacals*. Ryan and Joe thanked the women for the meal and followed Juan deeper under the overhang to a thick layer of grass mats. The hottest part of the day, yet it was cool under the sloping limestone canyon wall. Siesta time.

Ryan dozed for a few minutes, slowly becoming aware of the drone of voices. He opened his eyes. It was the four old women, eating and talking at the table. He closed his eyes again and thought about what it would be like tomorrow night at the ranch, telling Yolanda who he was and placing her under arrest.

He shifted uncomfortably on the straw mat and turned his thoughts to last night, to Yolanda's dark eyes and long black hair glistening in the firelight as they waited in the border canyon for daylight. He thought about how graceful and efficient she had looked on her grey mare, leading them across the river, and how she had unexpectedly looked back and waved to him as she led the two packhorses up the river trail alone.

Ryan took a deep breath and changed his position on the mat again. He forced an image of Yolanda with the pistol on her hip, then with it in her hand and tried to imagine her shooting Grady. The picture wouldn't form.

"*Es un valiente*, he is a brave one." The women were talking louder now. "Felipe says he stood up to Rodrigo, was ready to fight him and six of the Peruvians with machine guns."

"That sounds foolish to me, not brave."

"I hope they don't fight. This one comes with horses to take the cargo to the other side. The sooner it is gone, the sooner the devils will leave."

"What do you mean? They bring more every day, they will never leave."

"No, tell her, Fira."

"There was a fight with the *federales* somewhere in Colombia. They can't go back. Miguel and Felipe heard them talking when they took the firewood."

"Oh, *que bueno*! Then maybe they will leave soon."

"Not for a while. It will take a long time, a month, to move the cargo, even with thirty strong horses, my husband says so."

A month! Ryan sat up, almost hitting his head on the sloping wall. The four women stared at him in surprise. He looked over at Joe and Juan, both unmoving, asleep. He eased off the mats toward the women and stood up.

"It will take a month to move the cargo?" He looked from one face to the other, not sure which one had said that. The women glanced at each other. Finally Señora Bejarano shook her head.

"It is what Juan told me." She nodded toward her sleeping husband.

Ryan smiled, thanked them again for the meal, pulled his hat on and left. Back at the corrals, he saddled the dun, led her out of the corral and shut the gate. He would make a better impression on horseback; also, he wanted the guards to see and hear him coming.

Best not to surprise people armed with machine guns. He mounted the big mare, rode up onto the hard runway and nudged her into a trot toward the yawning cavern and the men who, a short time before, had been ready to cut him down.

The entrance to the cave was wide, funneling back into the undercut cliff a good twenty feet to a low, dark tunnel. The new horseshoes on the packed gravel left no doubt of his approach. Ahead, on his right, a group of the khaki-clad Peruvians looked up from a stack of large wooden boxes under the nearest airplane. Ryan did not bother to greet them. He kept the mare headed straight for the cave.

From behind the low stone barricade, the two guards leveled machine guns at him for the second time that day.

"I want to see the saddles and harnesses," Ryan said loudly in Spanish, swinging down from the saddle. "Is that them?" He pointed past the armed men to three jumbled piles just inside the wide tunnel. The guards did not respond, their round Andean faces expressionless.

Ryan led the mare past them and the barricade, into the big cave. Feeling their eyes on him, he snatched a rawhide-covered saddle from the first pile. It was heavy, brand new, with not a scrap of rigging on it.

Blankets and saddle pads made up the second pile, most still in clear plastic coverings. The third pile was harnesses, also new, neatly bundled into what he assumed were individual sets. He looked back at the pile of bare saddles. There was a lot of rigging to be done by tomorrow afternoon. He leaned over, pawing and poking at the harness and blanket piles, waiting for his eyes to adjust to the dim light. There was something else he had come to see.

Slowly, rows of waist-high pyramids began to take shape in the cavern gloom. Stacks of dark green duffel bags. He dropped the dun's reins and moved quickly farther into the cave, to the nearest stack. Three bags cross-ways atop three other bags, two cross-ways on those, two more on top – ten bags to a stack. He counted five rows, squinted into the darkness – how many deep? Ten... twelve... and more. He was sure there were more, but it was too far, too dark. Five rows across, twelve deep. He lifted a bag from the pyramid in front of him. It was heavy and solid. He heard footsteps behind him.

"*¡Deialo!"* Drop it! came an angry command.

Ryan glanced at the short Peruvian now beside him, hefted the duffel bag twice more and tossed it back on top of the others. About fifty pounds. Ignoring the machine gun and the sullen face, he stared back into the darkness.

"We'll be taking this out of here tomorrow," Ryan said, patting the duffel bag he had just replaced. Some of it anyway, he thought as he turned and walked back to the mare. "Tell the men to bring this equipment over to the corrals after siesta."

He gestured toward the stacks of gear as two men carried one of the wooden boxes from the airplane past him, into the cave. The black lettering on the box was in several languages, but the words "Danger – Explosives" and "C-4" jumped out from the other scrawling. Ryan led the mare out past the fortified entrance, stepped up into the heavy saddle and let the dun trot back toward the corrals.

His mind was racing. Ten duffel bags to a stack – five hundred pounds. Five rows across, twelve stacks to a row. By the time he crossed the runway, he had made the calculation: thirty thousand pounds. Rodrigo, that son-of-a-bitch Rodrigo, had thirty thousand pounds – fifteen tons of cocaine – ready to cross, and that was only what he had seen. There was more, he was sure, much more, farther back in the cavern.

17

The narrow band of cloudless sky above the canyon walls was fading as Ryan roped the last horse. He haltered the stout blue roan gelding and led him to the side gate where Joe and the others were working.

The four old men had surprised him. They were seasoned muleteers, remnants of Naranjo's old gang, and without question, knew their way around pack gear and pack animals. Even with a late start, they were almost finished. All the packsaddles were rigged, and this was the last horse to be fitted.

Ryan handed the lead rope to Felipe, opened the gate, slipped outside and walked along the stone corral walls toward the mouth of the canyon. Working with the horses and equipment had, to some extent, taken his mind off what he had seen in the cavern. He had been able to put it away for a while, but as the number of horses in the corral diminished, as he roped one after another and helped adjust the rigging, a disturbing thought had surfaced, an image of all the stacks of duffel bags that would still be in the cavern after every packhorse was loaded tomorrow. It was something that had to be considered.

Ryan rounded the outside corner of the corral and walked to the haystack, a thousand bales at least, sheltered by the inward slope of the canyon wall and near enough to the stone corral to be tossed directly into it. He climbed to a ledge of bales near the top and sat down. Pulling a handful of hay from one of the tight bales, he crushed the dried stems, then looked at them and smelled. Oat hay. Freshly cut and plenty of grain on it. He wondered where it had come from.

The thought caused him to look out over the corrals, toward the vehicles, the earth-moving equipment and the airplanes parked under the slope of the opposite canyon wall. All invisible from the air. Even the runway would hardly be noticeable between the steep concave canyon walls. All that, and fifteen tons of cocaine, so near the U.S. border. With resources to accomplish that, Rodrigo could have brought the hay from anywhere in the world. Ryan let the oat grains and straw fall from his hand.

This was a far cry from the one-shot deal he and Frank had thought it was. Juan had told his wife that it would take a month to move the cargo. What Ryan had seen in the cavern made him believe that Juan could be right. Yolanda had said she was bringing three more horses, along with the two that had packed the lard. That would bring the total up to twenty-four animals. Yolanda, Joe and the riding mounts plus one horse for trail gear. That left twenty packhorses to haul cocaine.

Crossing a load every other day, two hundred pounds per horse, would take a little over two weeks just to cross the fifteen tons he had seen – and there was more. Ryan shook his head at the thought of all that cocaine going into the U.S. on packhorses under a billion-dollar network of radar blimps. He found himself staring at the three airplanes parked against the canyon wall, facing the runway. Something else to think about. Two Beechcraft King Airs, both silver – one with red trim, the other with blue – big fuselages, bullet noses. Grady, Frank and he had once seized a King Air. They had waited two days for it at a small airfield east of Tucson. The hundred pounds of marijuana on board had cost the owner a million dollars' worth of airplane. Customs had kept the King Air, instead of selling it. It was probably still in use.

Ryan studied the third plane, an Aero Commander, also a turboprop, white, big and expensive, long nose, high tail. No doubt all three were equipped with the latest radio and navigational equipment, bringing the total worth of each to over a million dollars. All would be subject to seizure by customs the minute the first cocaine-laden packhorse crossed the river.

Ryan arched his back, rubbed his neck and rotated his shoulders. His instinct was to go for everything: the cocaine, the airplanes and Rodrigo. But things had changed since he, Grady and Frank had roamed both sides of the border almost at will. Working an investigation in

Mexico was complicated now. The State Department had to give its blessing, and that didn't happen without permission from the Mexican government. Notifying the Mexican government was the same thing as notifying Rodrigo and Naranjo. An operation of this magnitude did not take place without government complicity.

Ryan leaned back against the hay. Dusk was in the canyon now, but he could still see the planes, visualize the stacks of green duffel bags inside the cavern. Fifteen tons. Something unimaginable during the years that he, Frank and Grady were chasing grams and ounces of heroin along the border. If he thought for a moment that Customs would back him, not notify the State Department for two weeks, maybe three – long enough for him to get all the cocaine across – he would forget the reason he had come here and go for it. Grady would understand. Grady would insist on it... if he could.

A change of wind direction brought the sound of a whining, straining engine. Ryan looked toward the mouth of the canyon. In the distant twilight, what appeared to be a white bus dragged itself up from the rough canyon floor onto the end of the runway. Gears shifting, it came slowly on toward the ledge.

Ryan stared, puzzled. What the hell was a bus doing here? He jumped down from the haystack and walked to the front of the corral.

The bus slowed as it approached. It was an old school bus, one of the stubby, short models. It whined past him and lumbered to a stop at the foot of the earthen ramp leading up to the ledge. Ryan could see that it was filled almost to capacity with women.

He joined Joe and the four old men in front of the corrals. A window near the back of the bus dropped open, and a young woman in a bright pink dress leaned out.

"*¡Jose! ¡Hola, Jose!*" she yelled.

"Anita," Joe answered. He passed his lariat to Felipe and hurried toward the bus. The doors at the front opened, and the driver, a neatly dressed man in his early forties, stepped out and stood to one side as colorfully attired women poured out of the bus. Joe greeted all of them, some by name, some by suggestive remarks and gestures.

The driver was the only male on board. Something about him

sparked Ryan's curiosity, and he moved closer. The man was of average height, a little on the heavy side, dark straight hair and a narrow, neatly trimmed mustache. His jeans were faded and worn. The collar and short sleeves of his white shirt were frayed, and his brown boots dusty. Offhand there was nothing unusual about him, yet... something was not quite right.

Ryan felt a hand on his shoulder and turned. Joe had just introduced him to three young women, girls actually, not one of them past their mid-teens. Ryan asked where they were from. The one Joe had called Anita said they were all from the village of Paso de San Antonio. Ryan knew where it was from the map Frank had given him, but he asked about it anyway.

"*Alla, como....*" The smallest but oldest-looking of the trio pointed south.

"*Treinta kilometres,*" interrupted a young voice from a passing group.

"*¡Treinta, no!*" shouted the first girl in mock disgust. "*Cincuenta-uno y media,*" chimed in the girl clinging to Joe's right arm. All the girls giggled.

Ryan glanced up and caught the driver watching them. "How far is it?" he asked in English.

The surprised look on the man's face said that he understood. He straightened and cleared his throat. "A little farther than that." His English was good. "Sixty-five kilometers. Not far, but rough, very rough."

Ryan nodded, surprised at the articulate English. He looked the man over again, this time noticing the military creases. The old white shirt, worn and faded but starched, had a crease running down the middle of each pocket. The faded Levi's were also starched and creased. And the shine on the brown boots could be seen even through the fresh layer of dust. The driver of an old school bus in the middle of nowhere was very well cared for.

Rodrigo's men appeared, machine guns and semiautomatic pistols conspicuously displayed. The bus driver seemed surprised at first, then very interested. Not one of the Peruvians or the weapons they carried escaped his scrutiny. Obviously, this was the bus driver's first trip to the camp.

Not so the girls. They immediately mingled with the armed men and began to drift en masse up the ramp. Lights had come on up above. The bus driver looked anxiously at the departing crowd, gave Ryan a parting nod and hurried after them.

"Going to be a party, *Cuate*," Joe said in a low growling tone as he grabbed Ryan's arm and shook it. "Anita says this is the band." Joe and the three girls still with him were staring past the mouth of the canyon at a pair of bobbing headlights slowly advancing toward the ledge.

"The girls understand English?" Ryan asked quietly, also staring at the distant headlights.

Joe shook his head negatively.

"Take them on up to whatever's going on and see what you can find out about the bus driver." As he was talking he noticed the four old men making their way along the corral wall, headed home.

"The driver?" Joe gave him a puzzled look and glanced up the incline. The bus driver had reached the top of the ramp. He hesitated, looked around, then stepped out of sight onto the lighted ledge.

"Understand?" Ryan asked in English.

"Don't worry." Joe put his arms around two of the girls and squeezed them. "I find out everything." He grinned and started up the ramp. "You coming, Cuate?"

Before he could answer, the sound of shod hooves on packed gravel reached them. Ryan peered up the canyon into the gloom as the clatter grew louder. At first, there were only the showers of sparks from iron shoes, then he made out the lead horse and the slender rider, coming along the edge of the runway. "Take the girls on up," Ryan repeated. "I'll be along later." He turned, hurried to the corral gate and threw it open.

Yolanda rode in leading the long string of packhorses. She circled the rose grey back toward the gate and tossed Ryan the lead rope to the horses behind her. As Ryan caught the rope, light from the ledge above fell across Yolanda's face. It was wet, streaked with tears. She was crying.

18

The stallion colt trotted into the corral behind Yolanda and the packhorses, pranced the circumference of the stone wall and stopped in front of the closed gate leading to the cold water. He tossed his head and pawed the ground impatiently.

Ryan closed the gate behind him and looked up at Yolanda. She was in the shadow of the ledge now, head down, both arms braced against the saddle horn, her face no longer visible.

“Are you all right?” Ryan asked in English.

She nodded affirmatively but he could see her shoulders began to shake and hear faint sobbing. Ryan dropped the lead rope to the packhorses and hurried to the side of Yolanda’s mare.

“Come here.” He reached up, put his arm around her waist and tugged gently. She leaned over and he took her from the saddle easily. She buried her face in his right shoulder and began to cry uncontrollably. Ryan put her down and quietly held her.

“It’s the colt,” she sobbed several minutes later, “he’s all cut up.” Her voice broke, and she pressed her face back into his shoulder and cried.

Ryan pulled her closer. “He’s over at the gate, looking for a drink of water. He can’t be hurt too bad.”

“No, I saw him.” Her breath came in sobs. “I left him at the hacienda... he must have jumped the fence... got into some wire somewhere. He caught up with me an hour ago... He’s cut to pieces.”

Ryan held her for a while. The vehicle carrying the band arrived; its headlights flashed through the gate for a moment. Ryan heard the rattle of its dying six-cylinder engine. Doors opened, allowing the murmur of masculine voices and quiet laughter into the night. Guitar strings were struck accidentally and a *guitarron* – a six-string bass instrument like an oversized guitar – gave forth a hollow clunk as it was unloaded.

As the voices trailed away, Yolanda pushed herself away from Ryan and patted his damp shirt.

"Thank you." Her voice was thick. "I got you all wet." She wiped her eyes with the back of her hand and looked toward the pawing stallion colt.

"I'll get a light," Ryan said, dropping his arms from around her shoulders and stepping back.

As he opened the gate, he heard the soft whistle Yolanda used to call the mare and colt. He closed the gate behind him and hurried along the front of the stone corrals, thinking how good she had felt pressed against him. Then he reminded himself that she may have killed Grady, that in 36 hours they would be at the ranch with a load of cocaine and he would arrest her.

The new three-cell flashlight and extra batteries were in his saddle bags. The first-aid kits he had made up for the horses were somewhere in the nylon panniers. All of it, panniers, saddle bags, duffel bags and bed rolls had been left in front of the *jacal.*

First, he needed the light. Even the faint glow from the electric lights up on the ledge was absent beyond the corrals. The hut was a dark blob at the base of the canyon wall.

He felt along the thatched front wall with one foot until it struck something, then he squatted, feeling with both hands, hoping they would not find a scorpion or a snake. The thought made him pull his hand back when he first touched the slick saddlebag leather. He quickly unbuckled a flap and felt inside: fence pliers, the sawed-off handle of the shoe hammer, a small round tin of nails, a battery and... the light. He switched it on and rummaged until he had all three extra batteries. He shoved them into his hip pockets and turned to the nylon bags.

Just then a light came on across the runway, then a second and a third. Bright lights from propane or gasoline lanterns, exactly what he needed. Ryan walked swiftly to the runway and started across, flashing his light at the cavern.

"*¡Hola! ¡Hola, hombres!*" he called out repeatedly. Receiving no response, he slowed, continuing his approach cautiously until he was within the outer ring of light from three lanterns suspended from the overhang. He could see the short barrels of two machine guns pointing at his belly from the shadow of an alcove.

"I need one of the lanterns," Ryan said politely in Spanish as he slowly raised his hands to shoulder level. Two men stepped into the ring of light. Like the Peruvians he had seen earlier, these two were hatless, short and stout, with long, coarse black hair held in place with bright, folded bandannas. Both stared at him with cold mongoloid eyes. The man on his right wore a thick black mustache, khaki trousers and a light-colored long-sleeved shirt of coarse material. The other Peruvian was dressed as those in the corral had been, in new khakis.

"I need one of the lanterns to look at an injured horse." Ryan motioned with his head toward the nearest lantern.

"Who needs the light?" the mustached man asked in Spanish.

"Me, I need the light. One of the horses is hurt."

"Are you a doctor?" The same man asked gruffly. That seemed a strange question to Ryan.

"No, I am with the horses. One of them is cut up. I need a lantern to look at him.

"You have medicine?" The man raised his head slightly and looked down his nose.

"I have medicine," Ryan answered sharply, "but I don't have a lantern." He was becoming irritated.

The two men were motionless, staring blankly at him with their small narrow eyes, the yellow lantern light adding to their feral appearance. After a moment, the one with the mustache abruptly pointed his machine gun toward the ground by yanking on the nylon strap suspending it from his shoulder. "I will bring the light," he said as he stepped toward the nearest lantern.

Ryan led the way back across the airstrip.

At the *jacal*, he went directly to the two heavy bags containing the trail gear and took out two metal boxes that held veterinary supplies for the horses. Handing the Peruvian one of the boxes and a small bucket, Ryan asked him what his name was.

“Otero,” the man said.

Ryan introduced himself and led Otero to the corral where Yolanda was waiting.

“This is Otero,” Ryan said in English. “Apparently he comes with the lantern.”

Yolanda looked at the Peruvian, then back to Ryan. The lantern light exposed the tear-stains and her red, swollen eyes. She stared at him for a moment. The look told him there would be no more crying. Only her horse needed him now.

She turned without speaking and led the way to the center of the corral where the dark colt had been tied to the large snubbing post. Ryan could see now that the young stallion’s chest and legs were covered with dried blood. He handed Yolanda the supplies he had brought, took the bucket from Otero and walked to the gate leading into the other corral. He opened it, went to the flowing water pipe, filled the bucket with fresh water and returned to the other corral.

He dampened a small towel in the bucket of water and handed it to Yolanda.”First wash your face, then let’s get to work.”

One cut across the colt’s chest was deep and reached from shoulder to shoulder. The cut below was not as deep, but also ran the width of the wide chest. Three other slashes, a foot apart, ran horizontally across the front of each leg.

Kneeling beside the post where the colt was tied, Ryan aimed the flashlight beam along the young stallion’s underside. There were dried blood spatters but no wounds. He moved the light down, along the hind legs. More cuts, some deep, but no worse than those up front.

Yolanda was kneeling beside him. Ryan looked over at her. “Not pretty, but I’ve seen worse, and I have exactly what it takes to heal him up without a trace.”

♦ ♦ ♦

An hour later, Ryan was still trying to convince her. “Just keep this in the cuts.” He handed her a brown, half-empty, eight-ounce glass bottle and a smaller bottle they had used to apply medicine to the wounds. "And they'll heal without a scar."

Yolanda took the bottles and looked at him with doubt. She had wanted to suture the cuts.

"We can throw him down in all this dirt, sew him up..." Ryan had argued, "and I promise you infections and scars that will look like we laced him up with baling wire. I've seen animals clawed by mountain lions, gored by cattle, cut by wire and tug cables – terrible wounds – heal without a scar."

She had asked where he had seen all of this, and he had told her the truth. "Mexico, the copper mines near Cananea, southwest of Douglas." He had been born and raised there, his father being the on-site company representative in Mexico for Pyramid Copper out of Bisbee, Arizona.

He had told her that and went on to explain – as Paz Montejo, once the lead *muletero* at one of the big open-pit mines south of Cananea, had explained to him so many times – the medicine they were using caused wounds to heal from the inside, preventing drainage blockage and leaving no scars or hair loss.

Ryan leaned over and doused his hands in the bucket of now cloudy water. "No scars, I promise."

As he said it, he remembered that she wasn't going to be around to see if there would be any scars or not. He shook water from his hands.

Yolanda handed him a towel, still staring at the terrible but cleansed and medicated wounds on her colt's chest. Ryan dried his hands, leaned over, picked up a half-filled syringe sealed in clear plastic and a small brown bottle of combiotic penicillin.

They had spoken in English all night, except when they wanted Otero to move the light.

It grew brighter now, nearer. They both turned to see the Peruvian place the lantern on the ground in front of them and carefully began to roll up the left sleeve of his shirt. Ryan watched as the sleeve went up, past a coarse, blood-splotched bandage. The stiffened cloth was slowly unwound to reveal a festered, jagged furrow, running from thumb to elbow, across the top of Otero's thick, stubby forearm.

"Will you fix my arm now?" the deep voice asked in Spanish.

Ryan pulled the flashlight from his hip pocket and stepped to the shorter man's side. "What the hell happened to you? Why didn't you say something?" he asked angrily in Spanish as he moved the flashlight beam up and down the exposed bone. "You need a doctor! You need a doctor right now!"

"No doctor." Otero shook his head. "You fix it. Fix it like you did the horse." The oval eyes stared blankly at Ryan.

Ryan heard Yolanda catch her breath as she peered down at the grisly mass of torn flesh. She exhaled and turned away.

"Otero, you need a doctor," Ryan repeated. "Have someone drive you, or..." he glanced at the corral wall, in the direction of the airplanes, "fly you out of here to a doctor or you're going to lose that arm, maybe die."

"No doctor, no town," Otero repeated. "Rodrigo must not know." Ryan stared into the empty eyes for a moment. It appeared to be a bullet wound, several days, maybe a week old, and the Peruvian didn't want Rodrigo to know about it. That might be useful. Otero himself might prove useful before they left the ledge camp.

Ryan handed Yolanda the syringe and the brown bottle. "The colt needs a tetanus shot. It's ready to go in the syringe. I don't know how much of this stuff he gets, directions are on the label." He paused a moment. "Want me to do it?"

"I will," she replied quickly, leaning toward the lantern to peer at the yellow label on the small brown bottle.

"We're moving to the *jacal*," Ryan said, "going to need some hot water for this one." As he and the Peruvian headed toward the gate, a loud burst of accordion music, followed by whistles and whoops from the lighted ledge above, reverberated up the canyon. Ryan paused in front of the gate and looked back at Yolanda. She was swabbing a spot on the colt's neck with alcohol.

He spoke to her in English. "By the way, if we ever get the clinic closed tonight, Rodrigo has invited us up to the ledge... for something special, he said."

Yolanda shook her head. "By now Rodrigo doesn't remember anything he said or did today, yesterday or any other day. I'll bring the lantern as soon as I'm finished here."

Ryan wondered if that meant she was going up to the ledge with him or not. He followed Otero out of the corral and closed the gate behind them.

19

Ryan paused at the top of the ramp and surveyed the ledge in disbelief: strings of electric lights and a loudly rollicking mariachi band; armed, khaki-clad figures and spirited young women, laughing, shouting, dancing on a canyon ledge in the middle of the Chihuahuan desert.

Ahead of him, near the brink of the ledge, a long shallow cooking pit of grey mesquite coals lined with upright racks of roasting *cabrito* added a smokey haze and aroma to the festive scene. It was a carnival. Rodrigo must be out of his mind or have every official in Mexico in his pocket.

Ryan spotted Joe and his girlfriend seated at one of several newly constructed tables near the center of the ledge and made his way between the dancers and the cooking pit toward them, still trying to believe what he was seeing. The ledge itself was roughly the size of a football field, fairly level, and sheltered by the low, sloping overhang of the canyon wall.

Absent the present occupants and equipment, it would have the overall appearance of an ancient cliff-dwelling site. In front of him, past the tables, a large green canvas tent had been set up at the far end of the ledge, its peak almost touching the sheltering limestone overhang.

Out from the tent, near the edge of the cliff, was a small stall made of raw yellow lumber that gave the appearance of a bath and shower facility.

Near the back of the ledge, across from Joe and Anita's table, was the real eye-opener: a large, modern kitchen. Arranged in a convenient, semi-circle configuration against the back wall of the canyon were two chest-type freezers, two large refrigerators, ice machine, shelves, cabinets, sinks, water heater and a large chrome-trimmed cooking range.

Ryan was still staring at the kitchen as he greeted Joe and the girl. He sat down on the bench across from them. Joe finished the last of his beer and sent Anita for more.

"He's the *comandante*," Joe whispered when the girl was far enough away.

"What?" Ryan leaned across the top of the long wooden table.

"*El chofer*," Joe nodded toward a table several yards away. "The man who drove the bus, he is the *distrito comandante* of customs," Joe whispered again and motioned with his head.

"How do you know that?" Ryan looked to his left, in the direction Joe had indicated. The bus driver was there, two tables away, a girl with him. She was sitting very close, talking, smiling, her body moving in time with the loud music.

"Anita told me," Joe said, "and I have seen him, too, in uniform. He looks different now." Joe stared at the bus driver. "I have seen him at the checkpoints." Joe leaned closer. "He is the customs *comandante* from Muzquiz. His name is Suarez."

"What's he doing here?"

"No one knows." Joe leaned back, shrugged, tilted his empty beer bottle and peered inside it.

He looked in the direction Anita had gone, then leaned back over the table. "Anita said the store owner in Paso de San Antonio always drives the bus, but today, the *comandante* was with him. The store owner asked if anyone knew him. Some of the girls knew he was the customs *comandante*, but they were afraid. They said nothing. So the store owner got off the bus, and the *comandante* brought them here. The girls don't know why."

Anita arrived with four cold bottles of beer and another girl. Ryan stood up. The new girl was young, maybe sixteen, small, dark and very pretty in her low-cut red dress. Anita introduced her as Elva.

Elva smiled as she came around the table, helped herself to a bottle of beer and sat down. Ryan sat down, thanked Anita for the beer and took one for himself. In Spanish, he asked Elva where she was from.

Elva was seated in a perfect position. Ryan could look past her straight at Suarez. If the *comandante* had come for a good time, he didn't seem to be having one. His attention was not on the young girl at his side, the drink or the food in front of him. It was on everything else. He sat straight and stiff, eyes sweeping the ledge, pausing, probing, studying. Only his eyes and the hand holding a small black cigar moved.

"Arizona, Sonora, Baja California," Ryan answered Elva's question back to him about where he was from and looked briefly at her. Her answer to the same question had escaped him. He looked back at Suarez. What was he doing here? Why didn't he want the girls to know who he was?

"Elva, how often do you come here?"

"Once a week, sometimes two, whenever Uncle decides." Ryan smiled, nodded and looked away without asking about "Uncle."

Naranjo and the Colombian must have powerful connections. Every official in the state must be in on this high-profile operation. So where were the soldiers? And why was a customs *comandante* posing as a bus driver?

Ryan looked back toward Suarez. One of the Peruvians was leaving the *comandante*'s table with the girl. Suarez didn't seem to mind, or even to notice. He was still quietly smoking his cigar and watching everything.

"No, I don't dance," Ryan replied to Elva's question, as Joe and Anita walked toward the hard, swept-off area used for dancing. Past them, he saw Yolanda standing near the ramp. Spotting him, she walked in his direction. She had decided to come, after all.

She had seemed pleased earlier when he told her that the saddle and harness rigging was completed. That's when he had asked her about Naranjo, was he coming to see them off tomorrow? Her response had been friendly, too friendly, he'd thought at the time. "I have told him all about you, and he is looking forward to meeting you," she had said.

Yolanda stopped at the table, hands on her hips. "Still going to buy me a beer? Or am I too late?" She looked at Elva and didn't smile. Her long hair was freshly combed and still damp.

The swelling and redness was gone from her eyes, she looked as beautiful as she had that morning in the cafe.

"Never too late." Ryan stood up and worked his way out of the picnic-style table and bench. "Be right back."

When he returned with drinks, tortillas, salsa and roasted *cabrito*, Elva was gone. He set the plates and one bottle of beer down on the table and pulled two more bottles from his hip pockets.

"I never expected anything like this." Ryan made a sweeping motion.

"Mr. Rodrigo takes good care of his men – and himself." She nodded toward the west end of the ledge.

Still standing, Ryan turned to look in that direction. Rodrigo and a young woman had just stepped from the tent. Two more girls, giggling loudly, came through the door flap behind him.

Ryan glanced at Suarez. The *comandante* was staring at the foursome in front of the tent.

Ryan handed Yolanda one of the beers and sat down across from her.

"Looks like we're about to have company," she said.

Ryan looked back over his shoulder. Rodrigo was headed in their direction.

Ryan turned back to Yolanda. "Mr. Rodrigo wasn't too happy about my being here."

"He doesn't like gringos." She looked straight into his eyes and made a fake smile.

Rodrigo arrived at the table, a small burlap bag in his right hand. Ryan started to stand up.

"Keep your seat, Señor Shaw." Ryan sat back down.

"Shaw, yes, Señor Shaw." His eyes were wide, alert, darting from place to place.

"And Señorita Galvez, good evening." He turned back to Ryan, without waiting for Yolanda to respond and continued speaking in his strange-sounding Spanish. "Señor Shaw – I want to tell you how much I admire your handling of the old people today. I have never seen such work from any of them." He looked away, past the cooking pit, into the darkness. "I take it the horses and equipment are now ready?"

"Ready," Ryan answered in Spanish.

"Good." Rodrigo switched to English. "Get the Mexicans off their asses again tomorrow morning, and start moving... things." He shifted the small burlap bag to his left hand and made a saluting gesture. "Have a good evening." He turned from the table and led the three girls away.

Ryan watched after them for a moment. "You know," he said, turning to face Yolanda, "I don't think he much likes Mexicans, either." He looked straight into her eyes and made a fake smile.

She picked up her bottle of beer, sipped and smiled – a real smile – back at him. "He's so damn high on coke and God knows what else, I'm surprised he knows the difference."

"It makes his Spanish hard to understand, too."

"No," Yolanda disagreed. "It's a dialect, *Costeno*. It's spoken several places along the coast in Colombia."

Ryan nodded and sipped his beer, staring at her.

She raised her eyebrows. "What?"

"Nothing. I was just wondering how you knew that."

She shrugged. "Studied it in college, did some traveling, talked to people." She moved her finger slowly around the mouth of the beer bottle.

"Where did you go to college?" Ryan leaned across the table. They were having a normal conversation, as if on a first date and getting acquainted with each other, rather pleasant until his gaze wandered back to Suarez's table. It was vacant. Ryan straightened, glanced farther left toward the tent, to the right, at the dancers, back to the kitchen area, then at Yolanda.

She straightened. "Looking for your lady friend?"

For a moment Ryan didn't know what she meant, then he remembered Elva. "No," he shook his head and leaned back over the table. "I was wondering where Joe went." It was a ridiculous reply, and he could tell she thought so, too. "And in case you didn't notice, my 'lady friend' was just a kid."

"I noticed right away." She made it sound judgmental.

Ryan started to object, but decided to let it drop. Where was Suarez? He had seen people gathering just the other side of the dance area and wanted to look again, but then Yolanda would think he was looking for Elva.

"Where did you go to college?" he heard himself repeat instead of following his instincts to look for Suarez.

She gave him a puzzled look, sighed and started to answer, but was interrupted by screams from the other side of the dance area.The band stopped playing.

"*¡Corolio! ¡Corolio! ¡Santa Maria, corolio!*" one shrill voice rose above the others. Coral snake? Someone's found a coral snake, Ryan thought, picked up his beer, drank a sip, then looked past the band at a rapidly dispersing group of people.

Rodrigo was left standing alone, looking around, confused, holding something in his hands, He took a few steps, stopped, and stretched his right arm away from his body. Ryan could see a slender, brightly colored snake dangling from the Colombian's right hand.

"Damn, it's got him." Ryan slammed his beer bottle down, swung his legs out over the bench, and rushed toward Rodrigo.

Rodrigo began to flail the air with the snake still firmly attached to his hand. Ryan elbowed two Peruvians aside, reached into his right pocket, pulled out his knife, flipping the blade open and reached for Rodrigo's stricken hand.

Rodrigo drew back, giving him a dazed look. "My fighting snake," he said.

Ryan looked down at the almost two-foot-long twisting reptile, its small black head making chewing motions on Rodrigo's little finger. "A coral snake," Ryan shouted in English. "Coral snake, poison, like a cobra."

Rodrigo stared, unmoving.

"Like a cobra. It's going to kill you if we don't get it off." Ryan grabbed Rodrigo's hand, decapitated the snake, and pushed the knife blade, edge up, along the finger, slitting the snake's jaws and head. He pried the toothed parts off and wiped the wound with Rodrigo's shirttail. "Wash it off, get in one of your plane and get to a doctor." Rodrigo stared at his finger.

"Where are the pilots?" Ryan yelled toward the scattered crowd. Two Peruvians stepped forward. "Get him to a hospital, immediately,"

Ryan instructed them. " A big hospital, in Chihuahua or Juarez."

"No!" Rodrigo interrupted. "That will not be necessary."

He turned and placed his right hand on a nearby table. With his left hand, he pulled a long-bladed fighting knife from a scabbard on his left hip, positioned the blade over the last knuckle of the injured finger and ordered one of his men to strike the back of the blade. "*¡Pegele!*"

A Peruvian struck the top edge of the blade with the heel of his hand and the tip of Rodrigo's little finger rolled off the table onto the ground

Rodrigo straightened, slid the long knife back into its sheath and turning slowly around held his bleeding finger up for everyone to see. One of his men brought a towel from the kitchen area. Rodrigo, eyes glazed, wrapped it around his injured hand, sat down at the table and demanded a beer.

Ryan wiped the blade of his knife on the pant leg of his Levi's, folded it and slipped it back into his pocket. No one had noticed that its handle bore the same colors and pattern as the snake still writhing on the ground beside Rodrigo's severed fingertip. Ryan turned away from the gathering onlookers, wondering how Rodrigo had managed to get a coral snake attached to his finger. Then he noticed the small burlap bag Rodrigo had been carrying. It was lying on the ground next to a low circular adobe structure that appeared to be an old well.

Ryan stepped over for a closer look. It was only a walled-off area, about five feet in diameter. Inside, a small diamondback rattler and a scarlet king snake, crawling in opposite directions, passed and ignored each other in search of an escape route. The king snake's color bands were clear and bright: red, black and yellow. A different color sequence but otherwise it greatly resembled the coral snake.

Ryan looked at the small empty burlap bag and smiled. Old Juan, the snake catcher, certainly knew the difference. Ryan remembered the wry look on the old man's face when he said he had found Rodrigo a "good one." The coral snake must have latched on to Rodrigo's finger when he tried to remove it from the burlap bag.

Past the snake pit, a back portion of the ledge had long ago been walled off with large river stones, similar to the ones used for the corrals. Numerous narrow doorways and windows looked out upon the ledge from the front of the long, one-story structure. Undoubtedly, these were the homes the old people had been driven from by Rodrigo's drug-smuggling operation. Cots, sleeping bags, clothing and gear littered the area where Rodrigo's men were now quartered. Perhaps the old people would have it all back in a few days.

Ryan moved through the returning crowd, back toward his table, and saw Yolanda walking away from one of the tubs of iced beer.He caught up with her just as she set two drinks on the table.

Behind her, a figure came out of the tent, a blur, moving quickly into the shadows between the tent and the shower facility. Ryan thought instantly of Suarez. Whoever it was would have to come into the light again, near the brink of the ledge, or double back behind the tent and pass in front of the lighted kitchen area.

"Last of the cold ones." Yolanda made a gesture toward the beer on the table. "I can hardly wait to hear about the snake bite," she said without feeling as she sat down.

"Looked like they were pitting king snakes against rattlers," Ryan said, still facing the tent. He took a beer, drank, put his foot on the bench in front of him and leaned forward, watching as he talked. "I guess Rodrigo doesn't know his snakes very well."

Something behind him caught Yolanda's attention.

Ryan turned to see Joe coming from the direction of the ramp at a fast pace. At the same time, to his right, he saw Suarez come into the dim light between the cooking pits and the brink of the ledge. Suarez was leaning over, carrying something under his shirt.

"*¡Cuate!*" Joe shouted as he arrived at the table. "The horses are gone. The gate is down and they are all gone."

Ryan continued watching Suarez. The *comandante* moved quickly toward the ramp, not looking around or hesitating, just heading for the ramp. Slowly, Ryan turned his attention to Joe and stared. "The horses are gone?"

20

"La Mula," Yolanda shouted above the roaring engine and grinding transmission noises of the Jeep she was driving. Left hand gripping the steering wheel, she was pointing past him to the right.

Ryan looked up out of the dry wash they were riding through at the gray sky above the embankment on their right. Dawn was happening somewhere behind them on the other side of the mountain range they had been driving through all night in the open Jeep. On the skyline of the embankment, wedge-shaped protrusions and small hills of earth were all that remained of several ancient adobe structures.

He was tired, hungry and cold, and he really didn't care where La Mula was unless it was near Lalo Naranjo's headquarters, just east of the border town of Ojinaga, as Frank had shown him on the map. If La Mula was anywhere near there, it meant the Jeep ride had brought them roughly a hundred miles northwest of the ledge camp.

Last night, he and Joe had tracked the horses up the canyon with flashlights, far enough to realize that the animals could not be recovered before morning. Yolanda had commandeered one of Rodrigo's Jeeps and picked them up at the end of the runway.

"We can go south around the mountains and head them off," she said. They had dropped Joe off at the corrals and picked up their saddles. Joe would stay and make sure the horses didn't double back and get out into the wide valley.

It had all sounded reasonable enough. Yolanda had driven east past the old people's camp and turned south into the valley.

A short time later, she downshifted, turned west and pointed the Jeep's headlights up the first of what now seemed a thousand switchback trails, each one invariably carrying them higher and deeper into the mountains. Progress soon became a secondary concern; keeping the bouncing jeep upright was the main objective. Yolanda was good at it. She maneuvered, braked and shifted constantly, expertly, sometimes standing up in the open Jeep to see the ground ahead that had seemingly disappeared.

During the night's ordeal, Ryan had watched and admired her, remembering how good it had felt to hold her, to comfort and help her with the injured colt. She had kindled deep feelings he hadn't experienced for a long time. Feelings that had clouded his judgment last night.

The corral gate had been found lying flat, as if scuffling horses had leaned too hard against it. Could have happened, but then the horses had ignored the huge stack of oat hay. Instead of raiding the haystack or heading toward the scent of grass and mint in the big open valley a half-mile away, they had turned and gone back up the barren rocky canyon that had brought them to the ledge camp. Why would a bunch of loose horses do that? They wouldn't.

He should have looked closer around the gate for tracks other than hoofprints, examined the rope and wire fastenings on the trampled gate, but he hadn't done that. He had been too anxious to leave in the Jeep with Yolanda. If she had really intended to head the horses off, she was taking a long time to do it.

It was now clear to him that she had turned the horses out and started them back up the canyon to set up this all night mountain trek – but why? He looked over at her, then at the winding, sandy wash ahead, angry at himself for being tricked so easily. She was the last one to be alone with the horses, and her answers to questions about their own whereabouts and destination had been vague. Where were they going? And, did he want to wait around to find out?

With the dawn sky behind them, he knew the wash was taking them due west. Somewhere ahead, there had to be a road leading north. When they came to it, he would make her drive to the border.

"How are we doing?" Yolanda shouted above the engine noise. Ryan looked over and forced a smile. Under his denim shirt, the night's jostling had rolled the back of his T-shirt into a hard cylinder. He was leaning forward, unaware that his own undershirt was responsible for the dull throbbing just below both shoulder blades.

Yolanda smiled back, braked abruptly and turned the Jeep up the right embankment out of the wash and onto a greasewood flat. She leaned over, repositioned the axle-drive selector, shifted gears and leaned back in the seat. For the first time since leaving the ledge canyon, they were in normal high gear, speeding north along a stock trail weaving around boulders and patches of dense brush.

"What would you like for breakfast?" She shouted as mesquite limbs slapped against the dusty windshield.

"A big, thick steak, four eggs, hash browns and a pot of black coffee." Ryan replied sarcastically, dodging as another branch smacked against the glass in front of him. She laughed, downshifted and skidded the Jeep around a large pile of boulders and head-on into a jungle of thick, low mesquite brush.

Ryan ducked, braced his legs and grabbed the metal sides of the Jeep seat. Yolanda was obviously enjoying herself. He stared at her and thought about it. Could she so casually be taking him to someplace... unpleasant? Did she plan for him to just disappear the way Grady had? He didn't think so, but he wasn't going to bet his life on it.

He gripped the cold metal seat frame tighter as Yolanda accelerated and fishtailed through another stand of thick brush. Kidnapping her didn't sit well with him, but that was the only option left – the only way to find out about Grady.

He didn't like thinking about it, but if he did get her across the river, he could use what he already knew to arrest her on smuggling-conspiracy charges. A U.S. prosecutor might be talked into going along with that, at least long enough to get what they wanted out of Naranjo.

They broke out of the brush onto a freshly graded caliche road and turned east, back toward the mountains. It was full daylight now, but the sun was still behind the peaks now looming ahead of them. On the left, a half-mile away, a line of trees marked the far boundary of a cultivated pasture. The trees appeared to be salt cedars. That meant a stream – or river, possibly the Rio Grande. If it was, Ojinaga was behind them, probably on this same road.

Large red Brahman cows, some with small calves, looked up from the thick, green pasture as the Jeep sped by.

Suddenly, there was a man on horseback, alongside the road. Yolanda waved as they passed. He was armed. Ryan turned back to stare at the rifle under the right stirrup fender and the cartridge belt around the man's waist. Ahead, they were approaching three old metal-roofed buildings, one with an ancient gas pump in front of it. Ryan glanced at the Jeep's gas gauge. It showed empty. He pointed at it. "We're out of gas."

"For about half an hour." She nodded and sped on past the buildings.

"That was La Mula... my aunt's store." She looked straight ahead, waving at two more men on horseback who were riding away from the village. Both of them had rifles.

Ryan looked past Yolanda across the pasture at the line of trees. If they had just passed La Mula, then that was the Rio Grande. Ojinaga and Presidio were twenty-five, maybe thirty miles directly behind them. Just across the river was Texas State Highway 170, paralleling the river from Lajitas to Presidio.

He looked around him. No one in sight. He looked at the gas gauge again. Despite the bumps and dips in the road, the needle didn't move. The Jeep was running on fumes. It was time to end this, take her pistol, force her to drive the half mile to the river and cross with him. Ryan straightened in the seat and turned toward Yolanda. She gave him a puzzled look, then abruptly swerved the Jeep to the right, up a sloping driveway lined with huge pecan trees.

At the top of the rise they entered the flagstone courtyard of a sprawling Spanish-style estate. Yolanda stopped the Jeep in front of the main house. Two well-groomed, hatless men in dark brown trousers and white guayabera shirts came from the long covered porch toward them.

Each carried a fully cocked, nickel-plated .45-caliber semiautomatic pistol in a dark brown, hand-tooled holster with no safety strap. Wide cartridge belts and glistening boots matched the color of the holsters perfectly.

Yolanda turned off the ignition and looked at Ryan. "You did want to meet my grandfather, didn't you?"

21

The white bus backed away from the ramp, hesitated, then moved forward. Comandante Suarez turned the oversized steering wheel a full revolution to the right, heading the cumbersome vehicle directly into the early morning sun. At the end of the runway, he eased it down onto the rough track that had brought it to the ledge camp the evening before.

Suarez glanced down at the bundle near his left foot. He had wrapped the two packages carefully in his denim jacket, using his belt to strap the bundle to the exposed metal frame of the bus so it wouldn't slide around. He wished he could open the bundle and look at the packages again, but he couldn't, not with so many pairs of eyes behind him. He had looked last night, again and again, while thinking about what he had seen on the ledge and about what Monica had told him.

She had been to the ledge many times. She had been inside one of the big airplanes and Don Rodrigo's tent, and twice she had been inside a big cave across from the ledge.

He looked down at the bundle again, thinking about the white powder in one of the packages. If she said there were duffel bags full of cocaine in the cave, it was probably true.

Suarez looked up and realized how slowly he was driving, more slowly than necessary. He pressed the accelerator slightly and picked up speed. They were just clearing the mouth of the canyon, about to start across the wide valley floor. There was no sign of life. Nothing moved. It was something that had been bothering him.

Here, at the entrance of the canyon, here at least there should be soldiers. But there were none. Not here, not at the ledge. There were only the foreigners: the Colombian, his Peruvians and an American – a tall, green-eyed gringo who spoke like a Mexican. What was he doing here? Monica had never seen him before, or so many horses. Why all the horses?

Suarez shook his head. All the foreigners and horses, an airport, three airplanes, the equipment – who was in on this? The question had kept him awake all night. What officials were involved?

Exactly how something of this magnitude could be undertaken, even considered, without the military zone commander's endorsement, Suarez couldn't fathom. But it was happening. If the zone commander was part of it, his troops would be here. Suarez was positive of that. Finally, just before dawn, he had convinced himself that no officials were involved.

The sun was now full on his face. He glanced up at the round mirror that distorted but showed all the interior of the bus. A few girls were sitting upright, whispering. Others slumped against the windows or the seat in front of them. A few had apparently curled up out of sight. Most of them knew who he was. Monica had convinced him of that. It was something else that had kept him awake.

If his superiors ever learned of his trip to the ledge, they would assume he was involved in the Colombian's smuggling business and was deliberately denying them a share of the proceeds. He had no choice now but to report what he had learned. The report should go to area headquarters in Monclova, but it was the military zone commander, General Pagazos in Ojinaga, who wielded the kind of influence that could have someone reinstated to a former position with the Coast Guard in Tampico.

Suarez glanced down at the bundle again. Maybe he would only have to show one of the packages to the general, the one with the cocaine. Maybe, somehow, he would be able to keep the other one for himself.

22

Except for its construction of native rust-brown stone instead of traditional adobe and stucco, Lalo Naranjo's hacienda was typical of wealthy rural Mexico: large, rambling, red-tiled roof, terrazzo walks and steps. From the narrow, roofed porch that ran the length of the house, Ryan stared back toward the valley and the trees that marked the river, now more than a mile away. He and Yolanda could be there by now, crossing the river if he had not let the opportunity slip away.

He glanced briefly at the two armed guards converging on the Jeep. They had not searched him. He still had the .45 under his shirt. He turned and followed Yolanda past a carved wooden door into her grandfather's house. Ryan heard the Jeep behind him start up and drive away.

Passing through a small foyer, they entered a large, sunlit room with light-colored hardwood walls and dark red terrazzo tile. Sofas, overstuffed chairs and bleached-wood tables formed isolated clusters in several areas of the big room. The upholstered furniture was done in bright southwestern colors. Ryan was surprised at the contemporary look.

Across the room, a shriveled, dark-skinned man with long white hair was seated in a large, leather-covered chair near a window. He balanced a long, freshly lit cigar in the tray of an old-fashioned smoke stand, rose from the chair and came toward them. He had once been tall. Now he was stooped and gaunt but moved with unanticipated agility.

"I am Don Hilario Naranjo-Galan," the old man announced in Spanish as he extended his hand. His dark eyes were quick and probing. Ryan took the hand and met the piercing stare. Don Hilario "Lalo"

Naranjo, smuggler of liquor, marijuana, heroin and cocaine. Almost certainly a murderer, Ryan thought, but power was what he felt in the long bony fingers, what he saw in the small dark eyes, what he heard when the old man had announced his own name. Absolute power. This was the man to know in this part of Mexico.

"With much pleasure, Señor," Ryan said in Spanish. "My name is Ryan Shaw."

"My house is your house." Don Naranjo made a flourish with his hand to indicate how his entire home was open to his guest without looking away from Ryan's eyes. Yolanda gave her grandfather a perfunctory hug and kiss.

"Come." She glanced up at Ryan, "Have some coffee while I see about breakfast."

"Yes, have some coffee and eat, Señor Shaw." Don Lalo Naranjo gestured for Ryan to follow Yolanda. "Then we will talk."

A stocky, gray-haired man appeared in the doorway and led them down a short hallway to a small, brightly decorated room. Ryan and Don Naranjo seated themselves at a round table in front of a large bay window. Outside the window, there were no signs of civilization. No buildings or fences, only the low, craggy, rust-colored hill that had undoubtedly been the source of stone used for building the house.

"Señor Rodrigo had an accident last night," Yolanda said as she set one cup of coffee in front of Ryan and another before her grandfather. "He was playing with snakes, and one of them bit him." She sat down with her own cup. "A red, yellow and black one." She looked across the table at her grandfather.

"*¿Corolio?"* Don Naranjo looked back at her, raising his eyebrows.

"*Corolio,"* Yolanda nodded affirmatively. She told the story, talking fast, describing in detail the ledge party, the girls, the screams, the exceptional size and tenacity of the snake. Her hands and facial expressions told the story as effectively as her voice. She looked and sounded no different from any other woman with a story to tell. But she was different. There was a revolver buckled around her waist, and she had just delivered him to Lalo Naranjo.

Ryan felt eyes on him and looked up at the manservant who had led the way into the breakfast room. He, too, was an old man – perhaps as old as Naranjo – but with a more robust, outdoor look about him, like Juan and the other old men at the ledge camp. The servant was dressed the same as the guards outside but without the armament. He had been watching Ryan, and he did not look away when Ryan returned his stare.

The door to the kitchen opened, and a woman's voice asked how long the steak should cook. At the same time, a telephone rang somewhere in the front of the house. At first, that surprised Ryan; a telephone in rural Mexico was rare. Then he remembered that this was no ordinary residence. Of course, there would be a telephone at the hacienda of Don Lalo Naranjo. Ryan couldn't help thinking how interesting it would be to have a tap on this phone. The manservant was dispatched with instructions to tell the caller to call back later.

Yolanda went into the kitchen, leaving Ryan alone to hear Don Naranjo's version of the coral snake's trait of flattening the end of its tail to resemble its head. "You think you are cutting off the head of the little snake, Señor Shaw..." Don Naranjo glanced up as the manservant returned, then nodded and continued. "...and the other end bites you." The old man smiled.

Ryan had the feeling there was a message in this story and that if he figured it out, he wouldn't like it. They talked about Don Naranjo's red cattle he had seen from the Jeep and the types of mixed grasses in the cultivated river pastures until Yolanda returned with two large, steaming plates of food.

On Ryan's plate was a large steak topped with scrambled eggs. Tortillas and salsa were placed on the table by a heavy set woman in a white apron. Yolanda's plate was heaped with scrambled eggs and strips of crisp bacon. All of it looked and smelled delicious. This was all very... civilized, Ryan thought, wondering again why he had been brought here and why he hadn't been searched for weapons.

Suddenly he became aware of the silence around him. He looked up from his plate. Yolanda and her grandfather were staring at him. Had he missed something? The last thing he'd heard was that the best of Don Naranjo's red cattle, *los rojizos* he called them, were at another ranch.

"Grandfather wants to know if you think Rodrigo will recover."

"Yes." Ryan nodded, looking squarely into the old man's eyes. "The snake was removed quickly; then Rodrigo removed the part of his finger that had been bitten." Ryan held up his right hand, indicating the last knuckle of the little finger with the tip of his thumb.

Yolanda frowned and looked down at her plate. Don Naranjo continued to stare at him, nodding slowly as he handed his cup and saucer to the manservant with orders for a refill and the cigar that had been left in the other room. "You know about snakes, then." It was a statement, not a question.

"We have them in Arizona, the same kind." Ryan cut a piece of the steak, speared it with his fork, hesitated and glanced up at Naranjo.

"Please eat, Señor Shaw, I had breakfast earlier. Eat, then we will talk."

The telephone rang twice more as they ate. Each time Don Naranjo signaled the manservant to handle it. It rang again just as Ryan finished the last bite, put his napkin on the table and leaned back.

Don Naranjo did not signal the servant this time. Instead he pointed the damp end of his cigar in Ryan's direction.

"It's for you, Señor Shaw."

"What?" Ryan looked at Naranjo, then Yolanda. "For me?"

"For you," Don Naranjo repeated.

Yolanda looked at her grandfather. Ryan could see that she was as surprised as he was. He stood up. Don Naranjo nodded, and the servant led the way back into the big room to a corner table and the ringing telephone. Ryan hesitated a moment, then picked it up.

"Hello."

"Ryan?" It was Frank's voice. Frank was calling him at Lalo Naranjo's ranch? Ryan felt the back of his neck begin to tingle. He switched the phone to his left hand and turned. The servant was gone. The room was empty. He backed against the wall, staring at the doorway he had just come through. His right hand was already inside his shirt, cocking the hammer back on the .45. Frank was calling his name over the phone.

"Frank – what the hell's going on?"

"Ryan! Am I glad to hear you." Frank sounded relieved.

"Frank, what's happening?" Ryan pulled the pistol out.

"Am I glad to hear you!" Frank repeated. "I've been calling all morning. I don't know how much time we have, so just listen – ask questions later. Lalo knows who you are."

The words jolted Ryan. His body tensed.

"He thinks you're there on assignment, after the cocaine," Frank said, "and he wants to talk a deal." There was silence. "You hear me? You still there?"

"Yes, I'm still here," Ryan said quietly, his mind racing.

"He called me last night, put it to me plain and simple. He said if you weren't a federal officer, he was going to kill you."

"You told him who I was?"

"I had to, there was nothing else to do – but it's all right."

All right? Ryan thought. How can that be all right?

"He thinks everyone in the United States Customs Service is on to this packhorse operation, and he wants to make a deal."

"Go on," Ryan said. He was beginning to understand. Frank knew Naranjo better than he did, and Naranjo had been around long enough to know the consequences of harming a federal agent.

"He had me, the goddamned old son-of-a-bitch." Frank was sounding calmer. "If he's listening in now, he'll know you were just nosing around on your own, so tell me what's going on, and I'll be your insurance policy."

Ryan told him everything: about Yolanda showing up at the ranch and taking over; about Rodrigo, the ledge camp, airstrip, planes, equipment and the cave full of cocaine. As he brought Frank up to date, he began to realize the control he now had. He didn't have to kidnap anyone or bargain with an old man for his granddaughter's freedom. Don Lalo Naranjo was ready to deal.

"Frank, I'm going to hang up now. Stay by the phone. I'm going to see what kind of a deal he's talking about and call you back."

"Don't hang up!" Frank shouted. "Not until I tell you how to get out of there and back to this side of the river... just in case. If you don't call me back in an hour, I'll have a deputy out of Presidio pick you up at the place I'm going to tell you about."

While he was listening, Ryan shoved the pistol back inside his shirt and under his waistband. He left it cocked. As Frank described the escape route, Ryan wondered how he knew so much about the layout of Lalo's ranch. Aerial photos? Informants? Neither would account for the details he was now hearing over the phone. Frank must have been here. That would be an interesting story sometime.

"Frank," Ryan said after assuring him that he understood all the instructions. "I'm going to hang up now. When I call back, I'm going to tell you exactly what happened to Grady."

23

Don Naranjo stood up as Ryan came back into the breakfast room. "Good, you have finished. I think we will be more comfortable in the big room. The old man moved past Ryan.

Ryan stood near the table, staring down at Yolanda. He was disappointed. She was at the ledge camp last night when Naranjo made his call to Frank. She'd had no way of knowing he was a customs agent or what Naranjo had planned for him; still she had lured him here.

Yolanda avoided his eyes, pushed away from the table, stood and followed her grandfather out of the room.The stocky manservant gestured toward the hallway. Ryan fell in behind Yolanda. The telephone call had obviously been a surprise to her, too, but Naranjo would have brought her up to date by now, congratulated her for a job well done.

"And where do you think the horses are now... Miss Galvez?" Ryan asked in a loud, accusing voice.

"I thought you had seen them," Naranjo answered from the room ahead. "They are there, by the river."

Ryan entered the large room. The old man was standing beside the chair where he had been seated earlier. Ryan walked past him and looked out the window. In the distant pasture, near the strip of salt cedars, a spattering of reddish brown stood out against the backdrop of green. He hadn't seen the animals from the road. If he had, he probably would have mistaken them for more of the red cattle. He looked down at a large leather binocular case on the table beside him. They could still be cattle for all he could tell from this distance.

"They have been there since early this morning, resting and grazing." Naranjo picked up the binocular case, unsnapped the top and offered the glasses to Ryan. "The girl's mare brought them in last night."

As he pulled the binoculars from the leather case, Ryan looked across the table at Yolanda. She raised her chin, tightened her lips and glared back at him. No remorse there for the set-up. What did he expect, an apology? He had planned the same for her and she must know that now. He turned toward the window and raised the binoculars to his eyes. Turning the horses out to get him here had been clever. He wondered if that had been her idea or Naranjo's. He had a feeling it had been hers.

"To the right of the horses, at the base of the mountain, you will see the entrance of a canyon," the old man commented. "The place where you crossed the horses yesterday morning is exactly twelve and one-half kilometers down that canyon." He paused a moment. "Not exactly close, Agent Shaw, but much closer than you thought, no?"

Ryan didn't answer. He had just finished focusing the powerful binoculars. The horses were all there, grazing peacefully as the old man had said. He followed the line of salt cedars beyond them to the canyon opening. The mountain on the Mexican side ended abruptly in a sheer cliff. A flat-topped mesa north of the river, on the U.S. side, did the same. The canyon Naranjo was talking about appeared as a narrow crack between the two. Just down-river from the mesa on the U.S. side, about two miles according to what Frank had told him on the phone, the state highway between Presidio and Lajitas makes a southward curve and for several miles is only yards away from the river. That was information he didn't think he was going to need now. Ryan returned the binoculars to their leather case.

"Customs Agent Shaw." Naranjo waved him toward the nearby sofa and seated himself in the chair near the window. The manservant leaned over and lit the old man's fresh cigar.

"I apologize for the surprise telephone call..." He puffed on the cigar. There was no apology in his voice, Ryan thought, in the tilt of his head, or in the peculiar glint in the dark, round eyes. Don Naranjo had enjoyed springing the trap. He was still enjoying it. "But it saved time," the Don continued. "Now we can talk about our problems."

"What are our problems, Don Naranjo?"

The old man was quick to answer. "I will be perfectly frank with you, Agent Shaw." He turned the cigar in his hand, studying the glowing tip. "In this business with the Colombian, I have, at this point, lost everything." He glanced toward his granddaughter and leaned back in the leather chair. "None of the cocaine is mine. All of it belongs to Rodrigo. I was to cross it for him and be paid when it was safely on the other side."

He puffed the cigar and watched the smoke rise toward the ceiling. "There are other ways, many places that Rodrigo's cargo can be crossed, but time is running out... for both of us."

He looked up. "Chato!" He motioned the manservant toward a table across the room. "The newspapers." The man called Chato went to the table and returned with a handful of newspaper clippings. At the Don's signal, the servant handed them to Ryan.

"Your balloons are worthless," Naranjo said. "They have never worked, not even for one day, as you can see. One has crashed the others never left the ground. They are worthless."

Ryan looked through the articles. Two of them he had seen before, through the windows of vending machines at the Corner Cafe in Alpine. He glanced up at Yolanda, now seated at the other end of the sofa. She was watching him, motionless, nothing showing in her face. Ryan dropped the clippings on the sofa and turned back to Naranjo.

"The balloons will stop nothing." Naranjo shook his white-haired head and made a sweeping gesture with the cigar. "They don't even fly. But the Colombian, he knows only what the papers said about them in the beginning. He thinks they are working." The old man squinted, looking hard into Ryan's eyes. "The others think so, too, the ones who used to come to the old place. They all think the radar is here, along the border. He made another sweeping gesture with his cigar. "When there is really nothing. Do you understand?"

Ryan leaned back on the sofa and looked again at Yolanda. She was going through the clippings, newspaper articles that could reveal to Rodrigo that he was no longer stranded in an isolated canyon, that he didn't have to wait for packhorses to move his fifteen tons of cocaine, that all he really had to do was load it back into his airplanes and fly it into the United States himself. Naranjo had deliberately kept news of the failed blimp program from Rodrigo, but the Colombian could find out the truth at any time. That's what Naranjo had meant when he said time was running out.

Ryan looked back at the old man and nodded. "Yes, Don Naranjo, I do understand." As he sorted out the rest of it, he had to stop himself from smiling. Naranjo now believed that the entire U.S. Customs Service was onto his packhorse smuggling scheme and that a massive investigative effort was underway to take out the Colombian drug smuggler and his stockpile of cocaine. From Ryan's point of view, that put him in the driver's seat.

He studied Naranjo for a moment. The old man would be thinking the same thing, that he was in control. That was the reason Naranjo now sat calmly in his overstuffed chair, puffing a cigar, absolutely confident that whatever demands he made would be eagerly met by a government agency desperate to salvage its big investigation.

Ryan put on his best worried look and leaned forward on the sofa. "Don Naranjo, at this point, I have also lost everything."

"And that, Agent Shaw, is exactly why we are here." Naranjo straightened in his chair. "The best you could hope for now would be to report everything to Mexican officials. Rodrigo would escape with all the cargo he could load aboard his airplanes. The rest would be confiscated by the army. Someone, possibly even myself, would be forced to find a customer for it, and that customer would most certainly be someone in the United States."He gave Ryan an appraising look. "You are an experienced agent, Sefior Shaw. I'm sure you are aware of this process...."

"Yes, I know," Ryan agreed.

The old man's proposal was simple. "Agent Shaw, can you guarantee that after you cross Rodrigo's cargo, it will remain at the border canyon ranch until I have been paid for crossing it, and that my granddaughter will not be harmed or arrested?" It was what Ryan had expected, what he had hoped for.

Prosecuting United States Attorneys couldn't care less about the hired help if a source such as Rodrigo could be brought to trial. There would be no problem giving Yolanda immunity.

"Don Naranjo, I guarantee that the cocaine will not be seized until it has left the ranch and that Yolanda will not be arrested or charged." For a major Colombian trafficker and thirty thousand pounds of cocaine, any law enforcement agency in the world would back him up on this agreement.

"Then we have a bargain, Agent Shaw." Naranjo leaned forward and offered his hand.

"I have only two conditions." Ryan saw immediately that his words shocked the old man. The confident smile vanished, and a look of anger took its place as Don Naranjo slumped back in the chair. Ryan continued without hesitation. "First, Joe Montez is not to be harmed in any way. He is to be left alone to help me with the crossing."

"Ah yes, Jose." The Don's angry face relaxed, turned expressionless, but his eyes, staring blankly at the far wall, seemed to grow darker. "The one who betrayed me and brought you into my organization, your little finger."

Ryan had not heard the term "finger" used for snitch or informant for a long time. The way the old man spat the word out and the look in his eyes left no doubt that Don Lalo Naranjo had contended with "finger" problems before.

"I agree," the old man snapped, obviously not happy about this point. "What is your other condition?" Ryan turned toward Yolanda. She was watching him with noticeable concern.

If she had not harmed Grady, if neither she nor Naranjo had been involved in Grady's disappearance, the old man would tell him what he knew. If either of them had been involved, Naranjo would deny all knowledge of what had happened to Grady. Either way, it was time to ask the question.

Ryan cleared his throat and spoke slowly. "A week ago, a man went to the border canyon ranch, *la pipa*. Something happened to him there." Ryan saw Naranjo's expression soften, his eyes widen as he looked at his granddaughter. Ryan kept his attention on Naranjo, but he could see Yolanda relax and lean back on the sofa. Puzzled by their reactions, he continued. "The other condition to our agreement, Don Naranjo, is that you tell me what happened to that man."

"You are referring to Señor Grady Matthews, are you not?" Ryan was surprised to hear Naranjo refer to Grady by name.

"Yes, I'm talking about Señor Grady Matthews. What happened to him?

"Why don't you ask him?" The old man's eyes looked past Ryan.

Ryan turned slightly on the sofa and looked over his shoulder. Grady Matthews was standing behind him, smiling, leaning on a walking cane.

24

Without taking his eyes off Grady, Ryan found himself on the other side of the sofa. Grady leaned forward on the walking cane, and Ryan felt the arm not holding the cane close around him and tighten. “Good work,” Grady whispered as he hugged. “They wouldn’t let me near the phone.”

Ryan hugged back, delicately, staring with blurred vision from his tears of joy at the hardwood wall across the room. After a moment, he felt Grady’s arm relax, and he stepped back. Blinking away the mist, he helped Grady to the front of the sofa.

“Shot me in the belly, the son of a bitch,” Grady said angrily in English as he eased himself down next to Yolanda. He pulled the front of his shirt up from inside his pants and pointed to a small mended place in the tan material. “Went through two layers of belt leather right where the buckle fastens on.”

“Went through your boot tops, too,” Ryan managed to say in an almost normal voice as he sat down beside Grady, staring at the slightly off-color stitching in the shirt, still not believing what he was seeing and hearing. Since Sunday morning, when he and Frank found where the car had been parked and saw that the area had been swept clean, he had, without consciously thinking it, considered Grady Matthews to be dead.

“My good boots?”

“You must have had them in your hand. We found them in the trunk of the car.”

“That’s right, had ’em in my hand. Put on my jogging shoes,” he tapped the blue-red-and-grey leather shoe on his right foot with the walking cane. “Picked my boots up off the ground, and that’s when the son of a bitch shot me.” He turned to look at Yolanda. “Sorry, but that’s the only thing I can think of to call him."

Yolanda smiled, reached over and patted his knee."He went over the side of a cliff, you know."

Grady turned back to Ryan and looked pleased.

"I saw the wrecker pulling him out early Saturday morning, about halfway between Alpine and Fort Stockton," Ryan said. "He hit a deer, went through the railing and down into a...." He stopped. He wasn't going to wait for explanations to be doled out to him.

"What's going on here?" Ryan looked at Naranjo and Yolanda, then at Grady, and asked, "What the hell are you doing here?"

"I found him in the border canyon," Yolanda answered softly in English. "I helped him up onto the mare and brought him here." She looked at Naranjo. "Grandfather took him to the hospital in Ojinaga. They took out the bullet, and we brought him back here two days later."

"Conchas heard that a man he had been in a fight with in Pecos had died," Naranjo interjected. "He thought Senor Grady was a policeman who had come to take him back."

Ryan looked at Grady.

"I don't know what happened, exactly," Grady said. "He must have been aiming at my head while I was bending over, but I raised up and got it in the belly instead. I remember ducking around the car and going toward the butte, then along the fence back toward the road, but I saw him in his truck, patrolling the road. My belly was on fire. I could imagine the mess my insides must be in. I wanted some help, fast.

"I went back to the butte and down an arroyo that runs back of the ranch. There were horses in the trap. I penned four of 'em with a flake of hay. Couldn't find a saddle, but there was part of an old bridle hanging on the wall. I fixed it with some bailing wire, slapped it on a big sorrel gelding and headed down the canyon. Thought I could make the bridge and get up to the highway, but I don't remember much after leaving the ranch.

"He went past the bridge," Yolanda added. "I found him just north of the crossing."

Ryan looked across the table at Naranjo. "You took him to the hospital?" he asked in Spanish.

This time, Naranjo spoke in heavily accented English. “Many years ago, Agent Shaw, my wife was very ill. She needed medical care in El Paso.” He looked at Grady. “Señor Grady was at that time the *jefe* of immigration in Marfa. Somehow he learned of my situation and arranged permits for my wife and two of our daughters.” He smiled. “There was also a special permit for me, under another name.” Naranjo’s dark eyes were looking directly at Grady.

“I have always been grateful to Señor Grady for what he did, although I know he did it with the hope that I would become his little finger, that because of this favor, I would one day give him information, tell him something about someone.”

The old man raised the cigar to his lips. “But I never did,” he said between puffs. “I never told him a damn thing.” He lowered the cigar, stared a moment longer into Grady’s eyes, then turned and looked out the window.

“Never did,” Grady said, leaning back. “Never told me anything, but he and his granddaughter saved my life. I would say the favor has been returned. Now I would like to go home. I still have a stolen horse to find.”

“You are now free to go, anytime,” Naranjo said. “It was unfortunate that you happened upon Conchas and the packhorses. I couldn’t allow you to go back with that information. Now that Agent Shaw and I have come to an agreement, there is no longer a reason for you to remain.”

Ryan’s eyes wandered to the window and the valley beyond. If the first load of Rodrigo’s cocaine was going to be crossed tonight, the distant colored dots that were the runaway horses would have to be moved eight miles back down the river, up out of the gorge, and on to the ledge camp for loading. There was still plenty of time to do that, make the crossing and be at the old ranch house by morning with two tons of cocaine.

If he notified customs now, he would be ordered out of Mexico, and that would be the end of it. If this first load could be crossed – give customs and Texas state troopers a preview of things to come – maybe something could be worked out with the State Department, a delay... a mixup in notifying the Mexican government until everything had been crossed. That could happen.

He looked down at the walking cane and Grady's colorful jogging shoes. He had what he had come for. He could take Grady and leave now, drive to Ojinaga, cross the bridge into Presidio, and never come back.

His look shifted to Yolanda. She was staring at him.

25

The trail was rough and narrow, and often disappeared into the swift shallows of the Rio Grande. Yolanda and the rose gray set a fast pace. Ryan on the big dun kept pressure on the column of horses from the rear. At noon they reached the crossing where they had entered Mexico the previous morning.

Across the river, Ryan could see the wide, grassy entrance to the canyon that led to the old ranch. It was the only break in the steep walls of the river gorge for what Don Naranjo had claimed was exactly twelve and one-half kilometers.

Near the crossing, the string of horses doubled back, climbing the narrow trail along the south wall of the gorge to retrace their previous route. Soon they began disappearing over the rim.

Ryan followed, topped out and zigzagged down the switchback trail to the floor of the ledge camp canyon. There he paused, breathed a sigh of relief and looked back. The wedge-shaped slope was high, at least two hundred yards to the top and steep – steeper than it had seemed yesterday morning.

It worried him. The narrow, twisting trail was barely adequate for the small burro hooves that had helped carve it. Yet the horses took to it without hesitation, had skillfully negotiated it in last night's darkness. In a few hours they would do it again, this time carrying two hundred pounds of Colombian cocaine each.

Ryan's eyes traced the crooked trail from the rim down to the coarse sand at his mare's feet. The added weight would make a difference. Recovery from a misstep would be difficult. He stared at the slope a moment longer. It was no steeper than the National Forest trails east of Tucson where he had packed cement and sand for the Forest Service during two college summer vacations. He urged the dun on toward the departing horses. No steeper, he thought, but the park trails were five feet wide, the horses experienced, and an old packer from Yellowstone named Slim Johnson had seen to it that nothing foolish was attempted.

The sun was directly overhead. Ryan pulled the front of his hat lower Grady would be in Presidio by now. Frank was to meet him there, drive him directly to Alpine to the county hospital where Grady would get a thorough going over. Sometime tomorrow, Grady would be reunited with his stolen mare. Frank had given him the good news over Naranjo's phone. A state brand inspector had turned her up at a livestock auction in San Angelo. Frank had already dispatched someone to pick her up.

Ahead the horses were bunching up, three or four abreast now, not strung out the way the narrow trails had forced them to travel all morning. The young stallion was not among them. Isolated in the corral next to the ramp because of his wire cuts, he had been the only horse left after the big escape.

Ryan found that he missed the colt racing back and forth, herding, tossing his head and nosing the heels of stragglers like a wild stallion moving his herd. He had turned out to be an asset moving the horses from the ranch to the river, but he would be a nuisance to a loaded pack train. The high stone corral at the ledge camp was a good place for him. He hoped Yolanda would agree.

The thought of her caused him to look past the mass of horses ahead. She sat straight in the saddle, back arched, looking fantastic. She raised her arm and made a circular motion.

Ryan repeated the signal, removed the lariat from his saddle and searched the rock walls for something to tie onto. By the time he had the lariat strung across the canyon, Yolanda had done the same up ahead and was motioning him forward. They had hardly spoken since leaving the hacienda, only a few words about the horses, not enough to reveal how she felt about customs agents, especially one that had planned to arrest her.

His feelings about her were mixed. She had delivered him to Naranjo without knowing or caring what was going to happen to him.

She had also, without a doubt, saved Grady's life. He was having trouble reconciling these two events.

Ryan nudged the dun and followed Yolanda into an opening in the east wall of the canyon, down a long narrow passageway into a wide circular meadow completely enclosed by high cliffs. Yolanda trotted the grey on across the high turf grass to a grove of oak trees near the far wall. The cliffs were brown and tan limestone except for a thick stratum of greenish, slate-like stone near the top. Large, angular chunks of the slick, greenish stone cluttered the base of the precipice. Vapor rose from behind one area of the jumbled rocks.

Yolanda pulled her mare up under one of the big oaks and dismounted. Ryan rode on past her to the rising steam a few yards away. It came from a large, clear pool extending back under the base of the cliff. Numerous thick, table-sized slabs of the moss-colored stone had obviously been arranged by human effort to form a half-circle around the steaming water. Fine, reddish-colored sand danced along the bottom of the pool on the upward-flowing current of the hot spring.

"A few minutes in there will cure all your aches and pains," Yolanda announced. She walked past him carrying her saddlebags. Ryan turned the dun and rode back to the oaks, unsaddled, slipped the dun's bridle off and tossed it atop the saddle and joined Yolanda near the pool.

"How hot is it?" he asked.

"It varies." She was in the shade of the cliff, seated on one of the larger slabs. "Today it looks hot." She began pulling brown paper-wrapped packages from the saddlebags. "But you could stand it, probably feel pretty good." She nodded toward the other end of the slab. "Sit down and let's eat."

Tamales, fried *cabrito*, tortillas and green chilies. They ate in silence for a while, until she began to talk about her mother, grandmother and aunts bringing her and her sisters, brothers and cousins to the hot spring every fall to gather sweet white-oak acorns from the grove. "This is where I learned to swim." She looked at the water and smiled. "In the hot pool." She looked up at him. "There were Indians here, once. There are *metates* there." She pointed along a section of the cliffs. "Holes in the rocks, where they ground things.

Acorns, I guess. They came for the acorns too."

For the first time Ryan heard a slight accent. Probably because she was relaxed, the first time he had seen her that way. Probably tired and sleepy, too, like he was.

"Over there" – she pointed across the meadow – "is a big cave full of pictographs. One is a mountain lion, all yellow with a long, curled-up tail. It covers half the wall. I'll show it to you before we leave."

They finished eating. She wrapped the leftovers in a single bundle and reached for the saddlebags. Ryan picked them up and handed them to her.

She shrugged. "You haven't said much today." Her voice was soft.

"I'm tired," he said.

"You never say much. I thought you might be a little more talkative now that you know that I didn't shoot your friend."

Ryan thought about it while she stuffed the bundle into the leather pocket and closed the flap. He wasn't sure himself, now, if he had really ever suspected her. He decided to let it go, change the subject. "When did you find out who I was?" It was awkward, almost blurted out, something he hadn't intended to ask, not just yet anyway, but now it was out. Had she thought he was an informant, a "little finger" that her grandfather would have simply done away with?

She propped the saddlebags against the rock at her feet and looked across at him. Her brown eyes shined. "I knew who you were the minute I saw you at the ranch, day before yesterday." She smiled, pulled a pair of leather gloves from her hip pocket and laid them on the slab next to his. "About an hour after you bought those, and the ones you gave to Jose, I bought these."

Ryan looked down at her gloves, identical to his own except for the size. She leaned over, pulling her boots off as she continued. "Mr. Steiner told me all about Mr. Frank Marsh's friend, about letting him into the store Sunday morning, about everything he bought and about the badge in his wallet." She draped her socks across her boot tops and stood up. "I knew who you were as soon as I saw you in your new Steiner Brothers wardrobe." She smiled, walked around the slab to the pool and tested the water with her toe.

Ryan stared at the grove of oak trees. She had known all along that he was a customs agent, had told her grandfather when she took supplies to the La Mula store. Then Naranjo had called Frank just to be certain. She knew nothing was going to happen to him at the hacienda; she just didn't know Naranjo had set up the phone call from Frank. He felt like smiling. So he did, for almost a full minute.

"Joe said you had been away for a while."

He turned and saw her wading out into the water, her clothes on a small slab at the water's edge. He watched until the steaming water covered her shoulders and she began to swim toward the cliff.

Then he walked to the edge of the pool, took the .45 from under his shirt and lay it on the slab next to her revolver, sat down while he pulled off his boots, stood back up, and undressed.

♦ ♦ ♦

Customs Distrito Comandante Suarez was in full, freshly pressed olive-drab uniform, carrying a small blue-vinyl suitcase as he stepped toward the big bus that had just pulled up in front of the Paso de San Antonio village store. The gold Mexican eagle-and-snake medallion on his garrison hat flashed in the noonday sun. His brown boots glistened beneath the unavoidable layer of caliche dust. The *comandante* was aware that he looked foolish carrying the colorful, child-sized piece of luggage, but he was confident that no one on the bus would laugh or even so much as smile about it.

The door opened, and the young bus driver called out the remaining bus stops: "Manuel Benavides, San Carlos, La Mula, El Chapo, Barranca Azul and Ojinaga!" Seeing the uniform, the young man hurried to lower the volume of a mariachi-trumpeting radio on the floor in front of him.

"This bus passes near the army fort, no?" Suarez asked curtly in Spanish.

"Si, Jefe... Si, Comandante. I can't go in, but if someone wants off, I stop at the front gate."

Suarez grunted, stepped aboard and glanced down the aisle. There weren't many passengers. An old man behind the driver, three younger men near the middle, two girls and an old woman in the back. They were all staring at him and seemed concerned, especially the two girls. Suarez recognized them. He had driven them to the ledge camp and back.

He stepped off the bus and waved to Inspector Ramon who was waiting nearby in the commandeered van. Ramon nodded, waved and drove away. Suarez watched the van and its dust cloud for a moment, then looked down at the front tire of the bus and back along the side. This, too, was an old school bus like the one he'd driven to the ledge camp, a large one, brush-painted a bright blue. It was a thick coat of paint. The brush marks were deep, but none of the school-bus yellow showed through.

Suarez reboarded the bus. "What time will we arrive at the fort?"

"About six or six-thirty, Comandante."

"Don't forget to let me off." The Comandante didn't offer to pay. He walked back to an empty seat, sat down, and put the little blue suitcase on the seat next to him. It had come from one of the shelves in Señor Vicente Esteban's store. The only other colors to choose from had been red and pink. The little suitcase now contained the two packages he had taken from Rodrigo's tent. First he would show the cocaine. Perhaps that would be enough.

26

It was late afternoon when Ryan and Yolanda arrived at the ledge camp with the packhorses. Joe and three of the old men met them at the corrals. Within a short time, the six of them had all twenty-one pack animals saddled and ready for loading.

Ryan climbed the corral gate and looked the horses over. They were tired. The trek to Naranjo's and back with hardly any rest had taken its toll. Good enough, he thought. They would be easier to handle tonight. He stepped down off the gate, pushed it open and watched Yolanda ride out of the corral and up the ramp toward the ledge. Rodrigo had not yet made an appearance. He was sick from the snake bite, Marcos and Felipe had been told by the cooks. Yolanda would tell him they had returned and were loading up for the first trip.

Felipe and Joe brought two packhorses from the corral. Ryan closed the gate behind them. Juan, the snake-catcher, was not with the other old men today. According to the others, Juan and his wife had loaded their belongings on a burro and departed the canyon several hours before the coral snake incident last evening. Ryan smiled again at the thought of the old man selling the deadly coral snake to Rodrigo.

He took the lead rope from Felipe and, followed by Joe leading the other packhorse, started across the runway. There was a ton of cocaine to load. The thought brought back a feeling of uneasiness that had been pushed aside during the hot work inside the corral. The deal with Naranjo had certainly simplified matters, solved a lot of problems, but it had produced another.

The moon would be almost full tonight and well overhead by the time they reached the head of the canyon. Good for climbing up the steep switchback trail, good for descending into the gorge and crossing the river, not good for passing under the highway bridge. This would be a perfect night for a still-watch, a Border Patrol specialty, and the bridge was the perfect vantage point. Still-watch teams usually packed it in when the moon set. Ryan knew that; so did Yolanda. That was why she had made them wait for complete darkness before passing under the bridge two nights ago.

Cross the river and wait for the moon to set before going past the bridge – that was the way to do it, but Yolanda no longer thought so. "Why wait for the moon to go down?" she had argued. They are waiting for your orders, aren't they?"

"Of course," he had lied.

"Then we are safe," she said. "Why wait? We can make good time in the moonlight, go on to the ranch, unload and get some rest."

He'd had to agree or risk telling her the truth – that no one in the customs service knew he was in Mexico or anything about his agreement with her grandfather. They would reach the bridge with an almost-full moon overhead. If the Border Patrol were there, that's as far as they would get.

As Ryan and Joe approached the entrance of the cavern, two guards stepped out. Ryan informed them they were going to begin loading. The larger of the two men spoke in Spanish. "You are taking nothing without permission."

Ryan was hot, dirty, tired and in no mood for argument.

He glared at the man and motioned with his head toward the ledge. "Then go get permission."

The guard's eyes narrowed. He took a step forward, opened his mouth to reply, but it was the smaller guard who spoke.

"*Ya viene,*" he said as the clatter of hooves on the runway reached them.

Ryan turned toward the sound. Rodrigo and Yolanda were riding toward them. The guards straightened and squared their shoulders as Yolanda and Rodrigo pulled their horses up at the cavern's entrance. Rodrigo's face was ashen and wet with perspiration. His right arm, suspended in a sling improvised from a large towel, was held out, well away from his body. With his good hand, he took a handkerchief from his shirt pocket and daubed at his forehead.

"These people will take the cargo," he said in a low monotone, staring blankly past everyone. "You are to assist them in any way you can." The sorrel mare shifted her weight.

Rodrigo groaned and leaned forward in the saddle. Ryan thought he was going to fall and stepped forward to catch him.

Carefully, Rodrigo righted himself, eyes staring vacantly. Slowly, he turned the sorrel mare around and rode away. The large Peruvian mumbled a command that sent the smaller one trailing along behind Rodrigo.

Yolanda dismounted and came up beside Ryan. "The snake must have been chewing on him longer than we thought."

"No, he just didn't cut off enough finger," Ryan said as they both watched Rodrigo and the guard cross the runway. "What happens if he doesn't wake up in the morning?"

"I don't know," Yolanda answered quickly. "But the sooner everything is across, the better – and damn it, we're going to be short four horses this trip."

Ryan gave her a puzzled look.

"That's how many men he's sending with us."

Damn, he should have realized that. The growing stockpile of cocaine at the ranch would need protection. Now there was not only a pack train of cocaine to get past the highway bridge tonight, but four machine-gun-armed guards.

"There are supposed to be other saddles in here," Yolanda said as she walked into the cavern. "Where are the riding saddles?" she demanded of the guard.

The Peruvian pointed into the darkness. "There are no lights?" she asked.

The guard took down one of the propane lanterns, lit it and handed it to her. Leaving Joe with the horses, Ryan followed Yolanda into the cavern to a wide alcove on the right where they found stacks of English-style riding saddles, pads and bridles. Nearby were the four wooden crates he had seen the Peruvians unloading from one of the airplanes. Behind the crates, large rolls of what appeared to be fish netting had been leaned against the back wall.

"What's the net for?" Ryan asked.

"Hauling contraband," Yolanda quickly answered in Spanish. "An old *muletero's* trick," she added in English. "Something you don't learn summertime packing for the Forest Service."

She looked back over her shoulder and smiled. They had learned a lot about each other at the hot-spring pool.

Yolanda put the lantern down, hoisted two of the lightweight saddles and frowned. "I'd rather ride bareback." She squeezed past him, a saddle in each hand, and disappeared into the main cavern.

Ryan stared down at the black foreign words and big red C-4 printed on the largest of the three wooden crates. This was the plastic explosive used for car and airplane bombs. The two smaller boxes, one slightly larger than the other, were stacked on top of the C-4. Ryan hefted the smaller one. It was lightweight, labeled with Oriental symbols and had been opened. He set the box down and pulled up a loose slat. Small pellets of Styrofoam packing filled the box. He plunged his hand into the packing and pulled out the first solid object he felt: a small black box the size of a cigarette package, sealed inside a clear plastic bag.

Ryan could see three dials and two switches on one side of it. He heard footsteps approaching, shoved the device inside his shirt, pushed the raised slat down and picked up two saddles as the guard appeared.

"Bring four pads and four bridles," Ryan ordered as he pushed past the Peruvian.

A minute later, the guard was at the cavern entrance with the equipment. Ryan tied the saddles and other gear onto one of the packhorses, and Yolanda led the animal away.

♦ ♦ ♦

Loading the cocaine – two duffel bags on each side – went faster than Ryan had anticipated thanks to the three old men and the nylon fish netting he had been curious about.

"The way we loaded the burros with marijuana," Marcos had slowly explained when they started loading. With Juan gone, he had taken over as spokesman for the group. "In those days, we made our own net," he said, tossing a long section of netting across the back of the horse. He arranged it evenly, then pulled down, anchoring it on the ears of the packsaddle. "It was not as strong as this." He hooked his fingers in the net and pulled himself a few inches off the ground. "Sometimes it would break."

Joe helped Marcos and Felipe carry two duffel bags to the left side of the horse, double the net up over the bags and anchor it over the saddle ears. "I always carried extra net," Marcos continued as they netted two more duffel bags to the right side of the horse. "I lost a hundred kilos in the river once." They secured the two ends of the net together. "But it didn't matter," he laughed. "They caught us at the bridge. The Border Patrol caught us and took everything. Don Naranjo never knew I lost a whole burro load in the river." He chuckled, patting the netted duffel bags. "You're not going to lose any of this."

It was well after dark when the pack train moved out, with Yolanda and two guards in the lead and Ryan, Joe and two guards at the rear.

One packhorse had the trail gear; the other sixteen each carried two hundred pounds of Colombian cocaine. The stallion colt was left behind in the stone corrals. His shrill calls, distorted, reverberating off the limestone walls, could be heard well past the end of the runway.

The packhorses formed a single column and moved steadily, quietly along. It would have been a good time to bring Joe up to date, tell him that Yolanda and Lalo knew all about them, explain the deal that had been made, but the two Peruvians seemed always within earshot, and Ryan didn't trust their apparent ignorance of English. It could wait.

When the moon finally appeared over the east rim of the canyon, Ryan urged the dun up onto higher, rougher ground, around the line of packhorses, past the two guards and back into the narrow channel of sand beside Yolanda. Light from the almost-round moon lit her face as she looked over at him, smiled and reached back to the saddlebag on her right.

"How many times have you done this?" Ryan asked in English. The two Peruvians were several yards behind them, out of hearing range. The question caused her to hesitate before pulling a quart-sized thermos from the saddlebag.

"Officially or unofficially?" She unscrewed the metal cup from the bottle and handed it to him.

"Unofficially – just curious." He reached back into his own saddlebag and, after some rummaging, came up with another cup.

She looked toward him. "This is the first time." She said as she twisted the stopper from the Thermos.

"First time!" Ryan glanced back at the guards and lowered his voice. "You've never done this before?"

Yolanda smiled. "Nothing like this." She dried the stopper on the leg of her Levis, dropped it in her shirt pocket, reached across for one of the cups and filled it with hot coffee. She handed it back to Ryan and took the empty cup from him. "I have been up and down these canyons all my life," she said. "When I was old enough to ride, they let me bring things from the store in Alpine to the one in La Mula."

"You never got caught?"

"The border patrol ignored me. I was just a skinny little kid." She glanced down at herself. Ryan looked, too, remembered her wading out into the hot pool. Not a skinny kid anymore, he thought, but made no comment. "Then we moved to Fort Stockton," she continued. "I went to high school there, then went away to college and never really came back." She poured coffee for herself and looked over at him again.

"First time going this way with anything... honest." She sipped the coffee without looking away from him.

"Where have you been?"

"It's a secret," she said matter-of-factly, "even from friends."

For a few minutes, they drank the coffee in silence, listening to the sound of gravel crunch under the horses' hooves. "My grandfather prepared for retirement years ago," Yolanda finally said, softly. "He just never got around to it. He found a beautiful place where no one knows about him, or any of us."

"That's where you have been?"

"Yes."

"Going back?"

"Yes. I only came back for my mother. She is ready to go. I think grandfather is, too. He has already moved his best cattle and horses." Up the border canyon, Ryan thought, to the pens at the ranch, then trucked them out. That explained the ground-up condition of the road.

"I only got mixed up in this when I found out you were after him."

"I'm not after him anymore," Ryan said. "You did a good job taking care of him." He finished his coffee and pushed the empty cup toward her for a refill. She smiled and poured more coffee for him.

The narrow opening that led into the hot-spring meadow was just ahead. They both stared at it as they rode by. "Tomorrow evening, from this place," Yolanda said, "I think Jose can take the horses on back to the ledge by himself."

Ryan felt a warm rush. He nodded agreement. "Yes, I don't think he'd mind doing that."

Yolanda handed over her empty cup, took the thermos stopper from her shirt pocket and twisted it back into the mouth of the bottle. As he handed the cup back to her, Ryan looked up at the bright moon. The highway bridge was less than an hour away now.

27

Yolanda led the four guards up the switchback first. When all five of them had disappeared over the rim, Ryan began cutting packhorses from the bunch and allowing them, one at a time, to start the climb up the steep zigzag trail with their two-hundred pound loads. He was glad Yolanda had agreed to leave the young stallion colt at the camp. This was no place for his herding antics.

When the last packhorse had topped out above, Ryan followed Joe and his paint gelding, crisscrossing the face of the slope up out of the canyon and then down toward the Rio Grande.

Yolanda had posted two of the Peruvians on the upriver trail and, with the other two guards, was holding the crossing. As Joe and Ryan neared the bottom of the gorge, she started across the river. With a little urging from Joe, the packhorses followed. Ryan was the last one across. Joe, Yolanda and the guards were waiting, holding the horses in the wide mouth of the border canyon.

Ryan rode among the animals, located the bay gelding carrying the trail gear, snapped a lead rope onto his halter and led him up to Yolanda. The black hat shaded her face, but he could feel her questioning look.

"Rope off the canyon and take a break," he said. "I'm going to check out the bridge. There's always somebody who doesn't get the word. I'll be back in a few minutes." He moved away, leading the packhorse, before she could reply. When he looked back, she was stringing her riata across the canyon. He nudged the big dun into a trot.

If there was a still-watch team at the bridge, it would be a couple of border patrolmen waiting for migrants sneaking across the border. They wouldn't be prepared for a gunfight against machine guns.

Ryan kept the horses in a trot, eating up distance on the glowing strip of sand and gravel until a pickup truck crossed the bridge a hundred yards ahead. He slowed the horses to a walk. Time to move quietly, look like a smuggler. If anyone was in the canyon, the horses would let him know.

He stared at the bridge ahead. More than likely they would be up there. Either way, they would let him pass, then cut off his retreat before lighting him up.

He watched the dun's bobbing head as they approached the shadow of the bridge. The slightest movement, scent or sound, and its ears would respond, lock on. A small vehicle crossed overhead as they passed under the structure.

The mare's ears were working, searching ahead, to the sides, behind. Ryan and the two horses moved slowly on up the canyon.

Some 150 yards past the bridge, as the canyon made a westward bend, Ryan looked back. The canyon was empty. He rode into the shadow of what was now the south wall. Fifty yards later the canyon twisted north again, and he was back in the moonlight. He tied the packhorse to a small mesquite tree jutting from the rocky wall and rode slowly back down the canyon. Just past the bridge, he let the dun work herself into a lope toward the other horses.

♦ ♦ ♦

Yolanda and Joe took the lead. Ryan kept the four Peruvians at the rear with him, thinking he might have some control over them if there was trouble, but the bridge was passed without incident.

In the cool, protected silence of the narrow canyon, anxiety over the bridge passage that had been building all day and the adrenaline rush that had come with acting as decoy were soon gone, leaving Ryan with the same washed-out feeling he'd had all day Saturday after the marathon trip from Madrid.

His eyes burned and his back ached. There had been no opportunity to close his eyes last night, not bouncing around the mountains in the Jeep. No siesta yesterday, either, not after seeing the fifteen tons of cocaine. Night before last, he had slept a couple of hours, maybe three, as they waited for daylight to cross the river. That was the only sleep he'd had since Sunday night at Frank and Joan's. Three days and going on three nights with three hours of sleep.

He took a deep breath and arched his back. Holding up pretty well, he thought. He had always been good for two days and two nights with no sleep at all. There would be time for a nap at the ranch, maybe until noon, before a quick trip into town, meet with Frank and make the call to headquarters.

His head drooped forward, chin on chest, and he closed his eyes. They would unload the horses and put the cocaine in the barn; then he would roll the sleeping bag out on top of some of the hay bales and sleep. His hands slipped off the wide flat topped horn of the roping saddle. He straightened himself and looked back at the four Peruvians. They were ten yards back, two abreast. Ahead, the column of horses moved steadily, quietly. They were tired also.

Ryan put his hands back on the saddle horn, chin on chest, and again closed his eyes. A moment later, his hands slipped off again and again. Each time, he took a deep breath and put them back until the squeaking of a corral gate brought him fully awake.

The canyon walls were gone, and it was dark. What was left of the moonlight came from behind the distant peaks west of the border canyon ranch. Ryan followed the horses toward the faint, yellow glow of a flashlight in need of fresh batteries. He leaned back, searching the saddlebags for his own light. In the yellow beam ahead, he saw Joe on the ground, holding the gate open as the last packhorse entered the corral.

Suddenly, everything was bright. He saw Joe squint. Yolanda, ahead on the grey mare, raised her arm against the glare.

"Federal officers, don't move," came an electronically-amplified command.

Ryan raised his hands. "Federal officers, we're fed...."

He was cut short by a burst of machine-gun fire from behind. Some of the lights went out.

"Get down!" he yelled, leaned over and slid from the saddle.

More machine-gun fire came from the rear. Bullets ripped into the corral timbers around Yolanda as Ryan raced toward her and saw her suddenly go limp and slump forward in the saddle. Her mare's front legs buckled; then she recovered and reared. Yolanda toppled backward out of the saddle and onto the ground. The mare moved a few steps away and collapsed. Just as Ryan reached Yolanda, someone yelled a command, and a volley of gunfire erupted from the darkness behind the lights. Then it was quiet. Ryan felt Yolanda's neck for a pulse, leaned over and listened for her breathing.

28

Deputy Chief Jim Russell of the Marfa Sector Border Patrol was seated next to Ryan, talking in a low, hospital-waiting-room voice. Ryan's eyes were on the double doors where they had taken Yolanda. Neck wound and head injury, the paramedic had said. She was still unconscious when they arrived at the emergency room.

"Customs in El Paso said they didn't care about horses going south no matter how many there were," the deputy chief said

Ryan shifted on the hard wooden bench. Why didn't someone come out and tell him about Yolanda? He looked over at the deputy chief, remembering what he had said earlier about Department of Public Safety officials contacting a truck driver in Fort Stockton who had delivered a trailer load of horses to the border canyon ranch.

The truck driver had been in the cafe at Lajitas the day Grady was there putting up wanted posters for his stolen horse. The truck driver had mentioned several dun horses in the bunch he had picked up at a sale barn in Midland and delivered to the ranch. Ryan knew about that. It was the reason Grady had gone to the ranch looking for his stolen mare. He'd heard Grady go over all of it on the phone with Frank. He wondered how DPS had found the truck driver; then he remembered Frank saying the numbers on the scrap of paper found in Grady's car were probably a trailer license-plate number. They must have finally run that down.

"DPS requested that Brewster County Sheriff's Office send someone out to take a look around the ranch," the deputy chief had explained. "Couple of our men went with 'em and found all the signs: fifteen or twenty horses, penned, shod and gone south."

Ryan was watching two women who had just come through the

entry doors into the waiting room. Both were grey-haired. One was tall, slender and dark. The other was much shorter, not as dark, and heavyset. The tall woman had the same graceful bearing and thick eyebrows as Yolanda. Ryan was sure this was her mother. A nurse had recognized Yolanda when she was brought in, and Ryan had asked her to make the necessary call. The two gray-haired women hurried to the admissions desk.

"When we couldn't get anybody else interested," the deputy chief was now saying, "we put a couple of spotters at the bridge and waited. When they radioed in that close to twenty packhorses and seven armed men had just passed, we called the whole station out." The deputy chief waited a moment, then leaned back and was quiet.

The silence caused Ryan to again look over at the man beside him. Deputy Chief Jim Russell was a big man who appeared to be in his early fifties, with pale blue eyes and a deeply-lined face. He was wearing a rough-duty uniform: tan, three-and-a-quarter-inch-brim hat, olive-green short-sleeved shirt and matching trousers; black-leather river belt, holster and handcuff case; quick-load ammunition carriers and a Ruger .357 Magnum revolver with black-rubber target grips and black, double-soled Wellington boots. Rough-duty uniform was not unusual for a border patrol supervisor, not even a sector deputy chief.

Ryan was glad he had made the brief visit to Marfa Sector headquarters before going into Mexico. He was sure that meeting Russell and swapping a few stories with him and the chief was all that had kept him from going to jail tonight.

"Thanks, Jim," Ryan said, "for letting me ride the ambulance in." The ambulance ride was the least of it. He hoped the deputy chief knew what he meant.

Russell shrugged. "Sorry about the woman, and sorry your deal got botched up." He shook his head. "That's an awful lot of coke to leave over there."

"Nobody's fault," Ryan replied. "You made the right call." He took a deep breath and rubbed his forehead, picturing the stacks of duffel bags still in the cavern. "And it was the machine-gun fire that hit Yolanda, before any of your people fired a shot."

“A wonder they didn’t get you, too,” Russell said, “shooting wild like that.”

“They all dead?” Ryan asked, palms pressed against his face. He was sure he had asked that at the ranch.

“All of of ’em. Bunched up like that, they went down right away.”

“What did you do with Joe?” He hadn’t asked that before. He was ashamed that he had just now thought of him.

“Who?”

“Joe, the man who put me onto all this – little man, blonde hair.”

The deputy chief shook his head. “Never saw him. There was supposed to be seven, according to the spotters, but the four dead ones, you and the woman – that’s all we saw.”

“Little blonde man,” Ryan repeated. “He was on the ground at the gate when the lights came on.”

The deputy chief looked at him and shook his head again.

In his mind, Ryan could see Joe curled up in the brush somewhere, bleeding, dying. He stood up. He would go find him. Then he noticed the two women again, talking to the nurse who had made the call, talking about Yolanda, no doubt. Yolanda! Slowly, he sat back down, his eyes still on the women. “Jim, I’m going to need....”

Suddenly the double doors flew open, and a small thin man in hospital green was in the waiting room calling his name. Ryan stood up.

Dr. Carlos Mendoza smiled and introduced himself. “She’s going to be all right,” he said. “A small laceration on the right side of her neck – possibly a bullet crease – and quite a bump on the back of head, probably from the fall. I want to keep her here....”

“Excuse me, doctor,” Ryan interrupted. The two women were approaching. “Are you Yolanda’s mother?” he asked in Spanish.

“*Si.*” The tall woman gave him a curious look.

“This is Dr. Mendoza.” Ryan stepped aside and listened as the doctor repeated in Spanish what he had previously said in English, adding that Yolanda might remain unconscious for several more hours and should remain in the hospital for further observation. Dr. Mendoza gave a reassuring smile and departed.

Ryan took Yolanda’s mother aside, introduced himself and

explained that Yolanda was not in any trouble with the law. Yolanda's mother eyed him suspiciously as he talked, occasionally cutting her eyes toward the uniformed deputy chief. When Ryan had finished, she made no reply.

"Do you understand?" Ryan asked in Spanish.

"I understand," she answered sharply in English.

Ryan stared at her for a moment. She was not going to believe anything he said. Yolanda would have to explain it to her. "I have to leave now," he said. "When Yolanda wakes up, tell her everything will be all right and that I will be back soon." Yolanda's mother glared at him.

Ryan felt awkward. There was nothing more to say. He smiled at her, turned and walked back to the deputy chief.

"I need a ride back to the ranch." His thoughts were back on Joe. He could be hurt or, perhaps even worse, on his way back to Mexico, unaware that Naranjo knew he was an informant, a "little finger," and that Don Lalo Naranjo was not going to be happy about what had happened tonight.

Outside, it was still dark. Ryan followed the deputy chief to the green-and-white border patrol sedan parked near the emergency entrance. He had to find Joe.

29

Traces of dawn were appearing as Ryan climbed the corral gate where he had last seen Joe. Standing on the top rail, he wrapped his left arm around the tall gatepost and called Joe's name. Below, inside the thick cedar-pole walls, it was still pitch black.

He moved the narrow, powerful beam of light from the deputy chief's flashlight over the horses. They had been unsaddled and there was hay in the corral for them to eat. In the distance he could see through the slats of another gate that there were horses in the adjoining corral. One was a grey.

He turned, aiming the light where he had seen Yolanda's mare go down. She wasn't there. He called Joe's name again as he brought the beam of light back to the grey horse he had seen in the other corral. It was the rose grey, head down, not moving, but on her feet, not dead.

But what about Joe? Was he on his feet? Ryan moved the light back over the horses in the corral below him, looking for Joe's paint gelding, surprised at the number of uninjured horses. He'd had the impression that the Peruvians' machine-gun bursts had downed half of them.

The light found the paint. He was alone in the east corner of the corral near the barn, and he was saddled and bridled. Ryan eased down from his vantage point and made his way across the corral. As he approached the paint, something in the darkness beyond moved.

Ryan stepped to one side and pointed the light toward the movement. A figure, squatting in the dark corner of the corral, looked up into the light. "Cuate, you alone?" Joe whispered loudly in Spanish.

"Joe! Damn!" Ryan exclaimed. "You don't even look human hunkered down there." The little man was hatless, soaking wet and shivering.

"I've been in the tank, over by the windmill."

Ryan moved to him. "Are you all right?" He helped him up. "You shot or anything?"

"I'm okay, just cold." His teeth were chattering.

Ryan put his arm around him. "Come on up to the house. There's nobody there now but a couple of border patrolmen. They've got some coffee going. We'll get warm and fix something to eat."

Joe shrugged Ryan away. "Okay, okay, I can make it. I'm just cold," he said through clicking teeth. "I have dry clothes at the house."

They made their way out of the corral and into the barn. As they passed through, Ryan flashed the light over the piles of packsaddles, blankets and nylon netting. Good equipment, he thought. The horses had been good, too. There should have been more time. They should have been able to finish the job. The light stopped on Yolanda's saddle. It was over now – unfinished, but over. There weren't going to be any more trips.

He moved the light over to Joe. He was pulling a blanket from the equipment pannier. He pulled it around himself and moved on toward the door, his wet boots making squishing sounds with each step. Ryan untied the saddlebags from his saddle, threw them across his left shoulde, and followed Joe out of the barn. Last night's thirty-two hundred pounds was all of Rodrigo's cocaine they were ever going to get. Rodrigo would fly it out now, or as Naranjo had said, it would be confiscated by Mexican authorities and they would have someone sell it for them. Either way, it would end up in the U.S.

Ryan opened the door and followed Joe into the lighted ranch house. Two border patrol agents looked up from the kitchen table. The deputy chief had introduced Ryan to them before departing with the three pickup trucks carrying the seized cocaine. The two uniformed men put their coffee mugs down.

One was Hispanic, of average build; the other was blond, fair-skinned and big, taller than Ryan. He stood up.

"Keep your seat." Ryan motioned for him to sit back down. The big blonde border patrolman ignored him, stepped over to the stove and lifted the coffeepot from a low blue propane flame. "Looks like your buddy could use a cup of coffee," he said, filling a white mug and pushing it across the table. Joe thanked him, wrapped both hands around the steaming mug and sloshed on into the adjoining room.

The blonde officer set another cup on the table and filled it. Ryan dropped the saddlebags, sat down and pulled the coffee toward him. Harry Evans was the big one, he recalled from the deputy chief's hasty introduction, the other one was Mike Flores. Harry put the blue enameled coffeepot back on the stove and lit the gas burner in front of it.

"We were waiting for breakfast on you," he said placing a large iron skillet on the flame. "How do you like your eggs?"

Ryan could see a heaping platter of cooked bacon on the cabinet next to the stove. "Scrambled, and you can scramble Joe's, too."

"That makes it easy." The big blonde man tucked a dishtowel into his pistol belt and began breaking eggs into the black cast-iron skillet.

"Good coffee, Harry." Ryan commented, taking a second sip.

"Stronger'n stud-horse piss with the foam farted off," replied the big cook.

Ryan reflected on Harry's comment for a moment. Someone else he knew described their coffee the same way.

"We heard you told Russell there was fifteen tons of cocaine stashed over there," Mike Flores said from across the table. "Is there really that much?"

"It's there, all but the ton and a half or so you got last night." Ryan sipped again from his cup.

"They going to cross fifteen tons of dope with packhorses?" Mike sounded skeptical.

Ryan smiled. "No, *they* weren't. But me, the girl and Joe" – he nodded toward the adjoining room – "we were going to cross it." He went through the story quickly, hitting only the high points. As he finished, Joe came in, hair combed, in fresh Levi's, brown-and-white plaid flannel shirt and stockinged feet. Ryan introduced him to the two officers, and Joe sat down at the table.

Harry gave the eggs a final stir, dumped them into a large flat pan and slid it onto the table. "What were you going to do with the timer?" He leaned over and opened the oven door.

“Timer?”

“The one you’ve got over there in the saddlebags.” Harry slid the oven grill out and began spearing toast with a long meat fork. “We searched all your stuff.” He looked up and smiled.

“The timer.” Ryan reached down, picked up the saddlebags and unbuckled the flaps. He knew what Harry was talking about now, the black object from the wooden box in the cave. He had put it in the saddlebags to look at later but hadn’t had the chance. He took it out and set it on the table.

“It’s a good one,” Harry said, putting the toast and bacon on the table as he sat down. “Made in Japan. You can set it for one minute or for one week.” He spooned a large helping of scrambled eggs onto his plate and passed the pan to Ryan.

“I found a whole crate of them in Rodrigo’s camp.” Ryan took some eggs and looked across the table. “You know about explosives, Harry?” Harry had his mouth full but nodded affirmatively.

“He was with the Army Rangers,” Mike explained. “Knows all about bombs, dynamite, machine guns, all that stuff.” He took the pan of eggs from Ryan and smiled. “He’s also a pretty good cook.”

Ryan looked down at the device and thought about the wooden crates in the cave. No doubt the big one contained C-4 explosive; he could read that. If the smallest box contained timers, wouldn’t the other one be detonators? He looked across the table at the big ex-Army ranger who would know how it all went together. “Good breakfast, Harry,” Ryan said. “Good coffee,” he said again. “How long were you in Nogales?”

Harry gave him a questioning look, glanced at Mike, then back to Ryan. Ryan raised his coffee cup, held it for a moment, then smiled and took a drink.

Slowly Harry smiled. “You’ve had stud-horse coffee before?”

“A few hundred gallons,” Ryan said still smiling. “Is Willy still there?”

“Still there.” Harry nodded. “Old Willy is still there – two years ago, anyway. The Tubbs sold the ranch just before I left, but Willy got to stay on. The new people couldn’t get anybody else to stay up at that old-line shack."

Ryan looked down at his coffee and let his thoughts drift for a moment, from Rodrigo, Naranjo, the cave, injured horses and explosives to Willy Purvis, who had ridden the high pastures of the Tubbs ranch north of Nogales. No one walked out of Mexico and up the east side of the Santa Cruz Valley without Willy knowing about it. A good contact, but you had to drink a lot of stud-horse coffee.

"Just how far south is this cave with fifteen tons of coke in it?" Mike asked.

Ryan smiled. He liked the thought behind Mike's question. "Too far, Mike, too far, and it's guarded by a crazy bunch with machine guns just like the four they hauled out of here this morning." He turned back to Harry, who was busy with his scrambled eggs and bacon. Harry could tell him how to rig the explosives – but what about the horses? "You two feed the horses?"

"Stripped off the saddles, fed the horses, searched all your stuff and loaded the dope into the pickups. Now we're supposed to stay here until the customs people out of El Paso show up." Harry picked up his coffee cup and drained it.

Ryan steered the conversation onward. "I was surprised to see how many of the horses weren't hit. I thought half of them would be dead."

"Some of them are nicked up a little bit," Mike said. "But only the four we put in the other corral have bullet holes in them. A couple of them will probably be all right eventually, but the other two really ought to be put down." He shook his head.

"The rose grey didn't seem too bad." Ryan wandered from his intended direction. "Well, a couple of holes all the way through her neck. Nothing vital seems to have been hit there, but there's a hole in her right shoulder. I don't know about that.

"Get a vet out here, will you?" Ryan said. "And have him do whatever he can, especially for the grey. I would like everything possible done for her."

"You going somewhere?" Mike asked.

"Well...." Ryan began. He found himself at the jumping-off point sooner than expected. "I thought if you and Harry would help resaddle the packhorses, Joe and I would take the ones that can still move and get the hell back to down to Mexico before the customs agents from El Paso show up."

Joe choked on his mouthful of scrambled eggs.

♦ ♦ ♦

Thirty miles southwest of the ranch house, an army-green Ford Fairlane Dynasty, three Jeeps and four canvas-covered military trucks were speeding along a dusty caliche road. One of the two men in the back seat of the Ford sedan was General Claudio Pagazos-Zamano, Military Zone Commander for the Northeastern section of the state of Chihuahua. Sitting next to him was Customs Distrito Comandante Julio Antonio Suarez-Benavides.

At the fork in the road, ten or twelve kilometers back, Comandante Suarez had informed the general that they had taken the wrong turn, that the village of Paso de San Antonio was to the right, not to the left.

The general had only grunted. Comandante Suarez had no idea where they were going.

They passed a small group of buildings on the left side of the road, a gas pump in front of one of them. A few minutes later, the sedan suddenly turned right, off the dusty road, taking the convoy up a narrow driveway lined with large green pecan trees.

30

The sun was directly overhead as Ryan roped off the entrance to the hot-spring valley, rode across the meadow past the grazing packhorses, and joined Joe near the grove of oaks.

With the help of the two border patrolmen, they had managed to get gear back on the packhorses that were still able to travel, and had headed back down the border canyon before 8 a.m.

Ryan would have a lot of explaining to do later, but by then the remaining cocaine, thirteen-plus tons, would be under fifty feet of limestone rubble... he hoped.

Ryan dismounted and helped Joe lift the nylon panniers off the supply horse; then they both unsaddled and hobbled their mounts. The other animals would have to rest with their empty packsaddles on. Ryan motioned for Joe to follow. "Time we had a talk about all of this," he said, and walked to the long slab near the pool where he and Yolanda had eaten lunch the previous day. They both sat down.

Ryan took a deep breath and stared across at Joe. They had known each other for a long time. Joe would surely have been beaten to death in his jail cell if Ryan hadn't pulled the two Pima County deputies off him. Clearly, Joe was still devoted to him. Even after last night's disaster, here he was on his way back to the ledge camp simply because Ryan had asked him to come. It was time he knew the whole truth.

Ryan started from the beginning – the phone call at the embassy in Madrid – and explained in Spanish that he had come back to help Frank look for Grady, that nothing else had mattered. They had not even reported Rodrigo and Naranjo's smuggling operation because Naranjo had become their only remaining lead to Grady's whereabouts. Ryan told about Grady's encounter with Conchas, about Yolanda's finding him wounded and taking him to the hacienda. He told how sheriff's deputies and the border patrol had gone to the old ranch looking for Grady, found all the horse signs and set up on the bridge.

"That's how we almost got killed last night," Ryan said. "All my fault. I should have called from Naranjo's, told someone we were on the way."

Joe gave him a puzzled look. "Yes," Ryan admitted, "I could have called anyone I wanted to." His unspoken thoughts continued. And they would have ordered me out of Mexico immediately. And that would have meant no chance whatever to get it all: cocaine, airplanes and Rodrigo. Because he had wanted it all, four people were now dead and Yolanda was in the hospital.

He took another deep breath and went on to explain how Yolanda had discovered he was a customs agent and driven him to the hacienda where Grady was being held prisoner. He told about the deal with Naranjo, emphasizing the fact that Naranjo now knew that Joe Montez was an informant.

"They know everything," Joe said in English, shaking his head. "That is the reason Miss Yolanda was mad. All the way back, she said nothing to me, nothing." He continued shaking his head.

"Lalo is mad at you now, Cuate," he said after a moment. "He will think you lied." Joe looked up. "And Miss Yolanda, she will think you lied too." Yes, Ryan thought, looking toward the steaming pool... and she'll be right. Ryan looked back at Joe. He had almost gotten Joe killed, too. Time to cut him loose, get him out of this.

"I don't know what Rodrigo had planned," Ryan said. "Maybe some of the Peruvians were supposed to come back with us." He shook his head. "I don't know. By now Yolanda's mother has called Naranjo and told him what happened last night. How soon Rodrigo will get the word...." He shrugged. "I don't know that either. I may be riding into a hornet's nest."

He paused for a moment. "Joe, we took thirty-two hundred pounds of cocaine across last night. You've got a reward coming, a big one. The horses know the trail now. I can take them on from here. You go on back, get in touch with Frank, and I'll see you in couple of days."

Joe stared intently at him. "No! No good!" he said in Spanish. "Rodrigo will know something is wrong when you come back alone. If I am there, we can say Miss Yolanda went home again, took the missing horses and will come later, like the last time. That will give us time. When they go to sleep, you can blow everything up."

Ryan stared into the little man's pale blue eyes. One in a million, he thought.

Pulling the deputies off little Joe Montez was one of the best moves he had ever made. And Joe was right – Rodrigo would know something was wrong if he came back alone.

"Let's get some rest, Joe." Ryan's eyes were already searching the nearest of the white oaks for a suitable limb. He was going to need a good stout club.

♦ ♦ ♦

At the river crossing, only three miles north of the hot spring pool, Comandante Julio Antonio Suarez shifted painfully in the saddle. One other time in his life he had been on a horse, at a carnival when he was five years old. He remembered because of the snapshot his mother had taken. In the picture he was crying.

Chato, the old manservant from Naranjo's hacienda, looked up from the damp, disturbed sand and gravel at his feet. "They crossed into the United States yesterday or last night and have already returned, Lieutenant." He looked back down at the wet hoofprints, a troubled look on his face. "Perhaps less than an hour ago."

"Then we have missed a cargo," Lieutenant Robles commented. He was a slender man, a few years younger than Suarez, but wearing the same narrow, carefully trimmed mustache.

He had been placed in charge of the river detail consisting of himself, Suarez, Chato the guide and three enlisted men. "We will wait, as the general has ordered." Robles let his mare wade into the river shallows and drink. "Perhaps they will bring us something tonight."

"They will rest tonight and be back tomorrow evening, Lieutenant," Chato volunteered.

"How far to the ledge camp from here?" Suarez asked, grimacing as his horse shifted. It had been a rough trip for him. Most of it he had spent experimenting with various grips on the wide, flat horn of the Mexican saddle.

"Three hours," Chato replied.

"Then they could be back tonight," the lieutenant said. "There are many horses to feed."

Chato countered. "Many horses to load. Tonight they will rest and return tomorrow."

"No," the lieutenant said, firmly. "Unless they come tonight, they will not be back at all."

Suarez caught the lieutenant's eye, and for a moment they shared the same thought. Both had been left out of the ledge camp raid. Suarez really didn't care. He was thankful to have even a small part in the operation.

Last evening, in General Pagazos' posh living quarters at the army fort on the outskirts of Ojinaga, he had come very close to losing everything, being thrown to the wolves.

"I believe it is cocaine," the general had said as he looked up from his huge red-leather sofa and dropped the plastic bag containing a kilo of white powder onto the coffee table in front of him. "But you have only the word of a whore about the contents of the cavern. Even if there are duffel bags, surely they cannot be filled with this." The general pointed at the cocaine and yawned.

"As for the Colombians who have invaded Mexico, it will be looked into. In the future, I suggest you report such matters to your superiors in Monclova before making such a long trip to disturb my evening meal." The general's eyes had not been friendly as he rose from the sofa and nodded at the two soldiers standing just inside the door.

"But general," Suarez remembered the sickening feeling in his stomach, "there is more." He had never heard such desperation in his own voice, not even while talking to the young man on the yacht in Tampico Bay. Fumbling with the latches on the small blue suitcase, he had managed to get them open and dump the large, brown-paper package onto the coffee table before the soldiers reached him. The package had been opened before, and banded stacks of American twenty-dollar bills spilled across the table. The money was his last hope. As the general had so accurately pointed out, he had bypassed his own superiors and gone directly to the military. For that, there would be no acceptable excuse. There was also his unauthorized investigation, his unreported missing inspector and his encroachment on another customs district.

Staring at the money, the general eased back down on the sofa. Each of the fifty banded stacks was stamped "Silverado National Bank, Reno, Nevada," and each stack contained fifty twenty-dollar bills.

"$50,000," Suarez proclaimed, "and there is more, ten bags, ten green duffel bags filled with these packages. I have seen them in the Colombian's tent." General Pagazos continued to stare at the money.

Seeing the general's change in attitude, Suarez pressed on. "There is an American, too, General. He came yesterday with horses to move the cocaine." Suarez had decided that was what the horses were for. "I think he will move the money bags, too. I don't know when, but I think it will be soon."

General Pagazos picked up one of the stacks of money and slowly turned it over and around in his hand. Suddenly, he sprang to his feet, glaring into Suarez's face, his unmoving eyes barely visible between the narrowed eye-slits.

Suarez backed away from the angry face. Slowly, the general's expression softened. He smiled, looked over at the two soldiers and said, "Take the *comandante* to the officer's mess. See that he has whatever he wants; then show him to the guest quarters."

Suarez was puzzled by the general's sudden change in attitude. Then that morning at the hacienda, he had learned the reason why. The general had left him in the staff car and led an entourage of armed soldiers through the front door of the huge main house. Other soldiers had spread out behind the house and around the outbuildings.

Later, one of the soldiers who had gone into the house came for him and led Suarez inside to a large rustic living room where the general was standing with his back to a large unlit fireplace, as if warming himself. The general was a large, long-wasted man, fair-complexioned with light-brown hair and eyebrows. He was dressed like his men, in sage-green fatigues with matching short-billed cap. Unlike his men, the general's fatigues were new, starched and pressed, with two silver stars glistening from the top of each shoulder. Hands behind his back, the general glanced briefly at Suarez before resuming a study of the large, rough-hewn beams overhead.

"Comandante Suarez," he said, rocking back on his heels and forward again, "it seems that our host, Don Naranjo... you know Don Naranjo?"

"No, General, this is too far west, not my jurisdiction." The general gave him a brief, contemptuous look, then continued.

"Well, Comandante, so you will not be completely in the dark, I will tell you that Don Naranjo has been... ah... active along the border in this area for many years. This has been his home for as long as I have known him. The mountain camp you have described also belongs to him. It is part of his ranch. It was his headquarters in old days. Undoubtedly, he is responsible for whatever is going on there."

The general folded his arms and turned slightly to view the other half of the high ceiling. "As I was about to say, it seems that last night, Don Lalo Naranjo received word of our intended visit and immediately departed." He looked at Suarez. "I doubt that he will ever return."

He paused briefly, then continued in a softer voice, "I have always admired this place, hoped that someday it might be mine." He glanced slowly around the room, nodding his head. "And now, it is."

He again turned to face Suarez. "I will not forget, Comandante Suarez, that it was you who made this possible." He stared into Suarez's face. "Provided, of course, we find a cavern of drugs and the other merchandise."

The general walked to a large, black-leather chair near the window. "Can you ride a horse, Comandante?" he asked as he seated himself.

Suarez was city-raised, city-loving, did not like horses and had always been afraid of them. "No, General, I do not ride."

General Pagazos considered the answer for a moment. "Well, Comandante, it is a long, rough road around the mountains to the ledge camp from here. Even leaving immediately, we could not arrive before dusk. Better to take our time, spend the night in Paso de San Antonio and strike the camp at dawn."

The general leaned over, flipped up the lid of an ornate wooden box on the small table beside his chair and selected a long, dark cigar. He sniffed it, bit off the closed end and spat it onto the polished tile floor.

Suarez patted the sides of his trousers, located his lighter, pulled it from his pocket, stepped to the chair and lit the General's cigar.

"Thank you, Comandante." The general puffed the big cigar. "Now... there is a certain river crossing a few kilometers downriver from here. It is the place where the drugs and... other merchandise were to be crossed." The general leaned back in the big chair and raised his boots to a leather footrest in front of him.

"I know this crossing. There are no roads. It will have to be reached by horseback. I am told that there are six horses in the stables just down the hill. Four of my men and a guide are leaving immediately to intercept anyone – or anything – leaving the mountain camp before I secure it in the morning."

The general looked up from the big chair. "Comandante Suarez, I would like for you to accompany my men to the crossing. Your participation in the confiscation of any merchandise at the border would avoid any... jurisdictional technicalities that might later arise. Don't you agree?"

"Yes, General." He was being shoved aside, put completely out of the picture. But he had expected it. The general would raid the camp and take everything: airplanes, money, equipment and the cocaine. As an added bonus, if anything went wrong, if anything turned up unaccounted for, there was always Suarez, the customs official at the crossing, who could be blamed for letting it slip by. "Then, Comandante, you wish to join the river detail?"

"Yes, General, you can depend on me." One word from a border zone commander, and he could be on his way back to Tampico practically overnight. That was the real prize. He would not risk the general's displeasure, not even if he had to walk to the river crossing. Suarez remembered thinking that.

As he now stood up in the stirrups and winced, he wished he had walked. His butt was raw, bruised and on fire from the hard, unpadded wooden seat of the vaquero saddle.

"The canyon is there," Chato was saying as he pointed up the steep trail along the south wall of the gorge. "On the other side."

"Then we will go there, old man, and wait," Lieutenant Robles said. "Find us a place where we can see anyone coming for a long way," he ordered, patting the wooden stock of the AK-47 assault rifle slung from the horn of his saddle.

31

Up on the lighted ledge, a band was playing when the pack train arrived just after dark. Two pickups and an ancient flatbed truck were parked near the bottom of the ramp. Two of Rodrigo's Peruvians stood on the ramp in front of the truck, watching. Watching for what? One or more of their companions who had accompanied the load to the ranch?

Ryan led the horses past them into the corral and was greeted by the young stallion, snorting and pawing in the adjoining corral. He was going to be disappointed not to see his mother and Yolanda. Circling back to the gate, Ryan dismounted and closed it as Joe entered with the last of the horses.

"I will get the old men," Joe said, turning back toward the gate.

"We can handle it," Ryan replied. "Just strip the gear off and toss it in a corner. We won't be needing it anymore."

They were quickly done. So far, so good, Ryan thought. No crazy Rodrigo, no Peruvians with machine guns. Joe began pulling at the latigo on his own saddle.

"Leave that," Ryan said quietly, coming up behind him. "Take him and my mare back up the canyon and wait. I'm going up to see Rodrigo. If I don't come for you in an hour, go back to the ranch without me." He handed Joe the reins to the dun, opened the gate and let them out. When the darkness had closed around them, Ryan latched the gate and walked up the deserted ramp.

Rodrigo and two of his men were seated at a table near the middle of the ledge. Ryan walked up to them.

Rodrigo, wiping the corners of his mouth with a wadded handkerchief, did not look good. His face, covered with beads of sweat, was still colorless, and his head tilted noticeably toward his left shoulder. His right hand, protruding from the towel-sling, was heavily bandaged.

He belonged in a hospital. Easy enough with three airplanes a few yards away. Why didn't he go?

Rodrigo leaned sideways in order to tilt his face upward. "You're missing some horses," he said in English. "What happened?" His voice sounded stronger than yesterday and not friendly, but... he had said nothing about the guards. Again, only the horses mattered. None of the guards were supposed to return. Ryan tried not to show his relief.

"Shoe problems. The woman took them to Naranjo's. They'll be here in the morning." The expressionless face made it difficult to read Rodrigo, but his glare seemed to soften. Ryan added the topping. "We'll be moving two tons each trip from now on. We'll have everything across in two weeks."

Rodrigo's eyes closed for a moment. When he opened them again, the displeasure was gone. "I think you will enjoy the meal tonight," he said, as a way of dismissal. "Don Naranjo has sent us one of his prized steers."

Ryan turned toward the cooking pit near the brink of the ledge. "Smells good." Taking Rodrigo's cue, he excused himself and drifted toward the fire, feeling like he had just filled an inside straight.

The thick, round steaks, dripping juices into the mesquite coals, appeared to be loin cuts, but boneless Mexican-style butchering had precluded any such distinction. Whatever part of the carcass they had been carved from, they were going to be delicious. Ryan spoke to the cook, a plump old *señora,* and watched the meat sizzle until Rodrigo fell back into conversation with his men.

With a final comment to the woman, Ryan walked back to the ramp and hurried down into the darkness. A quarter mile up the runway, he found Joe with the horses, and the two of them rode quietly back to the corrals.

He then walked the half-mile back to the ledge, drawn by the steaks he'd seen. It had been a long time since breakfast with the two border patrolmen.

♦ ♦ ♦

Ryan finished a second large steak and a third bottle of cold Bohemia. He took the last bite of meat and judged it almost as good as the first. Aside from Naranjo's undisputed success as a narcotics smuggler, he also raised good beef.

Joe had eaten quickly and joined the dancers. Rodrigo had retired to his tent with one of the younger girls. Given the Colombian's terrible physical condition, Ryan had wondered why. He shook his head again at the thought. Maybe she would put him to sleep. Ryan turned up the brown beer bottle and drained it.

"They are from La Mula," Joe said in Spanish.

Ryan turned. Joe was standing over him, three brightly dressed women with him.

"The girls from La Mula are wild and strong." Joe's mouth was already puckered and twisted into his characteristic sideways grin.

Ryan looked at the girls. All the way from near where Naranjo's ranch is? After the wild Jeep ride through the mountains, he had taken time to study the map Frank had given him. As he had suspected, there was a road, a long meandering one, a few miles south of the ledge camp; it skirted south of the mountains, then eventually intersected a main highway south of Ojinaga.

Without question, the road was much better than the route Yolanda had blazed through the middle of the mountain range to confuse him. But still, it was a long and almost certainly rough and dusty way to come for a meal and an evening of entertainment.

"What are they doing here?" Ryan was still speaking in English, watching to see if the girls understood. "Why don't they just go to Ojinaga for their fun? They have mariachis there, don't they?" The three girls smiled blankly, nervously glancing around, not understanding.

"They came with the big truck," Joe answered, his crooked smile fading a little. "The one that brought the meat from Lalo's."

"What about the band and the other girls? Are they from La Mula, too?" Ryan looked toward the half-dozen couples now arriving at the smooth area used for dancing. Nearby, the three-piece band was assembling again: trumpet, accordion and guitar, each separately running their music scales.

Joe asked the girls where the others were from. "La Mula," they all answered.

"Wild and strong," Ryan repeated Joe's words and chuckled to himself as the band broke into a loud and fast *corrido*.

"Yes! Wild and strong," Joe shouted, his eyes sparkling a he clapped his hands in time with the music. "They are the black Mexicans, Cuate."

A young girl glanced in their direction as she whirled past. Joe tipped his hat and gave an ear-splitting yell. The three girls with him giggled. They were all exceptionally pretty: tall, dusky complexions, slender hands and fingers. Black American soldiers stationed along the border after the Civil War had defected to Mexico and settled there. Mexican and African ancestry had blended very well, Ryan thought.

A young Mexican man led one of the girls out to the dance area. A Peruvian took another.

Joe frowned down at Ryan. "You better get one fast, Cuate." He danced away with the last girl.

A movement to his right made Ryan glance in that direction. The young girl leaving Rodrigo's tent zipped the screened flap closed and came toward the music. She was intercepted by one of the Peruvians and ushered to the dance area. Ryan watched the dancers.

Following a series of particularly loud blasts from the mariachi trumpet, he heard a voice say, "Alpine." He turned toward a large radio on a table near Rodrigo's tent. It would play music for the dancers during the band's break and also tuned in news from the world outside the ledge camp.

"A spokesman for the U.S. Customs Service says it is the largest seizure of cocaine ever made on a U.S. land border." The announcer's booming voice promised more details were to soon follow.

Ryan spun around on the bench, stood up and headed for the tent, right hand inside his shirt, thumb cocking the hammer of the .45, fingers closing around the large, square grip.

All the chairs near Rodrigo's tent and the radio were empty. He looked back over his shoulder at the Peruvians around the tables, then at the dancers. No one was listening to the newscast.

At the tent he knelt, grasped a small nylon pull and straightened up, unzipping the door flap. Drawing the pistol clear, he stepped into Rodrigo's tent. On his right, in the dim light filtering through the lightly-colored tent fabric, Ryan could barely make out Rodrigo's form stretched out in the middle of a king-sized bed, propped up by pillows against a dark wooden headboard. He appeared to be completely naked under the breakfast tray that straddled him. Rodrigo looked up from the tray. Calmly, with no sign of alarm, he eyed Ryan and the pistol pointed at him.

"You heard the news?" Ryan asked in Spanish.

Rodrigo did not answer right away. He looked down at the tray in front of him. On it were two small piles of white powder and a short tube cut from a plastic drinking straw. Slowly, he picked up the straw with his good hand, placed one end in his left nostril, closed off the right with his index finger, leaned over and vacuumed up one of the piles of cocaine. He threw his head back and exhaled slowly.

"Yes," he finally answered, in English. "I heard the radio." He stared up at Ryan, leaned over the tray, placed the straw in his right nostril and sucked up the second heap of cocaine. Again he put his head back and exhaled. "Are you *policia* or an informer?" he asked as he closed his eyes.

"Customs," Ryan responded forcefully as he stepped nearer. "Do you have a gun?"

"No." Eyes still closed, Rodrigo raised his left hand and spread his fingers. "No gun."

"Move the tray and sit up," Ryan ordered as he moved to the foot of the bed. Rodrigo did not respond.

"Get up! I'm going to tie you up and leave," Ryan said louder than before. Rodrigo still did not move. "Get up," Ryan ordered again.

"Or what?" Rodrigo's eyes opened, staring wildly. "What more can you do to me, bastard? Everything is gone now. Everything. A lifetime."

Rodrigo moved the tray from in front of him, threw his legs over the edge of the bed and sat up. "Months, almost a year of this place."

Rodrigo lapsed into his strange, almost unintelligible Spanish. Ryan understood the "I am going to kill you" part of his rant

Rodrigo's left hand suddenly darted into the sling supporting his injured hand and came out with a sheathed knife. There was a quick motion and the leather cover shot past Ryan, thumping against the tent wall behind him. Rodrigo was holding the long fighting knife he had used to cut off his finger.

Ryan moved from the foot of the bed toward the door. "Drop the knife," he said. "There's no need for this. All I want to do is get out of here." Rodrigo stood up.

Ryan backed further away, keeping the .45 leveled at Rodrigo's bare chest. He moved his thumb up the pistol grip and pulled down on the safety catch to be sure it was off. He had made a mistake in allowing Rodrigo to snort the cocaine. Now, he might have to shoot the crazy coked-up bastard, and then he would be trapped. Everyone on the ledge would hear the shot and then see him come out of the tent. He wouldn't get far.

Rodrigo leaned to one side, reached out to the headboard to steady himself and shook his head.

Ryan glanced to his left at the rear wall of the tent. If he had to shoot, that would be the way to leave. He reached with his free hand into his pocket, pulled out his knife, thumbed the blade up and snapped it open as he stepped to the back of the tent. He knelt down, plunged the knife into the canvas and stood up, cutting a six-foot long gash in the tent. He could now duck out the back and circle behind the crowd that would be rushing toward the sound of the shot.

Rodrigo came straight for him, the long knife in his left hand, arm wide and low, ready to slash. Ryan saw the opening, stepped forward, pivoted on his right foot, leaned away from the charging man, and caught him square in the chest with a backward kick. He heard the breath leave Rodrigo's lungs, saw him stagger and double over.

Ryan moved in to finish it. Still gripping the butt of the .45, Ryan brought it down on the back of Rodrigo's neck. Nothing. Ryan hit him again. Still nothing. It was like hitting a sack of wet sand. As Ryan raised his arm to strike again, Rodrigo straightened, bringing his long stainless-steel blade into thrust position. Ryan backed away, tripped over something and fell face-up on the tent floor.

Rodrigo was quickly on top of him, his knee pinning Ryan's gun hand to the floor. Teeth clenched, eyes full of hate, Rodrigo brought the blade around. Ryan's left arm was moving up to block the knife, but there was no time, it would be too late.

Suddenly Rodrigo froze, staring at the floor above Ryan's left shoulder. Ryan felt the pressure on his wrist ease. He jerked his gun hand free and shoved the barrel of the heavy pistol into Rodrigo's neck. Rodrigo grabbed at the gun. Ryan pulled on the trigger.

Nothing happened. The flesh of Rodrigo's hand also on the gun had blocked the hammer. Ryan pulled harder on the pistol and twisted it free.

Ryan got to his feet. Rodrigo stood up and lunged toward him. Ryan stepped to one side, and the Colombian, slashing wildly, plunged through the opening that had been cut in the tent. Ryan stepped quickly to the slit. The pistol would fire now; the slide no longer pushed back by Rodrigo's flesh. Cautiously, Ryan parted the canvas with his left hand. It was dark outside, but he could see the brink of the ledge, only three feet away. He thumbed the safety lever up and shoved the .45 back into his waistband.

Rodrigo had gone silently – fifty feet straight down.

32

Ryan stepped back from the opening he had cut in the tent. As he righted the chair he had tripped over a few minutes earlier, he looked down and saw his pocket knife. He must have dropped it during the fight with Rodrigo. Lying in the webbed shadow of the screened door flap, the red-yellow-and-black handle looked like the coral snake that had bitten Rodrigo. That was what Rodrigo had stared at, what had caused him to hesitate.

Ryan picked up his knife, stared thoughtfully at the colored handle for a moment, then pressed the lock release, folded the blade and dropped the knife into his pocket.

He stepped to the door flap and peered out. The band was playing. People were dancing, talking, drinking and eating, still not interested in the English-speaking newscast on the radio now filling in the details on the Alpine drug seizure.

It was time to shut the radio off. He stepped out and flipped its power switch.

Ryan headed back into the tent to give it all a last look around. The tent was furnished like a hotel suite: carpeted floor, king-size bed, dresser, sofa, chairs, table and... duffel bags?

He moved quickly to the pyramid of bags in the dark corner. More cocaine? He pushed against one of the bags. Solid and lumpy. He unsnapped the hook fastener at the end of the bag and a large paper-wrapped package tumbled out. Ryan knew immediately what it was.

He picked it up. He had seen packages like this before in drug-smuggling seizures and arrests. He peeled back the heavy brown paper from one corner of the package and turned toward the light. This one was twenties, $50,000 worth.

He pushed the package back inside, closed the duffel bag and hefted it. Fifty pounds, over $150,000 worth. He stepped back. Ten duffel bags: $4.5 million... if all the bills were twenties. He had also seen packages of fifties and hundreds during seizures. Now he understood why Rodrigo hadn't wanted to leave camp, not even to have his snakebite treated.

He grabbed the bags and tossed them out through the cut in the canvas. The money was now on the canyon floor, fifty feet below.

Ryan looked around the ledge for Joe, saw him talking with two young Mexican men near the cooking pit, caught his eye and summoned him with a barely perceptible hand motion. Ryan pulled a bottle from the tub of ice at his feet and walked to a nearby table. He twisted the cap off the brown bottle of Bohemia and downed half of it.

"Cuate."

Ryan looked up.

"There are soldiers at Paso de San Antonio," Joe whispered as he sat down, glancing behind and around him. "They are at the hacienda, too." Joe leaned over the table, still looking furtively about. "The men who brought the meat, they saw the army trucks go to Don Naranjo's this morning, four trucks, all with soldiers in them."

Ryan stared, puzzled. Soldiers at Naranjo's? This morning was too soon for a reaction to the Alpine cocaine seizure. What then? No answer came to him. "How many soldiers at Paso de San Antonio?"

Joe shrugged. "Many... camped under the trees around the store. They are coming here for one of the Peruvians. That's what the people from Altares say."

Altares? Ryan recalled seeing the name but not its exact location on the map.

Joe continued. "They say that a Peruvian shot a man there last week, killed him." Joe leaned farther over the table. "The man who was killed was a customs inspector from Muzquiz. The inspector came to the cantina in Altares," Joe whispered. "There was a fight. The customs inspector shot the Peruvian in the arm, then the Peruvian shot him in the face. Killed him. The Peruvian said that if anyone told, he would bring the others, kill everybody and burn the village."

Ortiz! Ryan thought. The lantern bearer who didn't want Rodrigo to know about his injured arm. Then he remembered Suarez, pretending to be a bus driver.

"Then the shooting is the reason the customs comandante came to the ledge," Ryan said.

"I don't know, Cuate. I don't like any of this. I think we better leave now."

"Do the Peruvians know about the soldiers at Paso de San Antonio?"

"No," Joe answered. "Only the people from Altares know about the soldiers. The soldiers stopped them, told them to go back home; but one of their daughters is here, so they came another way. I think we better leave now."

Ryan considered it for a moment. Maybe this was a good time for Joe to leave. "All right," he reached across the table and patted Joe's shoulder. "Give me a few minutes, then meet me at the corrals."

Joe shook his head and turned away, still looking worried. Ryan turned and watched the dancers for a moment, thinking about Ortiz shooting the Mexican customs inspector. If the shooting was the reason the soldiers were coming here, why had they gone to Naranjo's?

No matter. He stood up. The soldiers at Paso de San Antonio would probably arrive at first light. He and Joe would be gone by then. Ryan looked one last time at Rodrigo's darkened tent, turned and walked toward the ramp.

♦ ♦ ♦

Joe held the flashlight as Ryan stuffed a large brown package into the saddlebag on the paint gelding. Joe had been even more eager to leave after hearing about Rodrigo. "$100,000," Ryan said as he buckled the flap down on the bulging leather bag. He walked around the horse to the other side. "You ride on out of the canyon and turn north down the valley, understand?"

"$100,000?" Joe whispered as Ryan stuffed a second package into the other saddlebag.

"Into the valley, turn north, understand?" Ryan repeated as he buckled the second flap. "North, then east along the river. I know the way to Lajitas. If you get into any trouble, call Frank."

"*Si*. Call Mr. Frank. This money is all mine, no?"

"It's all yours." Ryan handed him four banded stacks of twenties. "Drop this off at the old people's camp and tell them about the soldiers." Joe shoved the money into his shirt and mounted the paint. Ryan put his hand up. Joe gave it a quick, hard squeeze. "You are going the other way?"

"Yes. Now get out of here. Let Frank know where you are in a couple of days."

Ryan stepped back as Joe turned his horse down the canyon and rode quietly away. The moon was bright overhead. He would make good time.

The rest of the money was still in duffel bags, stacked far enough from Rodrigo's sprawled body that the horses wouldn't spook when it was time to load it. Two packhorses would be enough, five duffels of money each. They would be loaded and left up the canyon, ready to move out fast.

Ryan turned the flashlight on and looked at his watch. Almost midnight; three hours to wait. After loading the money, he would take two other horses to the cavern just before daylight, as if loading up for an early start. Going to the cavern any sooner would arouse suspicion. Ryan turned the light off and walked past the corrals to the big haystack, pulled one of the bales down for a step and climbed up onto the hay.

Set the timer first, Harry had said, then connect the leads and shove the detonator into the plastic explosive. Simple enough. Do it twice. Always have a backup, that was the rule, Harry said, in case something goes wrong with the first primer charge.

Ryan leaned back on the hay bales behind him. There would be no backup system for the charge placed in the cocaine cavern. There was only one battery. Mike wasn't sure how long it had been in his pocket weather radio. The radio had worked fine. Surely there was enough juice left to fire one detonator.

It had been quiet for a while up on the ledge. Ryan had hoped the band had stopped for the night, that the night's revelries were winding down, but the band came back strong. He pulled off his hat, turned and lay back on the hay, folding an arm under his head.

Tonight, there were two cavern guards as usual. He turned his thoughts to them and grew drowsy running scenarios on separating them. Getting them, one at a time, to the back of the cavern was critical.

The moon had dropped behind the rim when he awoke and turned the light on his watch again. Two a.m. Still too early. It was finally quiet in the canyon. No one was looking for Rodrigo – or him. He laid back and closed his eyes again.

When the morning chill woke him, he knew, even before looking at the watch, that he had slept too long. Three-thirty a.m. He grabbed his hat and vaulted from the haystack. His flashlight beam found the two halters; lead ropes; a roll of adhesive tape from the medical supplies; and a peeled, green-oak limb the size of a baseball bat that he had cut from one of the trees near the hot spring. He scooped everything up, stuffed the roll of tape into a hip pocket, switched off the light and walked to the corrals.

There was still plenty of time if he left the packhorses where the money bags were stacked instead of taking them farther up the canyon. He dropped the oak bat near the gate and went into the corral.

Moving quietly, he haltered the first two animals he could walk up to, threw blankets and packsaddles on them, adjusted the rigging, threw two sections of pack-netting across one of the saddles and checked the time. Four a.m.

Running late.

Quietly, in almost total darkness, he led the horses slowly out of the gate near the haystack, around the corner, between the corrals and the runway, past the flatbed meat truck from La Mula and along the base of the ledge.

♦ ♦ ♦

Almost an hour later, he repeated the saddling process on two other horses, adding the oak bat to the folds of netting. This time he led the horses out of the corral and up onto the runway. Shod hooves announced their advance across the pavement toward the cave. The sky was still dark, but dawn crispness was in the air. He was back on schedule. He switched on the flashlight so the guards could see him.

So far, so good.

Ten duffel bags of money loaded and waiting, just past the ledge. The dun mare saddled and ready, just inside the corral. Now to finish the job. He scuffed his boots on the runway and flashed the light around. Under the two dimmed lanterns, Ortiz and another, smaller, Peruvian were waiting for him.

"Ortiz, good morning," Ryan said. "How's the arm?"

The stocky Ortiz grunted and pulled awkwardly at the sling of the short-barreled Uzi with his left hand until the weapon pointed downward. He raised his bandaged hand, nodded his head and grunted again. The smaller man lowered his submachine gun and turned toward a nearby chair.

Ryan unhooked one of the lanterns with his gloved hand, turned up the gas flow and, still leading the horses, carried the lantern into the cavern. Near the first row of duffel-bag pyramids, he hitched the lantern bail to a ceiling hook and looked back. Ortiz was lighting a cigarette. The other man was slouched in the chair.

Ryan tied the horses to separate duffel-bag piles and slipped the green-oak bat from the folds of netting on the packsaddle. He leaned the club against the cavern wall, pulled the netting from the packsaddle, separated the two sections, draped one over the club and tossed one end of the other across the back of the horse.

Ryan looked again toward the entrance. The small Peruvian was still slouched in the chair. The glow of Ortiz's cigarette came from the far side of the low rock barricade. Ryan walked toward the opening of the cavern and stepped into the alcove containing the wooden crates.

The blade of his pocket knife loosened a slat on the largest box, and he pulled it up. His flashlight beam revealed white oblong blocks wrapped in clear plastic. C-4 explosive. He pried up a slat on the next-largest box. More Styrofoam pellets, like those around the timers. He reached in and pulled out two small clear bags. Inside each was a short pencil-sized metal tube with two electrical leads. Detonators, just the way Harry had described them.

Ryan exhaled, relieved. He pushed the two detonators into his hip pocket and walked to the cavern entrance. “I need help with the loading,” he said in Spanish.

Ortiz took a drag from his cigarette, raised his bandaged arm and looked at the smaller man. Slowly the Peruvian got up from his chair, slipped the nylon sling from around his neck, laid the Uzi in the chair behind him and followed Ryan back to the horses.

“Right here,” Ryan said, lifting a duffel bag and pressing it against the horse’s side. “Hold it right there.” The short man stretched, pushing upward against the bag with both hands. Ryan eased the oak club from under the netting against the wall, moved to the Peruvian’s left side, leaned slightly forward and swung the club. The heavy bat caught the small man squarely on the back of his neck with what Ryan hoped was moderate but sufficient force. The Peruvian collapsed without a sound, the bag of cocaine on top of him. Ryan rolled the bag aside, tied the man’s hands and feet, taped his mouth and rolled him up in a section of the pack-netting.

“Ortiz, come here a minute,” Ryan yelled in Spanish as he stepped into the dim recess. A moment later, he heard footsteps.

“¿Como?” Ortiz grunted as he passed. His machine gun was slung muzzle down.

Ryan stepped out behind him, pistol in hand. Ortiz froze when he saw the other man wrapped in the netting. Ryan grabbed the back of the stocky Peruvian’s collar and pushed the .45 into his spine. “Don’t move, Ortiz, or I’ll shoot you,” Ryan said forcefully in Spanish. He felt Ortiz stiffen. “Good. Now listen to me, carefully. There are explosives back there in the boxes. You know that, don’t you?”

Ortiz nodded his head yes.

“I’m going to blow this place up: the cave and all the cocaine. I’m going to tie you up, and I’ll take you and your friend with me when I leave, understand?”

“Yes.” Ortiz nodded and slowly raised his hands.

Ryan took the submachine gun and tossed it toward the back of the cavern, tied Ortiz’s good hand down to his crotch, taped his mouth, tied his feet and rolled him up in the other section of netting.

The crate of C-4 was heavy, at least a hundred pounds. Ryan carried it to the middle of the main cavern and set it down among the stacks of duffel bags. He flashed his light across the ceiling. Harry had said to look for a crack, some kind of fault or recess, and place the charge there. The dark limestone overhead was smooth, but in one place it sloped sharply upward, toward the back of the big room.

Ryan moved the crate of explosives to within a few yards of the rear wall, under the sloped ceiling, and took the timer and one of the blasting caps out of his pockets. Harry had already taped the small radio battery to the timer. Ryan set the timer for thirty minutes, connected the battery leads to the timer, then the two blasting cap wires to the timer. He made a hole in one of the putty-like plastic blocks of C-4 with his knife and pushed the blasting cap deep inside.

He shined the light on his watch. At six a.m. it should blow. Now, time to get out.

He hurried back to the horses, tied two nylon cords from the netting around the packsaddles and led the horses out, dragging Ortiz and the other Peruvian behind. As they emerged from the cavern, dawn was beginning to show above the canyon rim. Distant bobbing lights past the mouth of the canyon immediately caught Ryan's attention. He stopped, staring and listening. The faint sound of vehicle engines reached him, powerful, straining engines. The soldiers were on their way.

33

"Take the light." Ryan was standing on the runway over Ortiz. He had cut him free of the net and ropes. "Those are army trucks." Ryan pointed toward the mouth of the canyon. The Peruvian got to his feet and stared at the distant pairs of headlights.

"Take the light and go stop them. Tell them the cave is going to blow." The headlights were more than a mile away, but approaching quickly, fast enough to be caught by the explosion if they weren't stopped. Ortiz took the light and stumbled away into the darkness.

Ryan led the horses on across the runway to the stack of hay. The other guard, still wrapped in the net, had begun to moan and struggle. Ryan cut the net away and dragged him, hands and feet still tied, up to the hay. The sound of running footsteps caused Ryan to look back.

On the runway, a stocky figure, white bandage flashing in the predawn light, disappeared behind the corral walls, headed toward the ramp. "That son of a bitch Ortiz," Ryan said to himself as he strode to the corral gate and threw it open.

The dun mare was tied just inside. Ryan mounted and circled the inside of the corral, emptying it of horses. He didn't want to leave behind the means for anyone to pursue him.

The freed horses went straight to the stack of hay, and Ryan was unable to move them. Each time he tried, they circled back. He was about to abandon the effort and head up the canyon when he heard a familiar angry squeal. Horses peeled away from the hay ahead of the biting, kicking dark young stallion. As they abandoned the haystack, Ryan pushed them on past the corrals and up the runway. When the big colt charged past on the heels of the last straggler, Ryan followed him.

The approaching headlights were much nearer. There was shouting from the ledge, and Peruvians were streaming down the ramp, half-dressed, but each had a pistol and a short-barreled machine gun.

"That son of a bitch Ortiz," Ryan again said aloud, as he leaned forward and swatted a horse in front of him with the coiled lariat. The string of horses momentarily stemmed the flow of men from the ledge. None of them took notice of Ryan. All were intent on the approaching headlights and getting to the runway. In panic, they began dashing between the passing horses.

As Ryan followed the horses past the ramp and along the base of the ledge, he heard the sound of a turboprop engine. It was followed by another. He looked back. The runway was filled with Peruvians running toward the Beechcraft King Air, now rolling away from its parking place. An engine on the other King Air came to life, and some of the armed, half-dressed men veered toward it. Ryan was relieved to see that no one was headed toward the cavern.

Past the base of the ledge, Ryan reined up beside the two loaded packhorses and dismounted. In seconds, as the first airplane taxied by, he tied the lead rope of one horse to the tail of the other and remounted. With the money-laden horses in tow, he continued up the canyon beside the runway. The frightened horses ahead broke into a full gallop as the red-striped, silver King Air moved up the runway behind them.

Ryan held the dun and the two packhorses to a trot. The other King Air taxied past. Ryan looked back to see the Peruvians now running alongside the departing Aero Commander. Headlight beams of the approaching vehicles had now reached the far end of the airstrip.

Above the sound of airplane engines Ryan could hear gunfire. He turned his attention to the horses ahead, now strung out in a long column between runway and canyon wall, running full out ahead of the first airplane. Past the widened airplane turnaround area, the lead horses began disappearing around a bend in the canyon, the first of many narrow, boulder-strewn areas that prevented vehicle traffic going any farther up the canyon.

The red-striped King Air veered right inside the turnaround, circled the widened area and stopped in take-off position. The Aero Commander taxied past Ryan and followed the second King Air into the widened area. Immediately, the first King Air revved engines and came streaking down the canyon. Without hesitation, the second King Air followed.

Ryan tied the lead packhorse fast to the saddle horn, pulled the frightened dun to a halt and dismounted. They were now almost a half mile from the ledge, and no Jeeps or trucks could follow past the bend just ahead. As he pulled binoculars from the saddlebags, the Aero turboprop roared past.

Ryan lifted the binoculars. Three army trucks were now advancing on the heavy equipment. Peruvians left behind by the planes had taken refuge behind the bulldozer and dump trucks. Suddenly, a huge fireball rolled across the runway toward the ledge. Ryan felt the ground move and heard the dull thump of a powerful, muffled explosion. As he watched through the binoculars, a mountain-sized section of the canyon wall dropped, then slowly spilled out onto the runway.

The two King Airs veered to the left. The lead plane sheared a wing on the base of the ledge, spun around and went tail-first into the mass of rock now blocking the runway. The second King Air lost only the tip of a wing on the north wall but still followed the first plane sideways into the mountain of rubble. The pilot of the Aero Commender had time to reverse propeller pitch and was able to stop just short of the two wrecked planes. No fires erupted from the wreckage.

Soldiers poured from all three army trucks. Ryan looked across to the ledge. The tent was still intact. Rodrigo would have survived if he hadn't chosen to fight. Ryan turned the binoculars back across the canyon. A sloping wall of rubble now stood where the cavern had been. The cocaine was buried. Ryan put the binoculars away and led the three horses across the smooth turnaround and into the curve of the canyon.

♦ ♦ ♦

Customs Comandante Suarez turned restlessly, painfully, in the thin wool army blanket. Finally he raised himself from the ground on one elbow and looked around. The campfire had gone out. Lieutenant Robles, one of the enlisted men and the old servant from the hacienda were nearby, dark lumps in the shadows of the steep canyon walls. Overhead the strip of sky was beginning to lighten.

Suarez's bruised rear end was throbbing, the inside of his thighs burning, but something other than the pain had awakened him. A vibration of the ground. Maybe the two soldiers posted farther down the canyon had dislodged something. It was cold, and painful to move.

Suarez eased back down and pulled the blanket over his face. The general would be at the ledge soon, would take all the cocaine, all the money, and would forget about him. He would lose even the Muzquiz *distrito comandante* job and return to Tampico jobless and penniless.

He should have kept the kilo of cocaine and the $50,000 from Rodrigo's tent, maybe even gone back for more. Two or three of the money packages would have bought him any coast guard position in Tampico. He flexed his buttocks muscles and winced. He would be walking the rest of the way to the ledge camp.

♦ ♦ ♦

Moving the dun and the two packhorses at a fast walk, Ryan caught up with the loose horses a mile up the canyon. They had slowed to a walk, meandering, snatching mouthfuls of dry grass now that they were isolated from the sights and sounds of the ledge camp. Ryan moved ahead of them, looking back frequently.

He soon noticed that the wandering horses were keeping up with the steady pace he had set. Then he saw the stallion colt, bringing up the rear, nipping and kicking. At his approach, horses would race ahead of animals grazing in front of them, snatch a few mouthfuls of grass and again find themselves at the rear. This leapfrog pattern repeated itself as the young stallion pushed the horses up the canyon.

Ryan admired the spirited little stud and felt grateful toward him. The big colt was the sole reason he had been able to move the horses away from the haystack and up the canyon.

The dun mare moved along at the fast walk that had been set for her. Ryan looked behind him again, this time at the duffel bags. Five on each horse: two encased in netting on each side and one lashed on top with olive-green parachute cord. Everything looked tight. While loading, he had decided each bag weighed more than fifty pounds, maybe sixty. If so, the horses were overloaded. Maybe the bags had only felt heavier because he was loading them alone. He would check the rigging before starting up the switchback, maybe get two fresh horses if the bunch was still with him.

Ryan continued to stare at the ten lumpy bags. They contained at least $4.5 million of narcotics money, something he had no intention of leaving behind for corrupt Mexican officials. Yet in order to legally seize the money for customs, he would have to be a little dishonest himself, say that the packhorses carrying it had been found on the U.S. side of the river, wandering loose in the border canyon. It was an untruth he was prepared to live with.

By the time Ryan reached the narrow opening into the hot-spring canyon, it was full daylight, almost eight a.m. He had made good time. Only two miles now to the steep, crooked trail out of the canyon. The two packhorses were holding up fine, and he decided not to take the time to switch their loads to fresher animals. He wanted no problems going up the steep switchback. It was time to get rid of the trailing *remuda*.

He turned into the narrow entrance on his right. As he had hoped, three horses behind the pack animals followed him in, then two, then three more came through the crack in the wall, snorting suspiciously until they smelled the lush grass in the meadow. Then they poured through the opening, followed by the young stallion. Ryan waited until all heads were down, grazing, then led the two packhorses slowly back through the opening, into the main canyon. He was less than an hour from the river now, and eager to be across.

♦ ♦ ♦

Shiny depressions in the sand ahead caught his eye first, then he smelled smoke. Ryan reined the dun to a halt, tilted his head, and inhaled. It was a faint scent. He moved the mare nearer the canyon wall until he could feel a slight breeze on his face. The smell was stronger there – acrid, green-wood smoke. In front of him was a sharp bend to the right that would bring him within sight of the steep slope at the head of the canyon.

He moved the horses forward a few yards. The dun's ears pricked up, alerted, listening to something that Ryan was unable to hear. But he could see the boot tracks, fresh and glistening in the dry sand near the bend. He moved the mare closer, pulling up just short of the turn and looked down: Two sets of tracks, one slightly larger than the other, crisscrossed the canyon, and there were depressions in the sand where two people had sat leaning against the canyon wall. Nearby were cigarette butts and ants swarming over a dried tortilla fragment. No sign of a fire here – Ryan sniffed the air again – but there was one, not far away, and someone was boiling coffee. With the back of his neck tingling, he turned the horses around and quietly rode back the way he had come.

A hundred yards down the canyon, he leaned forward and put the horses into a trot. A few minutes later, without slowing, he swerved through the narrow opening, back into the hidden valley.

34

Old Chato sat on the driftwood log under the gnarled desert willow. As he had predicted, no one had come up the canyon during the night. If they had, the large fire that Lieutenant Robles had ordered his men to feed all night would have warned them away.

He eyed the men standing around him. The lieutenant was telling the three soldiers to finish their coffee and saddle the horses. Chato had saddled his chestnut gelding hours ago, just after the ground had trembled. Then he had walked down the canyon and awakened the two young soldiers who were supposed to be watching for an approaching pack train. Now he shifted on the log in front of the fire, turned and peered through the long leaves of the willow saplings behind him. It was light in the canyon, and late – later than the lieutenant had thought – when the high walls of the canyon had finally permitted enough light to rouse him from his blankets. No one would be coming up the canyon now. General Pagazos had attacked the ledge camp at dawn, when the ground shook.

Chato thought about the general, again hoping that his cooperation would be remembered. He had answered all the general's questions honestly and straightforwardly, and provided the general a clear picture of the smuggling operation: the new airstrip, the Peruvians and all the equipment. He told the general that he had worked for Don Naranjo since the old days, when they were both young men moving burro trains of liquor across the border into the quicksilver-mining camps. He told about the late night telephone call Don Naranjo had received from the general's own headquarters, how Don Naranjo had immediately left and would never return. He had even confessed that he, Chato, had been invited to leave with Don Naranjo, but had declined. His people had long been a part of the land around La Mula and he could not imagine life anywhere else.

Chato felt no guilt for telling the general what he knew. Don Naranjo, his friend and provider, had made a mistake in attempting to keep the new airport and Rodrigo's cocaine a secret from the army zone commander. Don Naranjo was gone, and there was no reason for Chato not to do the best he could for himself. He was hoping he would be able to remain at the hacienda. He wished he were there now, could be there when the general returned. General Pagazos would be tired and hungry when he finished with the ledge camp. If he were there, Chato would see to it that the general was well fed and made comfortable.

"Comandante Suarez," the lieutenant said. "Are you awake?"

"Yes." Across the fire from Chato, a blanket on the ground stirred. "I am awake," Suarez raised up on one elbow and grimaced. "But I am not riding today. You may have the men saddle my horse, but I will walk the rest of the way."

Lieutenant Robles looked down at Suarez and exhaled in disgust.

"The hacienda is nearer," Chato volunteered, "only half as far."

Suarez raised his eyebrows and looked at the old man. "Then I will go back." He twisted farther around, staring at the coffeepot next to the smoldering fire.

Chato leaned over, refilled his own empty cup and handed it to the Comandante. "I would like to go back with him, Lieutenant," he said, looking up at Robles. "From here, the canyon will take you to the ledge in less than two hours."

Lieutenant Robles frowned and exhaled again. "Whatever you want to do," he said sharply. "Whatever either of you wants to do." He tossed his coffee cup onto the ground and walked deeper into the willow thicket where his men were saddling horses. Chato smiled to himself and emptied the coffee pot onto the smoldering fire.

♦ ♦ ♦

Ryan watched from the opposite rim of the canyon. Smoke had been drifting from a willow thicket at the intersection of a small arroyo and the main canyon. Even with his naked eye, he could see movement behind the mat of slender leaves. Binoculars revealed only shadowy figures around the source of the white smoke. Trampled sand and gravel in front of the thicket indicated heavy traffic in and out of the arroyo.

As he watched, the willows parted, and a mounted Mexican soldier rode into view, a single gold bar on each shoulder of his sage-green shirt. What appeared to be a Russian AK-47 assault rifle was slung from the horn of his stock saddle. The lieutenant was followed by three other mounted soldiers, enlisted men in faded fatigues, all with M-1 carbines slung across their backs.

The four soldiers rode quickly down the canyon and out of sight around the bend. Ryan turned his attention back to the willow-choked arroyo. There was no movement or sound, and now, no smoke. If the soldiers went on past the entrance to the hot-spring valley, the way to the river would be clear.

Ryan eased back from the canyon rim and jogged back along the ridge. He wanted to see the soldiers go past the narrow crack that led into the little valley. If they didn't, if they noticed the fresh hoof prints and went in, they would find the packhorses and the duffel bags.

Ryan looked back over his shoulder. The slope leading out of the canyon was in sight, only a mile away, the Rio Grande just beyond that. Even if the horsemen spotted him, he could easily make the river before they wound their way back and forth up the switchbacks – as long as he remained on the rim.

Getting up the sheer walls of the little valley had been precarious. He had tied the dun mare and the two loaded packhorses behind a plum thicket and walked along the steep walls looking for a way up. Past the large hollow that contained the mountain lion pictograph Yolanda had shown him, a stratum of the hard, greenish slate that protruded from the brown limestone. Angling upward across the face of the cliff, it was a narrow, sometimes-broken footpath that led to the rim. Handholds were carved and pecked into the limestone cliff, perhaps by the same ancient people who had painted the large yellow, long-tailed mountain lion on the wall of the shelter.

Ryan stopped now, just above the entrance to the small round valley, breathing deeply, quietly. The four soldiers had already passed and were fifty yards down the canyon, horses moving at a brisk walk. Ryan watched until they blended into single dark blot. A final look with the binoculars showed only a distant bend in the canyon. He took a last deep breath, knelt, found the first handhold and lowered himself onto the narrow ribbon of slate.

Clinging to the rough limestone niches, he moved slowly back down the narrow, sloping shelf of rock to the floor of the hidden valley. His pace quickened as he crossed the open meadow, his stride growing longer the nearer he came to the wild-plum thicket where he had left the two packhorses and mare. He pushed through the spiny thorn-like brush, snatching lead ropes and reins, hitched the packhorses together, vaulted into the saddle and led them toward the narrow entry. As he put the dun mare and two packhorses into a trot, he noticed the stallion colt grazing with the other horses near the oaks. He hoped they wouldn't follow and crowd the narrow trail out of the canyon. The colt would eventually track his mother to the ranch or return to Naranjo's.

At a fast trot, Ryan and the three horses entered the narrow corridor. For a moment, the clatter of twelve iron-clad hooves in the confined space was deafening; then they were out into the main canyon. He kept the horses at a trot to the bend in the canyon, walked them past the willow thicket where the soldiers had camped, then put them back into a trot. He glanced back often at the empty, shrinking canyon until he came to the switchback slope.

There he stopped and dismounted. The packhorses stood quietly, sweat dripping from their soaked harness as Ryan tightened cinches, checked the netting around the loads and told them in a soothing tone what good horses they were. He adjusted the hitch connecting the sorrel to the bay's tail, making sure it would slip free if either horse lost its footing on the narrow trail. Satisfied with the rigging, Ryan stared back down the canyon for a moment. Assured it was still empty, he mounted and began the climb out.

It was a slow. deliberate process, back and forth across the slope. Halfway up, Ryan noticed fresh hoof prints and part of a round-toed boot or shoe track, headed in the wrong direction – upward. The soldiers, coming down the trail, should have made the last tracks. These were headed out of the canyon. He watched the trail ahead for more signs. Hoof prints, along with tracks made by a shoe or boot, were definitely pointed in the same direction he was going. Someone had led horses out ahead of him.

On the rim, Ryan turned the dun toward the narrow, sloping trail that would take them to the bottom of the Rio Grande gorge. From here, he could see the river crossing and the top of the big cottonwood tree that grew in the wide, green, park-like mouth of the border canyon on the other side. No one was in sight. He turned in the saddle and glanced for the last time at the empty ledge camp canyon behind, turned back and nudged the mare down the trail.

Below the rim, a cool breeze struck his face, bringing the moist smell of the river. Sounds of the shallow moving water grew louder as he descended. As he left the narrow trail and angled toward the crossing, he heard another sound – the low fluttering snort of an impatient horse.

It came from behind, too far left to be one of the packhorses. Ryan cringed as the dun's ears snapped toward the sound.

"¡Alto! ¡Manos arriba!" It was a man's voice, loud and not far away. Ryan felt the mare hesitate even before he tugged the reins. He focused for an instant on the river, the border, ten yards away, thirty yards wide, belly deep. Too deep for horses to run in. He raised his hands and turned slowly in the saddle to see a uniformed officer standing just below the sloping trail, his back to the canyon wall. A chrome or nickel-plated .45 was in his right hand. It was Suarez, the customs man from the ledge. To the *comandante*'s left, on a slender-necked sorrel gelding, sat an old man in a battered brown hat. Ryan recognized him as the manservant from Naranjo's hacienda. He was holding the reins of another sorrel.

"Hands up!" Suarez repeated insistently in Spanish, keeping the barrel of the .45 aimed at Ryan.

"I am a federal agent," Ryan said in Spanish as he raised his hands higher.

Suarez moved away from the canyon wall and glanced up the trail Ryan had just come down. "I'm a federal officer," Ryan repeated, "and

I'm alone." Suarez moved to within a few feet of the dun mare.

"Get down," he shouted in English. "You are under arrest."

Ryan looked again at the river, then down at the large black hole in the end of Suarez's pistol. Slowly he leaned over, and keeping both hands up in Suarez's view, slid down off the saddle.

"What do you mean, federal officer?" Suarez asked loudly. "You have a badge? You have identification?"

"No." Ryan turned to face him, hands even with his shoulders. "I left all that on the other side." He nodded toward the river.

"He is a federal officer," the old man said in Spanish, moving his horse a few steps nearer. "He came to the hacienda. Don Naranjo knew he was a federal officer, a customs agent."

"Customs?" Suarez looked confused.

"I came to look for my friend who had been shot by one of Naranjo's men."

"No." Suarez shook his head and stepped to one side. "You are crossing cocaine for the Colombian. I saw you at the camp. If you are only looking for someone, what is that?" He pointed toward the packhorses.

Crossing cocaine for the Colombian, Ryan thought. That's what one of the charges would be. The five duffel bags of money would be another matter if Suarez reported them.

"The man he was looking for was at the hacienda," Chato said, "another customs agent. He had been shot. Don Naranjo knew him, and we took him to the hospital."

Suarez's eyes shifted back and forth from Ryan to the packhorses. "It's not cocaine," Ryan said.

Suarez stared for a moment, then his eyes widened. "Move over there." He pointed toward the river. "Sit down and keep your hands up."

Ryan dropped the reins, stepped to a level area of loose gravel and sat down with his hands up.

The *comandante* walked to the packhorses and felt one of the duffel bags. His face brightened. "Bring your knife," he shouted to the old man. "Cut one of the bags down."

The servant rode up to the last packhorse, pulled a large hunting knife from the sheath on his right hip, cut the nylon cords holding the top duffel bag in place and rolled it off onto the ground.

Suarez backed up to the bag, straddled it, leaned over, unsnapped the fastener, and pawed two of the large brown packages out onto the gravel. He ripped one open. Bundles of fifty-dollar bills spilled out onto the ground. Suarez stared down at the money.

"I will wait for you up the river," the old servant said. Without waiting for a reply, Chato turned his horse up the gorge and rode away, leading the other sorrel.

A wise old man, Ryan thought. Now he would not be a witness to anything Suarez decided to do. "The army was at the ledge camp when I left this morning," Ryan said as he watched the servant ride away. "Rodrigo is dead, fell off the ledge, and the cavern has been blown up. All the cocaine is gone."

All the money, too, Ryan thought, as far as he was concerned, and he had wanted the money, wanted to be the agent who brought in the five-million-dollar dope-money seizure. If he had really only wanted to keep the money from corrupt Mexican officials, it would have been easy enough to destroy it along with the cocaine, or to have hidden it. If he had done either, he would be on his way to the ranch now, not sitting on the ground on the wrong side of the Rio Grande, wondering if a Mexican customs officer was going to shoot him or put him in jail.

He turned back to Suarez. The *comandante* was studying the packhorses. Counting the bags, Ryan thought, wondering how much money was there.

"About $450,000 a bag if it's twenty-dollar bills," Ryan said, "over a million, if it's fifties. I didn't want the Peruvians to have it." He made no attempt to make the last part sound convincing.

Suarez grabbed the lead rope to the first packhorse. "This money is the property of the Mexican government." He didn't sound very convincing either. He sounded like someone who was thinking about keeping some of the money for himself, maybe all of it.

"*Correcto*," Ryan nodded his head. "*Correcto*, and me? Am I still under arrest?" He was pretty sure Suarez wasn't going to put him in jail now. That would leave a witness who knew too much about the duffel bags. If the *comandante* planned to keep any of the money, he would have to get rid of the witness, either let him go or shoot him.

Suarez looked down at the spilled money, up the river, then back at Ryan. "You go." He motioned toward the dun mare. "Get on your horse and go back where you belong."

Ryan quickly got to his feet, walked past Suarez, retrieved the reins, mounted and rode the mare into the river. Halfway across, he looked back.

Suarez was standing over the duffel bag of money, still holding the lead rope to the packhorse. A movement behind the *comandante*, near the top of the gorge, caught Ryan's eye. He looked up. Horses were streaming down the incline – the packhorse *remuda*.

Suarez turned toward the noise behind him. Ryan urged the dun mare on across the river into the mouth of the border canyon, stopped and turned to watch. The horses came down the incline, showering rocks and debris below. Bringing up the rear was the dark stallion colt.

The lead horses veered off the trail, shied away from Suarez and moved a few yards downriver, snorting, pawing and drinking. Across the river, Ryan moved back to the edge of the water, where the horses could clearly see him and the mare. Suarez tugged on the lead rope, trying to move the two packhorses away from the crossing, out of the path of horses still clattering down the incline, but the bay gelding balked. The last of the horses came off the steep trail, the stallion colt squealing and tossing his head behind them.

One animal stumbled, slamming into the sorrel packhorse, knocking her aside and loosening the slip-knot connecting her to the tail of the bay. Free of the other packhorse, the sorrel hurried after the others, her head held to one side, keeping the lead rope clear of her hooves.

The big colt squealed and nipped the left hind leg of the bay packhorse. The offended gelding bolted, his shoulder striking Suarez squarely in the chest, knocking him to the ground and ripping the lead rope from his grip. Kicking and biting, the colt chased the bay packhorse into the bunched r*emuda*, scattering all of them into the river.

Through the spray thrown by the charging, lunging horses, Ryan saw Suarez stagger to his feet, hands empty, looking for his pistol. Ryan spun the dun mare around, kicked her into a full gallop and led the crossing horses into the border canyon. Around the first bend, out of sight of the river, Ryan slowed the mare to a walk and looked back. Suarez and Naranjo's servant still had their saddle horses, and the old man would know there was no way out of the canyon between here and the ranch.

But there were only horses behind him. Several trotted past him; others, heads still high, had slowed to a walk.

As he moved steadily up the canyon, Ryan kept close watch behind him. The canyon remained empty except for the r*emuda* of wet horses. Some were pausing now for mouthfuls of dry grass before moving on.

As he passed under the highway bridge two miles north of the river, the horses ahead spooked a family of javelinas. Ryan watched the big boar, a sow and five half-grown piglets hurry up the canyon and plunge into a large thicket of sagebrush. Horses snatched bites as they passed the thicket. The scent of bruised sage mingled with that of the javelinas.

How much time had passed since he last smelled that desert musk-sage perfume? On a dark lonely highway headed for Alpine, he knew, but his weary mind wasn't sure just how long ago that had been.

The two packhorses moved ahead of him, nine duffel bags still intact. He wouldn't have to lie about finding the money after all. These actually were runaway packhorses, found this very moment, wandering on the U.S. side of the Rio Grande with, well, who knows how much money. Maybe there were more fifties, maybe some hundreds.

Ryan could feel a huge grin growing on his face. He glanced down at his watch. In five hours he was going to be at the County Hospital in Alpine, sitting on the bed beside Yolanda, La Morena, and the smile on his face was going to be even bigger.

About The Author

Ray Summers knows the United States/Mexico border and its landscapes, culture, people, issues, wonders and merits almost as well as the back of his hand. For 30 years he served in Texas, Arizona and New Mexico as a Border Patrol, Customs and Drug Enforcement Agency agent. His service and his storytelling savvy imbues his first modern Western crime saga, “Border Canyon.” with a resonant realness that brings depth and impact to this fictional mystery/adventure set in the Southwestern borderlands.

A native of the Lone Star State raised in the West Texas town of Monahans, Summers grew up often on horseback, working on ranches and wandering the area’s vast wind-blown sandhills, exploring and collecting Native American arrowheads and other artifacts uncovered by the shifting sands. After graduating from high school in 1955, he briefly worked as a lineman for the local power company before attending trade school in Fort Worth and then signing on as a telegrapher and later station agent for the Santa Fe Railroad. Summers also served four years in the Air Force as a mechanic, crew chief and flight engineer on RB66 twin-engine jet bombers.

Ray began his federal law-enforcement career in 1960 with the Border Patrol and then as a special agent with the Customs Service, the newly formed Drug Enforcement Administration in 1973, and then the Customs Internal Affairs unit. During his decades as a criminal investigator, he served in Nogales, Arizona, and such Texas locales as Sonora, Del Rio, Houston, El Paso and Austin, and worked on extended details in New Jersey and New York plus temporary emergency sky-marshal duties mandated by President Nixon in 1970.

On his retirement from federal service in 1990, Summers became a private investigator conducting fraud, theft and arson investigations for various clients and private insurance companies. He married his high school sweetheart, Janet Wynona Cloninger, in August 1956. They have three children, Susan, Alan and Cathy, as well as one grandson, Zachary Shipp, and reside in San Angelo, Texas.

50921610R10139

Made in the USA
Middletown, DE
29 June 2019